# Silent Conversations

CW00743282

Alan Wall was born in Bradford in the West Riding of Yorkshire, and was educated there and at Pembroke College, Oxford. He is married with three children and lives in London.

ALAN WALL

# Silent Conversations

Secker & Warburg LONDON

Published by Secker & Warburg 1998

2 4 6 8 10 9 7 5 3 1

Copyright © 1998 by Alan Wall

Alan Wall has asserted his right under the Copyright, Designs
and Patents Act 1988 to be identified as the author of this work.

This book is sold subject to the condition that it shall not
by way of trade or otherwise, be lent, resold, hired out,
or otherwise circulated without the publisher's prior
consent in any form or binding or cover other than that
in which it is published and without a similar condition
including this condition being imposed on the
subsequent purchaser.

First published in Great Britain in 1998 by
Secker & Warburg

Random House, 20 Vauxhall Bridge Road,
London SW1V 2SA

Random House Australia (Pty) Limited
20 Alfred Street, Milsons Point, Sydney,
New South Wales 2061, Australia

Random House New Zealand Limited
18 Poland Road, Glenfield,
Auckland 10, New Zealand

Random House South Africa (Pty) Limited
Endulini, 5A Jubilee Road,
Parktown 2193, South Africa

Random House UK Limited Reg. No. 954009
A CIP catalogue record for this book
is available from the British Library

ISBN 0 436 20486 X

Papers used by Random House UK Limited are natural,
recyclable products made from wood grown in sustainable forests.
The manufacturing processes conform to the environmental
regulations of the country of origin.

Printed and bound in Great Britain by
Mackays of Chatham PLC

To
Philip Byrne

## Acknowledgements

I am grateful to the following people for their help: Gill Coleridge, Geoff Mulligan, Nathaniel and Anthony Rudolf.
The greatest debt of all is to Philip Byrne, to whom this book is dedicated.

Everything that moves falls still when it enters our lens. Then we switch the daylight off, and it starts to move again, as though for the first time. And that's our work, fashioning these wayward splinters of light, to entertain all those who come to watch the resurrectionists, here in our little room in the dark.

MIRO PELIKAN, *Film*, 1970


The whole of an archaeologist's life and work is a silent conversation with the dead.

PERCY HARDINGE, *Archaeology*, 1963


Ishtar: Sumerian divinity, related to Venus. The most passionately amorous of ancient goddesses, but also the most lethal in battle. *A Dictionary of the Past*, 1910

# 1

# Prima Scriptura

*Zend*

*On Ashley Simon's table stood three objects: a pyramid, a
marble egg and a tiny terracotta head of the goddess Ishtar. The
goddess had large bird eyes that were forever hungry with
amazement. She was four thousand years old.*

*Ashley stared at the three objects, as he did every day.
Between them he watched the dialectic of his life trace itself
out, for the egg has no edges, the pyramid no curves. The one
wombs life inside it, the other death. He lifted the egg into
his hand and thumbed its relentless chilly smoothness. It seemed
to him to be a defiance of all geometry. The pyramid reminded
him that one man, given a world to command, would whip a
million slaves to labour, if that might ensure his own survival
beyond death.*

*Then there was Ishtar. In the ravenous simplicity of her
features, perched there on her little block of perspex, she would
swallow the day entire and make it night inside her. How had
he ever come to be her devotee?*

JACK GOODRICH PUT HIS BOOK BACK DOWN ON THE TABLE
and stared again at the postcard that had dropped on to his
mat that morning.

We must meet urgently to discuss your novel, *About
Time*, and the film Miro Pelikan wanted to make of it.

HARRY TRENCH

Trench – Pelikan's faithful cameraman for his last ten films.
But where was he and how were they supposed to meet?
The postmark said Bexhill-on-Sea, so he must at least be in

England again. Jack pulled back the curtains and looked out. Relentless rain. It was eight-thirty on a Monday morning in Putney and rain in malevolent gusting thrashes soused the pavement. He had a view from his basement flat as clear as the dirty windows allowed. When he looked up he saw legs, some stockinged, some trousered, below them the clatter of puddles, while above was nothing but a skyful of droning rain as it veered and backed and slapped its malignant chill into flesh and fabric. Soon enough he would go out and take part: in the great thoroughfares of London he too would sink or swim. He looked at the writing on the white ruled rectangle laid on the table before him:

*Gypsy Swan*

He smiled bleakly, bitterly. It was right, he knew that this one simply had to be right. He had woken to those three syllables at dawn, another gift of sleep. His instincts told him to push for it: fourteen- to twenty-year-old market, hair-gel to match the fragrance, tube squeeze and aerosol spray. Neither puerile nor staid, but puckish somehow, the hint of elegy offset with horny adolescent insolence. The telephone rang. It was Jonathan.

'Have you done your copy?'

'Yes.'

'Can you come over?'

'Yes.'

'Sooner rather than later then. I've got a presentation on this one by the end of the week, remember.'

An hour later he joined the rain dance. He stopped beside the Jaguar with its shattered window. Fragments of glass lay across the passenger seat, though some had tumbled on to the paving stones like little diamonds in the rough. Inside he could see the wired gap where the radio had been torn out. He stared at the white crash helmet he held in his left hand. Yorick's black goggles looked blindly back at him. Jack reflected it was just as well he could no longer afford a car like this, otherwise he'd be the one who'd have to pay for its repair. He only hoped the sons of bitches had left his bike alone.

The bike was untouched but wet, its plastic and metalwork slimy and cold. Still, the engine throttled into life and he steered the bike out into the road. He was in Kew nine minutes later. He parked the Honda in front of Jonathan's house. The rain had suddenly stopped and sunlight already glazed the slaked streets.

This was where Jack would have preferred to live if things had turned out differently, in one of these little cottages threading the narrow lanes around Kew Green. Jonathan's tiny front garden was overgrown with cotton lavender, briar-rose and thyme. Jack stood shaking himself, caressed by the dripping honeysuckle leaves, and rang the bell. Jonathan opened the door and stared at the six-foot, drenched, black-leather blur in front of him.

'Come in,' he said. 'I've already watered the carpet this morning, so maybe you could leave some of that lot on the mat.'

Jack shed his wet outer skin, convulsing like a snake, and dumped it by the door. He had taken his crash helmet off with great care and counted the number of his hairs deposited inside. Today wasn't so bad. Then he opened his bag and laid the sheet of paper on the glass table while Jonathan went into the kitchen. Jack looked carefully, as he always did, at the pictures crowding the walls. Jonathan came back with a mug of coffee, which he gave him, then sat down at the table. He studied the sheet on the table in silence for a few moments.

'Gypsy Swan,' he said finally. There was scepticism in his voice. They had worked together for many years, and knew one another's manoeuvres. 'Gypsy Swan . . . You don't think it might be a bit too much of a cross between a box of matches and a sea-front fortune teller?'

Jack kept his eyes fixed on the small bronze minotaur by Michael Ayrton that crouched dumbly in the centre of the glass table. He said nothing, and Jonathan knew well enough what that meant.

'You're committed to it, then? I'd actually thought of Mondrian for the design, to be honest. Yellow and red squares on a black grid. A geometric purity. Sort of punk chess. But you reckon it should be pale faces and mascara, do you? Black stocking-tops and split skirts? Django Reinhardt twanging it out while the doomed pair tango?'

'It's just a mood I sense at the moment,' Jack said. 'Theatrical, a bit over-stated. Carnival time, but with a hint of mystery. I think they've grown tired of the shouts on one side and the silence on the other.' Jack looked around the walls again. A Hodgkin lithograph, a small, early Kitaj, a John Piper, two Mary Feddens and, in pride of place over the fireplace, an early Lucian Freud portrait. Jonathan had been shrewd. Seeing the downsizing that was about to descend, he had left the Knightsbridge design consultancy of which he had been a director. His colleagues had bought him out five years before at his own insistence. Now the Knightsbridge consultancy was in the hands of the official receiver. Two of its larger clients had removed their accounts a month after Jonathan's departure and handed them to him. They had been impressed by his readiness to work from home, cut overheads, employ freelancers and present them with smaller invoices. They even found it oddly satisfying to come and have meetings at his little house in Kew from time to time. After all, they spent half their lives sinking through pile carpets in five-storey office buildings.

Jonathan's small freckled face twitched in perplexity. Jack noticed again how absurdly youthful his skin always seemed, and how there was no grey at all in his dark curly hair. He was a stone lighter than he had been five years before when they had started working together. He seemed inexplicably untouched by anxiety. Jack found this comforting, but puzzling. When they occasionally turned up at presentations together, everyone assumed Jonathan was the younger man, but at fifty-five he was ten years older than Jack.

'All right then,' Jonathan said finally. 'With misgivings, I'll try it. What's the rest of the stuff you've got down here . . . wet look or dry . . . apply it in seconds . . . only a fingernail

6

flick lasts all day. She doesn't often spread her wings . . . in olden days they thought her song was music for the end of time. Lovely stuff, Jack, the poet still lives on inside, I see. Looks like I'll have to start again then. Out goes Piet with his Calvinist specs and in come the harlequins with cellos playing. Saint-Saëns.'

'This swan's not actually dying.'

'Best wait and see how the presentation goes before we decide that, shall we?'

Jack was staring through the rear window into Jonathan's small garden.

'Don't have any more work you could give me at the moment, do you?'

'That bad is it? I don't, I'm afraid. You could try these people, though, if you can face it.'

Jack read the card Jonathan had spun across the table to him.

'Who are they?'

'God knows. But they seem to have a deal to do some merchandising for Toni Inglish. So money should be flying round like hay at harvest time. I'll phone up and tell them I've managed to get Brewer's one-time main man for copy.'

'Main man?'

'It's so long ago, no one will remember how main you were, believe me.'

Jack rode back to Putney and walked round the corner to buy some milk and a paper. On the far side of the bridge, in the doorway of the closed-down curry restaurant with the legal notices plastered all over its windows, a pigeon was vigorously picking solid fragments from a splash of dried vomit. Pigeons. They only moved in when the pavements were already rich with gold. Nothing speculative about a pigeon: it was solid, well researched, residential.

Back in the flat again, he took that card from his pocket.

**Dale Freeman**
**Director**
**Freelands Marketing**

He didn't much like the sound of that. All the marketing men he'd ever met came wearing different guises, like the phases of the moon, and his instincts told him that Dale Freeman might be close to a total eclipse. He dialled the number.

'Oh yes, Jack, of course. Jonathan phoned earlier about you. You were one of the top creatives at Doyle's.'

'Brewer's.'

'That's right. Number one, I gather, till you threw the fetters off. I admire that. Anyway, we have some interesting material here, Jack. Your sort of quality is what we're looking for.'

'You've seen my work then?'

'Oh, almost certainly. You see, we have this amazing opportunity to market some high-quality merchandise for Toni Inglish. You know Toni, of course – you'd need to have been living on another planet not to. We're trying to go lateral on this one. Not just the usual venues of concerts and what have you, but a whole suite of possibilities.'

'How far have you got?'

'We've got plenty of ideas.'

'Any agency been involved?'

'No. The world's your oyster.'

'Have you got a designer, then? Or an art director?'

'No, Jack, at the moment you could describe us as being very much in the conceptual stage. That's the beauty of it, and where your input could be so crucial.'

Jack sucked the air in slowly through his teeth.

'Without any design concept or overall director, I'm not sure where I'm supposed to come in.'

'Top floor, 12 Villiers Street. Friday at nine. Suit you?'

'Well, I suppose we can at least talk about it,' Jack said. 'So I'll see you then.'

It felt all wrong. They had no idea what they were doing and wanted it sorted out on the cheap. Then they'd no doubt argue about his bill, however minuscule he made it. And why were they on Villiers Street anyway? That must be the wrong address for them, surely? A short rental, probably, for effect. He went into his bedroom and changed into his running gear. It was tow-path time.

Soon his feet were pistoning along, syncopated with his breath, the river to his right as he pounded past the boat-houses. He headed down towards the Harrods' Depository. Three miles three times a week. Every week. Otherwise he started to feel seedy. He needed to get nice and sweaty and to leak all the gunge out of himself; needed to scour out his lungs. Anyway, he enjoyed it as he hefted himself along, shouting abuse occasionally at the ragwort and the nettles, dodging the daily scatterings of dogshit. He had been built for better things than meeting Mr Dale Freeman in his offices in Villiers Street on Friday, that was for sure.

After he'd taken his degree in archaeology at Lancaster the woman at the careers advisory service had been frank. 'I imagine there may be the occasional dig here and there,' she had said doubtfully. 'Otherwise it's museums, I suppose, and there's an awfully long queue for most of those.' But Jack had wanted to write, and what's more he knew that he could. He'd already started. 'Ah, then we would usually recommend advertising,' she had said. Well, why not? At least it would take him to London. There were lots of jokes at Brewer's about his degree. 'Maybe you'll be able to tell us where they dug up the new MD.' But he worked away quietly on his book *About Time*.

When the novel was finally published, he had sent a copy to Miro Pelikan, who was filming in Provence; he could still remember the note he had received back:

> *You have written a book it is impossible to film. These are the only ones that have ever interested me. I find ways, as you must know, by leaving almost everything out. As soon as I am finished shooting here, we must meet in London.*

By then he had already been living with Philippa for years. That week he had asked her to marry him. She agreed with

9

the same patrician insouciance with which she seemed to agree to everything else, including sex. Well, come on then, she used to say, let's get on with it. No point dithering, after all. There was nothing furtive about Phil, she came from a different world entirely from his own. Jack tried to keep everything secret, even from himself. He sometimes wondered if Phil even knew what a secret was. She simply had no need of one. No need to hide, no need to apologise.

They were invited for the weekend down to her parents' house in Cornwall. He had only met Major Hubert Dawlish once before, but he still remembered clearly the tall straight figure, close-cropped grey hair, unblinking green eyes.

New Farm was perched on a hill half-way down the Helford estuary. It had been built by one of the more eccentric disciples of the Arts and Crafts Movement, Timothy Dalrymple. Somehow Norman Shaw's curving roofs and oriel windows had lost their symmetric sweetness in Dalrymple's enthusiasm to bring red bricks to the country.

New Farm had never really been much of a farm to begin with, but the sale over the years of its surrounding fields and the widening of a road along its eastern side meant that it barely even qualified as a smallholding any more. There was some poultry, and there were rows of broad-beans and lots of flowers, but mostly now there was a half-acre of well-mown grass sloping up to the house itself, which was shielded by a great copper beech that flamed into flickering amber whenever the sun arrived.

The house was briefly mentioned by Pevsner, who observed: 'An undistinguished building, a mere miscellany of nostalgic motifs, unified only by their desperation to escape modernity. It appears to have been translated from one of the drearier suburbs of London into the unlikely greenery of the west of England.'

The Major had shown this entry to Jack shortly after their arrival. 'Typical isn't it?' he had said. 'The ones who worshipped Hitler bombed our cities, and the ones we took in and sheltered go around insulting our countryside. With nice fat advances from London publishers, no doubt. I don't know what it is about Englishmen that makes us put up with all this.'

The green eyes stared at Jack and Jack had no answer to give them.

They went sailing in the twenty-five-foot yacht moored down at Mawgan. The Major pressed him gently about his skills. Jack could see the succession of disappointments in the older man's eyes as he registered that he could neither sail, nor fly, nor ride.

'Phil has a pilot's licence of course,' he said, swiftly coiling a rope on deck, 'but you'd know that.' He didn't. 'Handles a boat as well as any man. One of the best riders in her time too, even though she's sworn never to climb on another horse. Strange girl in some ways. It seems extraordinary that you didn't do *any* of these things when you were younger.'

'Well, I flew round Blackpool Tower once in a light aircraft with my father. It cost ten shillings each, I remember. And I rode the donkeys on the beach, from one pier to the next and back again. And once a year we went for a trip on the *Bridlington Belle*. Two hours on the waves. The rest of the time, back home, I rode my bike.'

The Major eyed him sceptically. 'I'd have thought you might have been better off joining the army, rather than going to university so soon.'

'You may well be right.'

On their last evening Jack had walked out into the garden with a glass of wine. Tangles of sound came from the birds in the hedgerow. The leaves of the copper beech snared the last rays of the sun. Hubert walked down the lawn towards him.

'I just wanted to say, I'm glad you're joining us.'

Jack turned and looked at him in genuine surprise. Hubert was smiling. It was as though he'd come to terms with all of Jack's deficiencies, and decided to make the best of a bad job.

'I could teach you to fly, if you liked. Never understood why Phil turned against these things. Something to do with class, probably, showing her solidarity with the needy. She read a lot of Marx at university, but then I suppose you did too. Sedition seemed to be very much the thing. She imagines we only have what we have here because I *exploited* people. Don't remember exploiting anybody. I could give you the names of quite a few people who exploited *me*. Some of them will always be needy, however much you give them. If you do want to – learn to fly, that is – then let me know. Kept my licence up to date. Phil says you never did get to Mesopotamia.'

'No,' Jack said, confused, 'unfortunately I didn't make it. Got to Israel and Turkey, but not Iraq.'

'Isn't that where most of it is though? Archaeology?'

'A lot, yes. There's a fair bit round here too, if it comes to that.'

'Not quite the same, is it? Like making do with climbing in Snowdonia, when there's the Alps and the Himalayas.'

Jack had never thought of it like that, but he took the point.

'It's just, if you liked, that could be your wedding present. A honeymoon in Iraq. Spent some time there myself. Still have one or two contacts in Baghdad. Anyway, there's time to talk about all that.' Phil was an only child, as was Jack himself, and he suddenly realised how badly the Major must have wanted a son.

'So, you plan to make your living in advertising now?'

'No,' Jack said. 'No, I plan to make my living from writing. You probably didn't know, but Miro Pelikan wants to make a film of my novel. I've already started work on the script.'

'Good man. Why doesn't Phil ever tell me any of these things? What's it about, your book?'

Jack hesitated. 'A man who wants to steal the past, I suppose. To own it, I mean, as though it were an art collection.'

'Does he succeed?'

'At a price.'

'There's always a price, Jack, I'm sure of that much. We owned half the world when I was growing up, and now we're paying for that. Through our teeth. I doubt if anyone could have done it much better, but one's not allowed to say that any more.'

Jack worked on his script throughout the preparations for their marriage, and throughout their honeymoon, which they spent in Paris rather than Mesopotamia: Phil didn't care for either the climate or the cuisine of the Middle East. She didn't mind him doing all the writing. In fact, he came to realise that she liked it. One of the things that had drawn her to him in the first place was his writing. They had met at a party at International House near Hyde Park Corner, where she worked teaching English as a foreign language. Jack had been doing some copywriting for a brochure they were preparing. Later, when they went for a drink, he had given her a copy of 'Ziggurat', the one story of his that had been published in the *London Magazine*, and the Ur-text of *About Time*. There was a social uneasiness in him that she immediately liked. It was emphasised by his working-class accent and the look of intelligent wariness forever in his eyes. He was, for her, exotic. Even mildly disreputable. A burglar in the mansion of culture, she had once said. She had been weary of her own kind for some years. They all knew one another's expectations and requirements a little too well for her taste. And she didn't like fitting in, particularly with anything her father suggested. She'd been thinking of finding work outside Britain.

The one thing she hadn't wanted was for him to be an advertising executive. It was all that dross which she had been trying to leave behind by becoming a teacher. She was prepared to marry a writer, not an adman or some promo-wallah with his head full of gizmos.

Jack worked so hard on his script for *About Time* that Brewer's sacked him. 'Fuck that lot anyway,' Phil had said cheerfully, 'you don't need them.' When it was complete, he sent the film script to Miro Pelikan. His advance from the book became his side of the deposit on a little house in Earlsfield, and he waited for Pelikan to contact him. Four months went by, then one day Jack read in the paper that

Pelikan had died. Suddenly. Unexpectedly. A heart attack in the middle of the night. The film died with him. Jack knew well enough that no one else would ever be likely to want to make it, but he tried anyway.

He had no money left. His novel, despite some sparkling reviews, didn't achieve many sales.

'So, write another, Jack,' Phil had said, bent over her preparation at the table. 'I'm earning enough to pay the mortgage. Just about, anyway. So sit down and write another. That's what writers do, isn't it? Write one book, then another.'

But he couldn't. He sat down often enough to try, but the blank paper stared him down. Somehow finishing that film script, and watching it disappear into Miro Pelikan's grave, had emptied him of any writing.

One day they were down on the Helford sitting on the Major's boat. One of his neighbours had joined them. Hubert was holding forth.

'Two months ago, Frank, I happened to be driving down through southern France. A little over the limit, I grant you, maybe even ninety, ninety-five. Something like that. One of those uniformed oafs on a motorcycle pulled me over. I was happy enough to say sorry, shake hands on it, but not a bit of it. Shouting things, throwing his hands in the air, wearing his shiny helmet and those ridiculous boots. Reminded me of nothing so much as Mussolini on his balcony. Do you remember? Could make out just the odd word from his jabber, enough anyway from my schoolboy Frog to under-stand it wasn't very pleasant. Finally I stopped him. Waved my finger in his face like this.' (The Major's hand became a metronome before them.) 'My dear fellow,' I told him, 'I wouldn't talk to me like that if I were you. I actually met de Gaulle in London during the war. You do remember *why* he was in London, do you? I think he'd probably have been the first to tell you, that if it weren't for the likes of me, you'd still be under the heel of the Hun. Bloody impertinence.'

They were all still laughing when the Major's neighbour asked Jack what he did. He was about to say he was a writer, when he suddenly understood, as though it were being etched in acid on his brain at that moment, that he was Hubert's unemployed son-in-law, being kept by his daughter. As soon as he got back to London, he started freelancing. And he had to work hard, harder than he'd ever worked at Brewer's. By that time, the only writing he did was his copy, so that he could pay his half of the mortgage. Which he did. But Phil seemed to look at him more and more as though he were a wounded veteran she'd taken on after a war; as though he were a large gesture she'd made once, then come to regret. He still wanted her, very badly sometimes, but he simply couldn't touch her. And she said nothing. She looked at him sadly and said nothing.

One night he didn't come home at all. They didn't discuss it. It became one night a week, then more often than that. Only once she said, 'Mind you don't catch anything, won't you?' He did though. The Adam and Eve Clinic in Hammersmith. So that's why they'd left Eden – looking for penicillin. But by that time they had stopped making love entirely, so he kept everything to himself. Afterwards his nights out became more frequent.

'Why don't you just bugger off completely?' Phil said to him one day. Her foul mouth was a point of honour with her, something else she could do as well as any man. He supposed that the Major had made her into the son he never had. 'It would make it easier for me when I do the shopping. I can't be doing with all this coming and going, Jack.'

So he went. For two months he vanished. When he returned, exhausted and humiliated from his escapades, they shared a bed again as though it were for the first time. She didn't say anything, but then she never had said anything. 'What do you want, Jack? Do you want me to keep telling you I love you? I'd never have taken you between my legs if I didn't. If I don't cry out, that's because of who I am. Stoic first, woman second. Remember my training. My father wouldn't even admit I was a girl until I was fifteen.' For weeks it seemed they'd finally come through. He stared at that extraordinary face with the large beak of a nose and her hacked blonde hair, tied up at the back in a couldn't-care-less straw swathe, and he wondered how he'd ever convinced himself he'd wanted anyone else. And then it all began again. He'd developed a taste for variety between the sheets, and now the taste demanded satisfaction.

'I can't stand it,' Phil said finally. 'You just can't keep your zipper fastened, can you? I had no idea you were like this.'

'I wasn't like this,' he had said.

'Oh, I see, it was me, was it? Didn't moan and groan enough when you gave me one. I've done my best at trying to love you, Jack, which might be a little harder than you think. But if I'm not enough, then go. I'm not the faithful doxy who'll sit at home knitting while you go round screwing everything that moves.'

'We'd have to sell the house,' he had said quietly. He was sick of it all too. As sick of himself as she was, but he couldn't stop himself going out there.

'So let's sell it then.'

He moved out once more, and a month later Phil phoned him to say she was pregnant. He moved back in. Their daughter was born. He tried, he really did try. Then, when Dotty was one, he started going back out to the bars and the streets where he'd gone before. When Dotty was two he moved out again, and this time he stayed out.

Now as he pumped back up through Bishop's Park he could see the bridge, and to the side of it the mansion block where he rented his basement flat, for far too much money. The mortgage and the rent between them had begun to add up to more than he was bringing in each month. For he had promised, not just Phil but himself, that she would not have to sell that little house in Earlsfield, or have to go begging to her moneyed parents. This working-class boy from Oldham would make sure his daughter was raised in that house, even if he couldn't manage to live with her mother any more. And he had kept his promise too, until now. Dotty was already ten years old. How could that be? How could a whole decade fall out of a hole in your pocket like that? It was absurd.

But this was the worst time he'd had. He was depending on Jonathan more and more. Life as a freelance copywriter seemed to get worse all the time. He had to find some money from somewhere. And that was why he would be turning up with a tie on, and a smile pasted over his face, to meet Mr Dale Freeman on Friday morning.

●

Friday 8.45 a.m. Embankment Station. He had arrived a little early so he could stand and stare over the water for a few minutes. The first film of Pelikan's he had ever seen had been *River*. As he stood there, he remembered the images of the wharves further down; he could still see those extraordinary shots of the Thames, with smoke and fog rolling over its back, as though it were a shiny and dangerous creature which men clambered over at their peril. It had been a short early film, no more than thirty minutes, and it was, like most of Pelikan's best work, in black and white. The voice-over had been written by Prévert as a long free-form poem. As the lighters and barges cruised gravely upstream and down, the words glanced away from the silver images and then settled back again to accrue about them. Jack had spent a whole weekend five years back with his new Leica, climbing up and down those wharves, trying to capture just one view of the river as Pelikan had seen and held it. But when the film was developed there was nothing. There were only clips of lifeless inconsequence frozen in time. And it wasn't the forty years between that had made the difference either, but his own eye, that stagnant pond. He began to see how, when a great director peers through a lens, he rearranges the world around it, and reality spins for a while into a different orbit to aid his little journey. But Jack was no director, though he had improved as a photographer, largely by studying the stills from Pelikan's films. Pelikan was dead though. And Jack's appointment with Dale Freeman was in three minutes' time.

He knocked on the door at nine precisely. There was a flurry inside and then the door opened. A woman of about

17

fifty stood smiling at him. At least, he took the expression to be a smile. So caked in cosmetics was her face that she could have been wearing a stoical grimace, or the melancholy resignation of a circus clown. Then came that voice. Phil had that voice too, when she was minded to use it, which was not often. As though a skilled tongue were licking ice-cream from the naked surface of your mind. Irresistible to working-class boys like himself. Once anyway. Silk sheets wrapping round your ears, like mummy cloths.

'I've come to see Dale Freeman.'

'Did you make an appointment?'

'No, he did.'

She shrugged incomprehension and indifference.

'You can come in and wait, but there's no knowing when he'll turn up.'

That make-up's surface shimmered again. It looked like desert sand with the sun's mirage behind it. Her hair was black as a crow's and gleamed with aerosol varnish.

He followed her into the office. The word office didn't somehow cover its air of slovenliness and resonant catas-trophe. It didn't look to Jack as though it had been long inhabited either, but every stainable surface had already been stained. Ash had scattered over the desk-top papers like a *memento mori*. The woman sat down again at her desk and picked up the telephone she had left off the hook.

Jack stared through the window down at the gardens and the river beyond them and listened with growing amazement to one side of whatever the conversation was.

'Yes, well I felt a little bit like that myself this morning, my darling, but you seemed very keen at the time, didn't you? Mmm, but I didn't say no, did I? In fact I have the feeling I didn't say anything at all except a long sort of dreamy sound with an O in the middle.'

Her voice was a dizzy swoop through the altitude of her vowels.

'Yes, and I hope that lotion doesn't stain because those sheets were Harrods. Mmmm thighs, I know, mmmm, I think it's called the wrestler's clinch.'

When she had finished the call she turned and blinked at him twice, like a white-faced owl sending a signal. The mascara was anthracite black and the face powder brittle snow.

'Husband?' he said, weakly, feeling called upon to say something.

'Somebody's, yes.' She was gazing at the top of his head. She pointed. 'Is that a style?' she said at last.

'No,' he said. 'That's alopecia areata. It comes and goes.'

'Is it coming at the moment then?' she said. 'Or going?'

'I'd say it's hesitating.'

'It's very . . . what's the word I'm looking for?'

'Asymmetrical?' he offered uncomfortably.

'Erratic, I suppose. It's whopsical.'

Thirty minutes later, as Jack was on the point of leaving, Dale arrived. He clattered through the door with a pile of newspapers in one arm, a cigarette in his mouth. He saw Jack and can-canned his fingers in a little wave towards him.

'You the guy from the *Evening Standard*?'

'No. I'm Jack Goodrich.'

'Jack Goodrich. Jack Goodrich. Now don't tell me. You're the man from Abbott's.'

'Brewer's,' Jack said. 'A long time ago.'

'Can't have kept you waiting so long you lost your job, surely?'

He laughed and Jack stared at him in silence. Tall, slim, immaculately turned out in his sports jacket and expensive jeans. And above it all a mop of blond curly hair that trickled across his forehead with winsome insolence and floated around his ears in a wheatfield of lavish unconcern. The hair was straight out of Botticelli, his eyes were blue, his cheekbones high. He looked as though the world was his, and he knew it. I could just leave now, Jack thought. Money, though. Money.

'Let's get started,' Dale said, pulling photographs, CDs and a video out of his drawer. 'This is what we're looking at. You interested in modern music?'

'Some of it.'

'Toni Inglish is the best, I'd say. More of a Wagner man myself, but I do see the point when they call her the female Bob Dylan. I'd never really studied her songs properly until I had this proposal.' Dale waved some papers at Jack. He could make out only the letterhead saying Toni Productions and the words *Dear Dale* . . . 'But this is serious stuff. Makes me proud in a way to be asked for my contribution. They've never really done any heavy merchandising, you see. Toni's not interested in that sort of thing. Very much the pure artist. But, frankly, these days you can't afford to play the virgin – money penetrates everybody. So my plan is to look at the whole range of possibilities. Obviously on-site sales for concerts, T-shirts, hats and so on. But I believe there's another angle. There's a big fan club for Toni, although again it's not something she spends her time on. But there's a mailing list here of over a hundred thousand worldwide. And I want to look at a direct-mail campaign.'

'Direct mail,' Jack said sadly.

'That's right and you're a bit of an expert on that, so they tell me.'

'I think you should consider an agency, you know, if you're planning on an international direct-mail campaign . . .'

'Don't like agencies, sir,' Dale said definitively. 'I'm a freelance spirit myself. Like yourself, as I've been told.'

'Maybe you should use Jonathan then,' Jack said idly.

'Who's Jonathan?'

'The man who recommended *me*.'

'Oh, *that* Jonathan. May well do. We may well do, it's been on our minds. Take this stuff away, Jack, the video, the CDs, some of this promo stuff, examples of the treatment the other stars have been getting. Have a think. Chat away to Jonathan if that's the way you guys normally work. The concert merchandising's one thing, but I do feel the heart of this may turn out to be the direct mail. An earring maybe, just a single one, the way she wears one herself. Maybe a pendant, but no medallions. No hairs on this chest. Possibly a ring. We could be looking at a half-sheet flyer, a single gate-fold, maybe even a six- or eight-page brochure. We have to think about strategies at the moment. They told us you were an ideas man, Jack. Famous for it at Abbott's . . . and the other place as well, obviously. So take it all away, and have a little ponder. We're probably talking big bills here, if we can pull it in the right direction. There'll be enough to interest all of us. Phone me next week, after you've had time to brainstorm and . . . whatnot.'

Jack left and Dale Freeman asked his assistant, Marilyn, to get the bank manager on the line for him. She was pressing the return button on her computer with metronomic regularity and increasing irritation.

'Are you sure?' she said.

'I'm sure,' Dale Freeman said, turning the pages of the newspaper and lighting another cigarette. 'He's going to have to talk to me sooner or later.'

•

That Saturday Jack did not, as usual, collect his daughter from Earlsfield to take her out for the day. She was doing something with her friends. 'We could go somewhere on Sunday instead,' he had said.

'No, Jeremy's taking us to Chessington tomorrow.' Jeremy. Then Phil came back on the line.

'The cheque doesn't seem to have come through yet this week,' she said. 'Why can't you just make out a standing order, Jack? It's only eight years now I've been asking you.'

'Sorry. Slight problem at the bank. Don't worry, I'm sorting it out. Who's Jeremy, by the way?'

'We're going to have to have a talk, Jack. Soon.'

That afternoon he climbed into his running gear again and set off down the tow-path. Jeremy. Going with his daughter to Chessington. Dotty looked startlingly like Phil. He could never look at her without thinking of her mother. What was it that had driven him out, all those years back? He had never worked it through, not even in his own head. He had undergone two month's unsuccessful therapy, and the therapist had become intrigued by the physical characteristics of the women he slept with.

'What is interesting is that none of them are ever like your wife,' she had said.

'Maybe I felt like a change.'

'A lot of changes. But most men prefer a particular physical type, and you have yourself confirmed that small blondes like your wife were the ones that most excited you. So why all these brunettes? And tall women with red hair? And small women with black hair and big breasts, when you really prefer small women with blonde hair and small breasts?'

She drove relentlessly on to the conclusion that all his one-night stands with women who were not his physical type amounted to a plea to Phil to do the one thing he didn't believe she had ever done: love him. 'Why are you still married?' she had said. 'You've not lived with your wife for years and yet you've not divorced her. Perhaps you've been waiting for her to beg you to come back. To say you're the greatest lover in the world. Instead of saying, what was it you told me she used to say after passionate coitus?'

'I'm completely knackered now,' Jack said quietly.

'Maybe being married to her gives you the guarantee you need that you won't have to marry any of the others.'

That therapist had irritated him – she seemed so sure of herself. Anyway at twenty pounds a session three times a week, he couldn't afford it. So now he ran instead.

Once when Dotty was sick he had stayed at Earlsfield overnight. He had crept in at midnight. Phil's bedroom was filled with her smells, a great crowd of mingled perfume smells, her clothes strewn about everywhere. He'd forgotten what a rip inside himself that craving for her could be.

'Not now, Jack,' she had said. 'Not *now* for Christ's sake.'

Back in the shower he scrubbed and rubbed but kept his head well clear of the thrashing water, until finally he thought, 'Ah, why bother?' and let the hot stream drill into his scalp too. Afterwards, all dried out and with a whisky in his hand, he took the comb and stared at his head in the mirror. It seemed to be shifting to Mohican mode – there was a reasonable brush of brown tangle down the middle of his head, but riddled, patchy baldness on either side. More gently than a mother takes the tweezers to a child's splinter, he inserted the teeth of the comb into the cratered field of his head. Hair came away with each finessing sweep. Ah, dear God, he thought to himself, if it goes on like this I'm going to have to get a night job. As a solitary watchman. In a coalmine.

He walked into the other room, picked up *About Time* from the table and opened it at random.

> *The first time the nature of his powers had focused was when Ashley Simon had held the flint in that museum on the school trip so many years before. Suddenly his hand was of immense power, describing the terror of an elliptic arc through air over so many thousands of years, and as the deer's skull shattered underneath his blow and blood leaked into the silk cape of his fingers, he had passed out.*
>
> *Hallucinations, the psychologist explained. An acute neurotic disturbance leading to hallucinations. But the woman had no real interest in their truth or their power, these hallucinations, or why they had ever been bestowed upon him. If what we hallucinate actually happened, or will come to happen, then what comfort can be found in those clinical syllables? Whoever can travel in time has few companions.*
>
> *One day he saw angry light blazing around the hands of the school secretary. He hadn't understood until he heard the headmaster call out to her to get someone on the phone for him. Her hands flared with the numbers he didn't dial for himself, alight with that network of his hated communications. By the time he came out of the office again, the quiver and lick of the flames had ceased; there was now merely a dull and leaden apparition, a halo with all the electricity rotted. But what a voltage of hate lay in those fingers.*
>
> *He didn't talk about it any more. He watched uncomprehending as his own powers grew. At university he spent a month inside Freud's mind but found his greybeard science as clipped and diagnostic as the old man's features, staring out of those pictures on the covers of books. There he sat in Berggasse 19 in Vienna surrounded by the emblems of the psychic past of man. Roman and Greek gods mingled in therapeutic silence with Egyptian falcon-headed deities and*

*Etruscan warriors. But Ashley gazed at the photographs
and saw more power emanating from the heads of the gods
than from their tight-faced interpreter. The only thing he had
in common with Freud was a gift for mesmerism.*

*Once he had risked speculations on such things, though
without saying that he himself had any such powers, with his
favourite professor, an antiquarian and a bibliophile whom the
other students found tiresome and mildly crazed. The
following day two books were dropped on to his table in the
library without comment. They were* Manual of Psychometry
*by Professor James Rhodes Buchanan and* Nature's Secrets
*by William Denton.*

*Both of these books were more than a hundred years old,
and as Ashley turned their pages he felt that someone had at
least tried to describe what he knew to be true inside him, for
both these men had explained how experience encodes itself
in the inanimate. Not everyone can read the runes, but for
those who can there is no amnesia in the rocks, no silence in
the sands, no oblivion among mountains. All objects speak
more vividly, with more carnival exuberance, of time's shapes
pressed into them than any but the most articulate of men.*

*Ashley lifted up the effigy of Ishtar and pressed it gently to
his head. He could hear the wailing of women, feel that hot
and fetid darkness tightening about him, hear the priest's
invocations from the top of the ziggurat, and sense the death
of the man the knife was angled over. He shuddered with the
orgasm of fear as the blade cut through his belly and tore
down without swerving into his genitals. Ishtar was never far
from death, she thrived on it, it was her element. One of
them anyway.*

*He put the little statue back in place between the miniature
pyramid and the stone-cold egg. Once on an icy scree in Scotland
he had laid a hand on the rubble beneath him and suddenly
everything was blank, a white-out had screened history entirely
from the picture. Man was gone, all except for the one intruder.
Beneath him, alertness accruing to chronology in its massive
shoulders, a mammoth started its thunderous trundle towards
his bivouac. He could still feel the ice age of that desolation,
he carried it about with him, dangling like a phylactery which
contained his sacred texts, all his echoing devotions. What
would be would be.*

24

Yes, what would be would be. He closed that book of his. He picked up the card from Harry Trench again. Must meet urgently to talk about your novel, *About Time*. And the film Miro Pelikan wanted to make of it. He felt the panic of hope inside him. He tried to steer clear of hope these days for it confused him. There wasn't even any point in his going out, he told himself; he told himself this once a month, though. The last time he had danced, a few weeks ago, fleece from his shifting tonsure actually fell on to his face, trickling down his nose. He looked at that statue of Ishtar on the front cover of *About Time*, and at the round-faced owls, bleak with wonder, gazing out from among the lions. Anyway, the diseases were growing stronger every year and seemed less and less baffled by science. In time viruses would inherit the earth. Have one night of pleasure, even one hour, ten minutes, and your flesh could wither on the bone, like a dying tree. He had had enough of it: it was time to stop. What a world his daughter had been born into. He was receiving the tonsure, so he might as well become a monk. And in any case, what would be would be.

He would watch that video of Toni Inglish, though it was the last thing he felt like doing. Money, though.

One minute into the video, Jack couldn't understand how he'd managed to miss her. This one was real. Because he so avoided the babble of the rock rigmarole these days, he had let something of genuine importance pass him by.

She was not tall, dressed entirely in black, and with her blonde hair shaved. What was that? Gulag chic? Death-camp kitsch? Joan of Arc before the immolation? She sat down at the piano and started singing. And as she sang, he saw the small tattoo of a phoenix in flames on her neck, in among the thread of her veins. She played the song solo, with her own spare accompaniment. It was her reprise of the life and music of Roy Orbison:

It's six in the evening
Grey cloud and raining
And I've just remembered how long you've been gone

So I walk to the juke-box
To dial up a memory
I press a few buttons
To hear a few songs
And as I stand black-shawled
Naked as mirrors
His voice sails across like a bird through the smoke
Singing it's over and love's gone for ever
That love is the darkest of all the dark jokes

Your baby doesn't love you any more

The zoom kept probing her. Black dress. Black stockings. Black shoes. This stage was a hospital ward. Terminal. Then in a frenzy she was hammering the keys. The only moment of fullness in her half-anorexic body was her breasts. No one was being invited in, though. No gentlemen callers looked welcome. The skin on her face tightened to pale junkie parchment each time she sang. Then it was over, as cleanly and unobtrusively as it began. She stood up from the grand and bowed slightly. Her voice had been ice and warmth at once, early June in late December. The video was about to show her next number with the band, but Jack switched it off. He simply didn't want to hear any more now. He went over and picked up his guitar. He found the song's sequence of changes, but there had been some especial exacerbation there, some conflict she'd found between note and note, chord and chord. The song's curious electricity rasped and crackled between A minor and E minor, shifting through variants of C and F major as it ran its troubled course. He put the instrument down again. And he knew that he couldn't stay inside alone that Saturday night: it wasn't a good feeling.

He went on the underground.

He'd read an announcement about the Caine Mutiny – it was Dave David's latest venture.

The place had only been open for a week, but it was full enough by the time he entered. There were enormous pictures of Bogart from the movie, clicking the ball-bearings in

26

his hand and sweating paranoid fear. Behind the bar stood four men wearing Bogart hats. Two large video screens at each end showed the film itself, but out of sync with each other, and with the sound turned off. The sound was the latest studio-enhanced lament from Swarm about the brevity of love. And echoing about were the fashionable creatures of London, colliding happily into one another's bodies.

One of the aggressively cheerful barmen poured him a glass of white wine and he climbed on to a stool. Another five minutes passed before Dave David made an appearance behind his own bar. At six-foot five in his freshly pressed pink and white shirt, he stood there smiling. He had a way of nodding his head gently all the time, as though quietly agreeing with himself about everything. His dark brown hair was shaped expensively to his head. His large hazel eyes darted about the place, with the intentness of an eagle on its ledge.

Dave had made himself famous years before with his Goliath clothes shops in Kensington and Chelsea. They were reported on and gossiped about as much for the illicit goings on in the dressing-rooms as for the cut-price *avant-garde* of the rags. Dave was photographed drinking champagne from the bottle in the back of his Rolls, taking his clothes off with Suzie Bobtail, the singer he twice married and twice divorced, and diving into Salvador Dali's swimming pool while the Spaniard held aloft a live lobster. For a while the press loved him, then they lost interest, and the banks started to have their doubts too. Dave made a lot of money, but he spent even more and finally went belly up. Now he had opened his bar and his special number for an hour each evening was to insult any candidate who came within shouting range. The punters loved it.

Jack had been staring with growing confusion at the décor. What had at first seemed to him some unfortunate stains on a part of one wall he now realised was a global decoration scheme. The stains were everywhere. Then he heard Dave explaining to one of his boys behind the bar.

'So I told the interior designer, I want blotches over each

wall the colour of vomit. Could you give me a pantone colour for that, she said. I said, I'll give you a sample, darling, if you don't agree to reduce that estimate.'

Dave still kept enough of his East End accent to preserve an air of entertaining menace. He seemed to hear everything being said all along the bar, even through the murk and blather of the music. One of those tall wide-boned boys, whose bodies look designed to fit into officer's uniform, was trying to win the interest of the woman sitting next to Jack. The boy wonder didn't, however, seem to be having much success.

'The name's Chris,' he was saying in the cultured yawn that had become the fashion. He flicked back the golden spray that lay across his forehead. 'Chris. With two s's actually.'

Suddenly Dave swooped on him.

'Chris with two s's,' he yelled. 'What like piss? Well what are you going to buy the young lady to drink then, Chrissssssssss?'

The audience was shouting approval and the lady in question rocked back and forth with the cigarette between her lips. Long thin black-stockinged legs. Black patent high-strapped shoes. A leather skirt with no interest in making it far down her legs. Chris(s) had fallen silent. After a few minutes he left. Obviously a rookie.

'Stupid git,' Dave said, grinning at his boys. 'Trying to pick women up by telling them there's two s's in his name. I've got two v's and three d's in my name but it doesn't mean I've got VD two and a half times over, does it?'

'Have you, Dave?' one of his boys shouted.

'Haven't looked today,' Dave shouted back.

Suddenly over the sound-system as Swarm faded out, she was there again. He was listening to Toni Inglish, her voice playing at being a whore over some major seventh chords.

I'm streetwise and sassy
Blissed out and hip
Dangled and chained down and frilled

28

> Marilyn, quarrelin'
> Black-stocking thighs
> Sex caviar champagne chilled
> I'm that once in a lifetime
> Magical night.
> And I'm everything which your own wife's not quite

'That's Toni Inglish, isn't it?' he said, to the lanky elegant woman next to him, but Dave was on to it.

'The sphinx speaks,' he said, bobbing his head before Jack. 'Yes, that's Toni all right. Know her, do you?'

'It's just that I'm doing some work for her at the moment . . .' His voice petered out as he realised the absurdity of the claim.

'They all are, mate, believe me. All the boys who come in here are doing a job for Toni and all the girls are doing a job for Swarm. Your secret's safe with me, squire. Nod's as good as a wink for yours truly.'

He was off again down the bar and the music continued. Jack couldn't stop listening to it, despite the giggles of the barmen.

> Desperate eyes promise perfume and sighs
> Erotica shades in the snow
> Men's dirty lies and those endless black skies
> And streets filled with users and losers below

The hopelessness in that voice was real. What am I doing here? Jack thought. I'm too old for this – I've been too old for this for a long time. The stool was high and Jack came down from it with a greater clatter than he had expected. His head jerked forward over the bar. The woman next to him cried out in a long tortured wail, 'DAAAAVE!'

Dave David danced swiftly back down the bar.

'What's the matter, darling?'

'His fucking hair's gone in my Bolly.'

Dave peered into her glass. It was true that a few of Jack's hairs, with startling precision, had left his head and landed in her champagne. All three looked at them floating there sadly in the fizz, like unwanted guests at a party.

'What you need is this, Charmaine,' Dave said removing her glass and filling another one with Bollinger. 'And you, sir,' he said to Jack who was already fighting his way out, 'need one of these.' He held aloft the hat he had lifted from the head of one of his barmen. It took too long for Jack to make his way through all those people to the door, and that song kept floating over him as he pressed and pushed.

Over an hour's walk back to Putney, but he didn't feel like taking the underground or using a bus. When he arrived at the flat, he walked over to the table and picked up the photograph of Phil and Dotty. Cars were streaming by outside, their motors blurring into a foggy hum of sound. Small groups were leaving the Star and Garter, throwing jagged edges of laughter across the street, like glasses they were finished with. Then he put the photograph back in its place, between the pyramid, the marble egg and the tiny figurine of Ishtar.

•

Now that she was sure Dotty was asleep, Phil slipped into the bedroom and changed. She took off everything and put on her white silk shift. The tips of her breasts were clearly visible. The shift only just reached the top of her thighs. Then she went back down to him. He looked, and then he looked again.

'Lovely,' he said, 'your daughter. She's lovely.'

'Yes.' He peered down into the oily reflections in his cognac, but she knew the hands in his mind were full of silk. She knew that he could still see the white milk of that shift flowing over her breasts, whether he looked or whether he didn't.

She walked across and took the glass from his hands.

She raised one leg until it pointed to the ceiling-rose around the light-fitting. And then she raised the other. She whispered with an urgency she didn't feel, Finish it, it's time now. She used to say that to Jack. Sorry if I've kept you up, he had muttered once. They didn't understand how women connected when they needed to, connected to the small manic rages of men's passion or, more importantly, to the limestone riddle of their own need. A cavern measureless to man. All women were that, even the ones who lied through their smiles and their moans.

Halted finally, he lay there hot and seamed inside himself. She went into the bathroom and turned on both gold-gleaming taps. A gush of water and a cloud of steam. She tugged the shift off and looked in the full-length mirror as it began to fog. God, you are so beautiful. Never seen anything so. Been with many women in my life, Phil, but I must tell. Oh my darling. All their voices, all their pleading self-interested voices, Jack's among them, though she didn't know why, because he'd never said anything at all, crawling one over the other like a cold wet knot of worms when you heave up the big stone. Which one of you is going to be the silver at the back of my mirror? Or is there no shape at all to the time of your life?

She lay in the water and ran her finger up and down herself. She laid her palm flat on her belly and kept it there.

Jeremy then. Jeremy who was five years her junior. Who had been married once before. To June, whom he took on knowing she had breast cancer. June, who had had one breast removed by the time they had been wed for nine months, and the other one a year later. June, whose chemotherapy made her lose all her hair, from her head and between her legs, even the little wisps on her upper lip. The chemo-therapy, one of whose side-effects was to make her sweat, particularly at night, producing a permanent acrid smell about her. This was unusual but not unknown. He had found this hard. He also found it hard when, sometimes in the night, he reached out for the traces of her breasts, and found only stitches, small wounds, little troubled mounds. Earthworks above a burial. He found it even harder when she would sob slowly, fearful at his disappointment, turning away from him into the darkness on the far side of the mattress. Jeremy, who when his wife died at the age of twenty-nine, soldiered on for six months (they all admired him for it, women offered, but he always refused) and then collapsed. Lying in his bed at night weeping, the sheets sometimes soaked with urine when he awoke. Incapable of going out for days at a time. Walking into shops, then leaving, unable to ask for whatever it was he needed, or even to remember what it was he had needed. Who would suddenly be disgusted by a terrible smell, then realise it was coming from inside his own clothes. Staring through the window of the flat they had bought in Barnes as the boats oared up and down on the tide. Unreal. Ghosts jammed in the hull. Shouts from nowhere to no one. Jeremy. Who had then risen from his bed, opened a photocopying shop in Sheen, another in Putney, one in Fulham and now a fourth in South Kensington, and who drove a Jaguar XJS (that, at least, would definitely have to go, she thought). Who at thirty-five was dark-haired, handsome in a plump sort of way, besuited, solicitous, proper, and desperate for a new wife who didn't simply die on him. Desperate for a bed full of life. Whose chin was a shiny blue acetate where the razor made its daily scrape. Striped shirts. Silk ties. Copies of *Country Life*, to plan the future. Jeremy, who adored Dot, and whom Dot would get to like more and more. Whose propriety made him unerotic, but he wasn't to know that. So terribly ready to please. He wasn't demented like Jack, hammering half-hatefully at sex as though lost in a tunnel he was trying to drill his way out of. Thank God for that anyway, she supposed. One Jack had to be enough for any lifetime. But she was going to have to concentrate on finding Jeremy in bed. Or helping him find himself, assuming she could maintain her interest in the project long enough. He talked to her there, pleaded, cajoled and whimpered, as though she were a new client. As though he were a doctor and she needed curing. And maybe he was. Maybe she did. She couldn't remember what her life had been like before the plague called Jack Goodrich had arrived in it. Maybe Jeremy had come to remind her. Was that possible? It was about time.

When she went into the bedroom again, he was lying there on his back looking at the ceiling.

'Can I stay the night this time?'

'If you want to start staying the night, you'll have to make an honest woman of me.'

He leaned up on to one arm and looked across at her, confused.

'You said you'd never divorce him. For Dotty's sake.'

'Maybe I've changed my mind.' Jeremy. Could she only go to bed with men whose names started with a J?

'You'll marry me then?'

'Aren't you supposed to gaze into the limpid pools of my eyes while you say that?'

'You'll marry me?'

'Yes, I'll marry you, but right now I'm completely knackered, so roll over, will you, and let me get some bloody sleep.'

•

Jack woke in the morning and counted the hairs on the pillow. Thirteen. He got up immediately and walked into the bathroom. He stared at himself in the mirror. He didn't look past himself or behind himself. He didn't half-close both eyes, or concentrate on the area below the bridge of his nose. He stared hard at the mangy pelt of his head. A lawn in a drought. A rug worn thin from too many feet. He took a deep breath and he started.

It was only stubble over half of his scalp, but it was hard all the same to razor it away. He kept stopping and drenching his head with hot water and lather, then he would begin again, edging into the tuft and bramble with his sharp steel blade. It came away, some as though it was glad to go, some as though it was rooted through to his brain. But, sector by sector, he sheared his head. At the end it was pink from the surprise of it and cut flowingly in three places. He rummaged in the mirrored cupboard and found some Elastoplasts. And there he was. Done. And he felt better, felt as though he'd met some commitment, entered finally the little monastery of himself.

Dale Freeman was jammed into the underground carriage, grimly clutching his newspaper. He stared at the picture on the front of it, but found it impossible to take in any of the words. Hisses and whimpers were leaking from the headphones framing the skull next to him. The head jabbed forward intermittently, like a bird's when it beaks away an intruder. Too many people, too little space. Blessedly, the carriage half-emptied at Holborn. He was about to start reading when he saw the ragged figure jump aboard. The man immediately began hammering his guitar with frenzied ineptitude and wailing how the summertime was coming and the leaves were sweetly blooming. Neither of these statements was any truer than it was tuneful. The autumn was coming and the leaves had started dying. Seventy feet underground at the start of a London morning, what difference did it make to anyone anyway?

Twenty minutes later an interested pigeon could have looked through the second floor of a building at the end of Hatton Garden and seen, through the grey-tinted glass, Dale Freeman hold up in triumph his document from Toni Productions and smile his way through his pitch. The pigeon would have seen the smile of the first ten minutes start to tighten, and the gestures of the arms grow a trifle angular, as Dale engaged a more combative tone. After a while the document from TP was actually being brandished at head height, as though one side in a conflict were giving an ultimatum to the other. Had the pigeon sat out the entire thirty-minute session, it could have observed Dale Freeman rise finally from his chair and spit out what looked like words of contempt to the three motionless gentlemen he had been addressing, before finally walking from the room with some vigour.

Outside, Dale took the mobile out of his case and hammered a number into it.

'Ferdie? No go with them either. Spineless sods. Where can I meet you? *Where?* You're paying then.'

From the pavement outside the Savoy, the scene was clearly visible. The older man rose from his seat and embraced Dale Freeman warmly, took him in his arms, as a father might his son after a long absence. Embracing the prodigal again.

As the waiter arrived with a pot of coffee, he could hear the end of Ferdie Lockyard's story.

'In that bloody great house that Dick's got on the outskirts of Jo'burg, they'd converted a room for the *au pair*, a little Dutch piece called Nina. Anyway, on the night of the party, there's suddenly this scream. We all go rushing in, and there's Rob Pickard stark naked in the *au pair*'s bed. Pissed as arseholes and fast asleep.

' "Why didn't you scream when he first got in?" says Dick's wife.

' "Well, at first I thought it was just Dick again," she says. Christ man, he'll still trying to straighten that one out, I can tell you.'

Dale laughed – too loudly. He'd heard the story before. He leaned forward.

'I've got to get some serious money, Ferdie.'

The older man shook his head.

'I went down fifty grand when Tempus corked, remember. God alone knows what's going on in the dear old S of A at the moment. First time in our life the Mint's not had an issue to do.'

'You haven't done great Jewish dentists yet,' Dale said quietly.

'Well, it would stand a better chance than a commemorative medal of Mandela for the townships, wouldn't it? Not much point looking at *those* customer profiles.'

'Toni English, Ferdie. It could be the biggest thing any of us have ever known. I admit I made a mistake with *The History of Time*.'

'A big one. I'm still filling the hole that mistake made.'

'It *should* have worked. I mean, if the distribution . . .'

'Freelands Marketing?'

'Separate limited company.'

'Thank God for limited liability, eh Dale? What's the deal with Tempus now?'

'Technically solvent.'

'Technically?'

'Let's say we had a friendly audit.'

'Charles?'

'Charles. Since the part-work can no longer be sold through anyone else's retail outlets, we reclassified it as material that we are planning on retailing through our own outlets. Which are being negotiated.'

'Reclassified at the full retail price?'

'Exactly, so all that material constitutes quite an asset. On the books.'

'Not for long.'

'Long enough for me to sort things out.'

'What about the debts?'

'The biggest ones were incurred abroad. All the printing was done in Thailand.'

'Long way for the arm of the average debt collector to reach.'

'Exactly.'

'So, your company doesn't have to go into liquidation then, it just has a little cash-flow problem.'

'Couldn't have put it better myself.'

'Still not going to help me get my money back, is it?'

'Toni Inglish will get all our money back.'

'Can't do it, Dale. My partners wouldn't wear it. Old times notwithstanding.'

'I can at least use Tim Tasker for some designs and prototypes?'

'How were you planning on paying him, out of interest?'

'From the proceeds, when they start coming in. And I'd thought of approaching Dell's for some printing.'

'I'm not giving out any guarantees on you, Dale.'

'But I can you use you as a reference, can't I? Come on, Ferdie, for fuck's sake, your oldest friend's son is going down the hole, and you won't even give me a trade reference.'

'All right. A reference to each of them, if they ask. A

slightly cagey reference. But no guarantees. I'm just not sure I can afford you any more, Dale. I'm not sure you inherited your father's luck. How's your mother, by the way?'

'My stepmother, if you don't mind. Seems to shed two years for every one I put on. She's beautiful, serene, elegant, Parisian. And making damn sure no one else can get near the art collection.'

'There's no deal?'

'No. Miserable bitch. She's hanging on to the whole lot. Under French law, we can't touch her. Only hope she gave my old man something of what he wanted before he went up in smoke.'

'As I remember it, she did,' Ferdie said dreamily, smiling again finally. 'She had your old man in flames long before he ever arrived at the crematorium.'

●

Jonathan Hamble stood in the middle of his cellar and looked at the black marks charcoaled on to vast white sheets about him. These new ones were all of Mark, whose aptitude for gymnastic contortion permitted a snake-like fluency of pose. He had shifted him over from front to back, from top to bottom and vice versa, forced him to topple though the orbiting omega squat of himself. In one he stared down at the tail of his unquiet being as it started rising, as though he would like to swallow it whole and complete the circle. Minotaur, hovering over the crouch of his sex, trapped in the labyrinth of his own confusion. The telephone rang.

'Can I come across and talk to you?'

'I've a lot on, Jack.'

'This one's interesting. Honestly. You've got to have a look. It would only take ten minutes.'

Jonathan had only just emerged from his cellar when Jack arrived. He was handed the video. 'Let's watch this together.'

They sat in front of the screen as Toni English leaned over her Martin and sang.

Through sad London windows
I see the moon glow
Like a sad poet did
Two hundred years ago
All will be new
When springtime comes through
So why can't my heart just be still?

By now the fiddle and accordion had joined in, but it was impossible to focus on anything except the pallor of Toni's features.

'She's there, isn't she?' Jonathan said after a few minutes.

'Oh, she's there, all right. What is it, do you think?'

'The glamour of death, I suppose. What's she on?'

'Everything, if you believe what gets written. It's mostly gossip and rumour but if you can drink it, swallow it, shoot it up or even have it administered by the district nurse, she's on it. Every so often she goes to some clinic to detox. Usually lets herself out before her time's up and settles down to some serious retoxing. Amazing gifts, though.'

'She writes all the material?'

'All of it. Words, music. Plays piano and guitar. Even plays a penny whistle on one of them.'

'So what's your Mr Freeman's number on all this?'

'Can't understand where he comes in at all. I'd have thought it would all be bigger. Couldn't D and B him, could you?'

'You're going to pay for it are you?'

'You could take it out of the next job.'

Jonathan took the card from Jack and faxed through the request. Twenty minutes later, the reply came back that no returns had been made at Companies House: Freelands Marketing had existed for two years, but no information was yet available as to its financial standing, turnover or credit rating.

'So how do they get into Toni Inglish?'

'Maybe she has a soft spot for him.'

'No. I would have said that Dale Freeman was definitely not Toni Inglish's type. He's too pretty altogether.'

'Maybe he supplies her with dope.'

'That would be more likely. But I don't think Freeman's *quite* that bent.'

'How bent is he then?'

'Don't know. The whole thing could fall apart, couldn't it?'

'Could do. Or the millions could be rolling in. Hard to say, isn't it? As per usual in our business.'

'Would you work on it with me?'

'Not really my line, you know, Jack. Pendants. Earrings.'

'That's why they'd want us. No agency overheads. They might be talking about big money, but they don't have it now, I'll tell you that. Those offices have only been rented recently. They've got one woman in there and she seems to spend most of her time offering a telephone pornography service.'

'I'm not doing months of work on credit.'

'But you'll look at it?'

'I'll look at looking at it. What have you got?'

'See her throat? Look, that tattoo.'

'Nice touch.'

'Well, that's it. The phoenix. That's the theme. Happens to be the title of her first and most famous album too. Have cut-aways of her head from below in little cameos. Show the phoenix, her neck, or the side of her head all shaved like that. But don't portray her on the product at all. Use the phoenix as the motif on all the jewellery and clothes. She *is* the phoenix.'

Jonathan looked at him and smiled.

'You should have shaved it all off before,' he said, tapping him gently on his raw scalp. 'If you'd stayed at Brewer's, you'd probably own the place by now. It looks good by the way. Looked like a squirrel's nest before. Now it looks . . . coherent.'

'I thought, if she can do it, why can't I?'

Jonathan worked all that day on some drawings. The shaved head and the phoenix on the neck: he liked them. He kept watching the video. He liked her too. She was real. So much of his work was concerned with unreality. He had only that week completed a new set of designs for a fragrance Bizarre would be launching for the spring market, and that was enough unreality for a while. After twenty minutes he forgot he was working and simply drew. It still happened, now and then.

They turned up on Wednesday at Villiers Street. This time Dale was there when they arrived. They positioned the mood-boards and some of Jonathan's drawings around the room. He had captured something: the black and white austerity of her appearance, the sense of keening grief that characterised so much of what she sang. And the phoenix. Everywhere the phoenix. Jack read out his copy. At the end Dale started clapping, leaning back in his chair.

'Brilliant. Absolutely brilliant. And the phoenix is perfect, we could go logotypical throughout on that one. There you are, told you we didn't need an agency.'

'So we've been taken on then, have we?' Jonathan asked briskly.

'Definitely, John. The winning team.'

'Jonathan.'

'Sorry?'

'The name – it's Jonathan.'

'Suit yourself.'

'Can we just talk briefly about billing?'

'Don't see why not.'

'I normally bill on a monthly basis. Jack comes in as part of my billing. Any problem with that?'

'None at all. Why should there be?'

'Fine. So what's the next stage?'

'I've got to see my designer and production people, and go and thrash out a few quotes with my printer, then I can get you properly started. Give me a week at the most.'

Outside the building Jonathan and Jack looked at each other.

'Well?'

Jonathan shrugged. 'Search me, Jack, can't work it out at

all. Anyway, we've come this far. Might as well do him a month's worth.'

●

The next morning Dale Freeman swung into the cobbled courtyard and climbed out of his TVR. He levered the knocker on the old coach-house door. A black lion's head. Little waves of mane. There was a series of shouts from inside and then the door opened. She stood there before him, her face enshrined in a look of undisguised hostility. She was sacked in what had once been a floral dress. Primavera after an apocalyptic meal. The dress had all been smeared with something white, flour or clay. There was a crow's nest of brown hair no comb would dare to break its teeth interfering with. And on her unstockinged feet a pair of authentically ill-cut homemade leather sandals. Dale was silent for a moment as he took her in. His marketing mind was impressed by the power of the image. This was wholemeal woman. Before him stood the summer solstice, the ritual circuiting of Glastonbury Tor, nature's first rough stab at a goddess of fecundity.

'Yes?' she said for the second time, a little louder now.

'Yes,' Dale echoed finally. 'I've come to see Tim Tasker. Would you be Mrs Tasker?'

'My name's Fielding,' she said. 'Sally Fielding.'

'Sorry, I thought you might be Tim's wife.'

'I didn't say I wasn't Tim's wife. What I said was, my name's Sally Fielding.'

It struck Dale that he'd probably entered the danger area of patriarchal assumption. He slipped through neutral to reverse as swiftly as he could.

'Is it possible to see Tim Tasker?' he said and smiled. The smile was not returned.

'Come in.' He followed as she stepped through the debris of what he supposed must be the kitchen. She stood at the top of the stairs and shouted 'Tim!' Then with an even more heroic bellow, 'TIM!'

'Coming,' replied a lugubrious voice from downstairs. It

was a deep voice, a true cellar of a voice. She was gone. Tim emerged finally. He was taller than Dale, and thin, in what had once been a white T-shirt. An enormous black beard sprouted from his bony face.

'Tim? Tim Tasker?'

'Yes.'

'Dale Freeman. We share a colleague in Ferdie Lockyard.'

'Yes. You need some designs done and some prototypes made.'

'Exactly. Though the design work has already been partially done by my creative team. What do you think of these?' Dale took out Jonathan's drawings.

'Let's go down into the workshop.'

They went down wooden steps into what Dale supposed had once been the ostler's cellar. Shrivelling pale rubber casts were strewn everywhere. Patina powders tumbled out of dirty cups like dead volcanoes. In the corner white paint had spewed out of a tin and been left to harden. On the shelves, in no sort of order, were the repro effigies. Rodin's thinker, Degas's little dancer, busts of Churchill, a whole galaxy of thick creamy disks that looked like medieval seals.

'Slightly chaotic,' Tim said, without apology.

'Nature of the trade I suppose,' Dale said with a collateral smile. One professional to another. 'Doing a lot of repro work, I see.'

'Yes, well it pays the rent,' Tim said grimly. 'Hardly why I spent those years studying as a goldsmith though.'

'This project should let you spread your wings a bit. What do you think?'

'The phoenix is interesting. Blue wings. Red flames. Could be enamel. I could use turquoise and a substitute ruby for your prototypes. Production's obviously a different matter. So you have a pendant, a ring, an earring, and a brooch.'

'That's what my creatives have come up with at the moment, Tim. Toni herself might have some input. And of course anything you yourself might want to originate could end up in the production brief as well.'

The telephone rang.

'I suppose I could start on it this week. I hope you don't mind me raising it, but . . .'

'Billing,' Dale said merrily. The telephone continued ringing. 'No, I like to have these things clarified myself at the outset. Saves quarrels later, I always say. I'd expect a standard monthly invoice for work completed from you. That fair enough?'

'I suppose.'

'Any worries, contact Ferdie. He'll stand for me.' The telephone still rang.

'I see.' The look in Tim's eyes suggested to Dale that he had grown used to not being paid. 'I've done a lot of work for the Union Mint over the years, of course. Ferdie always found my quality was higher than anything he could ever get over there.'

The phone drilled on and Dale saw with relief that Tim needed to do this work as badly as he needed him to do it. He droned on out of the sepulchral depth of his chest, low and husky. She had appeared at the top of the stairs and was staring down at them both with a look of massive incredulity. Tim had his back turned to her as he hung on Dale's every word. Dale pointed tentatively over his shoulder, as one might tactfully observe the return of a long-gone parrot to a distracted pirate. Tim turned his sad face round. Her voice now achieved a level not reached before. Each ring of the phone seemed to increase its volume.

'Did you hear the telephone?'

'Yes, Sally, I heard it.'

'Then why didn't you ANSWER THE FUCKING THING?'

The phone stopped ringing. She turned and trundled off. 'Good God All-Fucking Mighty,' they heard her muse as she receded. Tim's expression had not shifted, not even by a fraction, and he now redirected his fixed melancholy features to Dale's face.

'Not married long,' Tim said at last.

'Yes, those are magic moments aren't they? Well, I'd best

be getting back I suppose. When do you think you'll have something for us?'

'A week perhaps. I'll do some models, so you can get the feel.'

'There's my card, Tim. A lot of people in London are going to be waiting to see what you come up with here.'

Outside in the courtyard he lowered the hood on his car. It was warm enough now for an open drive.

'Nice car,' Tim said, in what seemed to Dale a tone of outright criticism.

'Yes, isn't it? That your stripy job over there?' Dale nodded in the direction of the blue and white Deux Chevaux, with the removable tarpaulin roof.

'Yes. Good old workhorse. Everything *we* need anyway. No need to impress anyone.'

'Your place is it?' Tim asked, nodding towards the coach-house.

'Belongs to Sally's parents actually. Peppercorn rent. Let's us get on with things.'

'Got the picture. Good. Right then, Tim. Over to you.'

He turned the car into the lane outside and blipped the throttle. Each to his own, he thought. Certainly wouldn't do for us all to be alike.

Ferdie was feeble. He'd lost his balls. He could still remember hearing the two of them, Ferdie and his father, going on about how they launched Kleiber Publishing, and how they'd have gone down for half a million if it hadn't all come off. Now he was whingeing about a measly fifty grand. *The History of Time* had been a good enough idea. A part-work series of fifty issues, to go out weekly over a year. He'd put six months' work into it. But they couldn't arrange proper distribution to the retailers in time – that was his one big mistake, he should have started on that earlier. Now he had a warehouse full of dated material sitting in Wiltshire. He realised he shouldn't have dated it either. Just Number One, Number Two . . . then he could have relaunched. All those beautiful pictures of Chinese water clocks and eighteenth-century chronometers, all those diagrams, from a shadow falling on a dial to an atomic clock. All his lovely photographs and captions. There was no justice in the world. No justice.

And his stepmother wasn't going to budge. The Matisses, the Picassos, the Braques – she'd got the old man to add a codicil to his will, and Dale was now effectively disinherited. That's the way it was beginning to seem, despite all the legal bills he was receiving for pursuing the matter. He accelerated as the road cleared. God, he loved this car, the way it handled. He turned off City Road half an hour later.

Along its own reach of the canal, Dell's Printing Works stood in a village-sized warren of nineteenth-century buildings. Dale parked the car and walked into reception.

'I've come to see Tom Dell,' he said to the woman in the booth.

'What's your name, love?'

'Freeman. Dale Freeman.'

She threw a switch and announced into the microphone, 'Dale Freeman in reception for Mister Tom.'

Mister Tom, he thought. Would he be led in by a faithful retainer on his pony? Round the walls were oil paintings of the Dell family, going back over the two hundred and fifty years of the company's history. Tom arrived – brisk, besuited, and angular. He came straight over to him.

'Dale Freeman? Tom Dell. Come up to the showroom.'

As they sat down, Tom shouted through the window for two coffees. Dale stared around the room at the rainbows of coloured printing behind the perspex bands. Calendars, Christmas cards, birthday cards, pregnancy cards, commiseration cards. Turner, Constable, Van Gogh, Rembrandt. And a whole bookshelf full of silvery city reports. Sleek, no-nonsense age-of-technology appearance, jammed tight with audit figures and projections. Promises. Predictions.

'So, how's Ferdie?'

'Oh, much of a muchness, you know.'

'Still chasing women?'

'Yes, but more of them get away these days.'

'How did his Gandhi issue go?'

'Very well, apparently. There's a big Indian community in South Africa, very keen on the Mahatma. He was a lawyer there of course, as a young man.'

'Shouldn't think he'd have had much luck marrying any of Ferdie's daughters though, would you?'

'He'd have needed a *very* special mailing list in his bag.'

Tom Dell laughed. Make them laugh, his father had always told him, and they already trust you.

'What we've got is this, Tom. A deal with Toni Productions to merchandise for Toni Inglish. A lot of it will be on-site obviously, but I believe a direct-mail campaign, using the considerable fan-club subscription, could yield real dividends — and be repeatable, maybe twice a year.'

'How big is it?'

'Over a hundred thousand worldwide. The beauty of it of course is that we don't have to translate. All these kids study English from Toni's albums anyway. I need prices on three things: a flyer, a gate-fold which is reasonably solid — say 100 gsm — and a full eight-page brochure.'

Tom Dell was already scribbling down notes on to his pad.

'Quantities?'

'You'd best give me ten thousand, fifty and a hundred for each. Just so I know where I am.'

'When do you need this?'

'Soon as you can, Tom. My creative team has already come up with the concept, which Toni herself loves, and my designers and prototype people are working day and night even as we speak.'

'You've got a card?'

'There you go.'

'I'll need trade references.'

'No problem. Just contact Ferdie. He backs this one a hundred per cent.'

'Then we don't have to worry. He must still be good for the odd million or two.' (Only if he's counting them in lire, Dale thought.) 'Must be getting a bit uncomfortable though. Jo'burg's the gun capital of the world now, so I hear.'

'That's right. They're negotiating with the government, though. A commemorative for Mandela. So I shouldn't worry too much about us — we're all pointing in the right direction. I can take a few of these samples, can I?'

'Help yourself. Give me seven days and you'll have your quotes.'

'Great, Tom, I'll be off then. Amazing place you have here.'

'Too big, I'm afraid. Going to have to slim it down a bit.'

'Downsizing?'

'As they say.'

'Well, we're all at it.'

As Dale Freeman drove away he thought, Right, now all I need is a direct-mail house.

•

Hooligan winds were kicking the river up on to the stone struts of the bridge. Jack could hear the squall growing more confident outside his window. He turned up the video of Toni Inglish and watched her singing.

> These kings of dawn mists and Bayswater battles
> Who haunt the dead streets at the edge of town
> Lifting up bruised pleading faces towards you
> As they dance on unsteadily down
> In somebody's house they're alive in a photograph
> In somebody's heart they're still wearing a crown

He suddenly realised what it was: she had no mask on. Even compared with the other musicians around her, who angled smiles or scowls towards the lenses, she was naked. She could actually tell the truth. He switched it off and took a book down from the shelf. It was Miro Pelikan's *Film* and some memory had just been triggered. He turned the pages. There it was again in the Introduction:

> *Why do I film so much in black and white? Because they made the rainbow into a propaganda machine. One Bonnard nude leaking its colours into the bath has more life to it, more*

*true motion to it, than all their polychrome confections. An*
*old photograph of Franz Kafka, his two eyes like black lakes*
*the century has drowned in, now that is film. No, I don't*
*like actors: why must I pay people to stand in front of my*
*camera pretending to be real, when all the time they are real?*
*Even the people I work with I have to help to be real again.*
*I take bandages from their eyes and rags from their mouths.*
*I say to them, Look carefully and silently into my lens and it*
*will make you honest. Don't turn away sunlight. Don't spit*
*out the water. Don't wear your skin as though it were somebody*
*else's clothes. Something you can see in any of my films —*
*men and women learning how to taste their own words, how*
*to put their fingers to their faces and find flesh there as though*
*for the first time.*

He switched the video on again. Everyone else was in colour. Toni Inglish was in black and white. Junkie white and dog-day funeral black. Her hair wasn't the colour of wheat, but bone. She was real, that was for sure, but she had chosen an expensive vocation. Or maybe it had chosen her.

●

Phil dropped Dotty with him that Saturday afternoon. He handed her the cheque. Gypsy Swan had been accepted.

'Sorry about the delay,' he said. 'How's Jeremy?'

She beckoned him out into the hall while Dotty started taking down her books from the shelf.

'I want a divorce, Jack.'

The strange thing about Phil was that she never looked any older. Maybe a line or two around the eyes, but that was all. It was the same creature in front of him that he'd first fallen for.

'I thought we'd agreed.'

'People agree things, then change their minds, Jack. You agreed to be true to me alone, to cherish me with your body and your mind, remember, then you went around screwing everything in a pair of tights.'

'Not everything,' Jack said as he turned away and looked up the stairwell to the main door. Bleak light was seeping through the leaded windows. 'That therapist said they were all substitutes for you, which is why none of them ever looked like you. She said they were all distorted versions of my wife.'

'Well, there was a version of your wife at home, in an empty bed. Undistorted. And there still is. I think I have a right to fill the bed again.'

'And Dotty . . .'

'She loves you, Jack. And you love her, I know. But you're not *there*. One day a week isn't *there*, either for her or me.'

'Jeremy,' he said.

'He's all right. You'll have to meet him soon. You'll still be her father.'

'So will he.'

'You should have thought of that before you started it all. This is my life, and Dotty's. You had ten years to come back in.'

'I tried once, remember, you said, Not now.'

'I was still smelling from your daughter's puke. I hadn't slept for twenty hours. Not now wasn't not ever. Never could cope with any kind of rejection, could you, Jack? Any hint of it and you were off, to find somebody new to adore you. What is it with you working-class boys, that you end up so terrified of the grown-ups ever getting cross?'

'Jeremy I take it comes from another neck of the woods.'

'Rugby and Cambridge. He owns some photocopying shops.'

'Your daddy will be pleased.'

'He was pleased enough with you, and so was I. You don't know anything about Jeremy, so don't start with your easy assumptions. He might even have had a harder time of it than you have. Can't imagine that, can you? What is it you're so scared of? You put down your pen and took up your prick instead. You stopped writing at the same time you stopped screwing me. Ever thought of that? I'm disappointed at who I am too, Jack. You're not the only person in the world who'd prefer to be different.

'I'll pick Dotty up at six.' She ran a finger over his scraped

scalp. 'Strange how tender it all is. You must feel the wind.'
Then she was gone.

The door opposite opened and Martine smiled at him.
He sometimes wondered if she didn't sit on the other side
of her letterbox permanently, listening to whatever went on.

It was a quiet afternoon. They looked at books together.
Sometimes he had to stop reading and pretend to do something in the kitchen. Buster Keaton's *The General* was on the
television. They sat and watched it. He put his arm around
her shoulder as they looked at that face, at the white desert
of its features, the unmoving thin lips, and the two great
lenses of those eyes, staring back without even the complicity
of a smile. A mask out of Greek tragedy. When Buster
pistoned up and down on the wheel-rods Jack suddenly
understood what he was doing, by not seeming to move a
muscle. Chaplin had wriggled and writhed his way through
*Modern Times* to show how human he was compared to the
machinery dwarfing him, but Buster Keaton said, If you're
ever to survive this, you'll have to become as hard as the
steel itself.

'You seem sad, Daddy.' Those eyes, exactly the same blue
as her mother's, though she wore her hair longer, as he'd
tried to have her mother do years before, but she couldn't
be bothered. Hack it off, keep it out of the way, tie it up
with a strip of ragged cloth.

'Do you like Jeremy, Dot?'

'He always brings me a present.'

'And he takes you to nice places.'

'Yes, he always plans trips.'

'Do you see him in the mornings when you wake up?'

'I did last week. Why don't you and Mummy live
together?'

'We kept falling out, love, you know that. I've told you
before. Sometimes grown-ups can't stay together, that's all.
We shouted at each other all the time.'

'You don't shout at each other now.'

'We're not in the room together long enough to shout at
each other now. Anyway, we've done every type of shout

that people can shout. At least twice. We finished all the shouts off.'

'Is Jeremy going to marry Mummy?'

'Maybe, but I'll be your daddy for ever. Remember that.'

She leaned up to his face and kissed him.

That evening he went running. Kick it all out. Just kick it all out of yourself. But it wouldn't go, it only sank in deeper.

When he came back, he slumped down in a chair and asked himself out loud, 'What would you have done with it, Miro? What kind of scenario would you have made of my book?' Maybe he *had* written one. Maybe Harry Trench would have it in his pocket. Where the hell was he?

Jack picked up his copy of *About Time* and left the flat. He could still write like this, if it came to it, couldn't he? Ten years of writing garbage didn't mean that garbage was all he could write. He wished he could remember where his copy of the film script was, so he could see what he'd done with it. Could he write another now, if that's what Harry Trench required? On the underground were two men in their thirties sitting side by side. Slack trousers and bomber jackets. Both had shaved heads – he seemed to be starting a fashion, or perhaps Toni Inglish had already started it. One of them was going through the listings with a pen in his hand.

'So what's on at the ICA?' the other one asked.

'*Whaling for Her Demon Lover.*'

'What's that then?'

'A feminist remake of *Moby Dick*, it says. Susannah York plays the Ahab figure.'

'Eh?'

'I'll read it to you. "In a brave piece of acting, which goes some way towards making up for her retrograde love scene in *The Killing of Sister George*, where she was a woman pretending to be a man's idea of a woman making love to a woman, she here delivers with all due gravitas, the denouement, in which the whale is seen to be all that is repressed in the Unconscious of Western society." '

'Sounds like they've taken the dick out of *Moby Dick*.'

When Jack finally arrived at St Paul's, he took the same route he used to take when he worked at Brewer's, all those years before. Smithfield Market. In his first week he had stood at the corner of Charterhouse Street and stared down with astonishment at the gutter. It was red and mottled with fragments of small corpses. Chicken claws, splinters of mink bristle, eyes he couldn't identify, all bobbing about in viscous coagulating blood. He had looked upon this little Tiber and noticed, amid the mire of animal confusion, four or five semi-conductors gleaming.

'There's a computer business up there,' one of the secretaries had explained to him. 'In among the meat boys.'

He walked down Cloth Fair. That had been Ashley Simon's house there, that was where the man he had invented needed to live. On the top two floors of one of the houses overlooking the churchyard of St Bartholomew. Sometimes he would step quietly down into the church and sit in the nave, behind one of those squat stone columns from which the Romanesque arches flourished. Sometimes he'd even listen as a man's voice chanted in the chapel. So many men in this religion: God the Father, God the Son, and (threaded through the beads of the years) all those chanting priests. The women were all virgins and martyrs. They tempted but they did not crucify. When the crucifixion started, they all knelt at the foot of the cross weeping and praying. Even the prostitute was there, having given up her tempting vocation. He wondered though if anyone could truly tempt you who could not crucify you too.

Sometimes from his windowsill, over the top of the four heads of Ishtar that perched there, Ashley had stared down at the winos gathering among the tombstones. Tins of strong beer, unshaven faces, coats matted from refuse and vomit. There was one with a beard half-way down his chest who never seemed to speak. The others would sing sometimes, in shaky unison at the gifts of life, at the sudden arrival of the sun. At other times they squabbled and cursed, stumbling over to the gravestone nearest to his window, where they urinated. Whatever bones lay under that slab were rained on every day of the year, even in the meanest drought.

Jack walked over to the gravestone. The Mitchell family – he remembered now. The bones had been there for two hundred years. One of them was a little girl; it had struck him at the time.

Ashley would often walk from Cloth Fair over to St Bride's. He was intrigued at the way the Enlightenment church (all airiness and illumination and the faith of reason) stood above the crypt with its Saxon and Roman stones, and its metal ('Safety for the Dead') coffin, to keep those corpses out of the hands of Resurrectionists. That horror of post-humous dismemberment. Shards of medieval glass and charred stone fragments still remained from the Great Fire of 1666. There were even oyster shells discarded long ago by Roman fingers.

And when the bombs came down to burn it out again in 1940, Enlightenment rationalism had created that technology, thrashing about up there in the heavens, but the flames burning out the leaded windows that night came from a darkness as fetid as anything any Saxon or Roman had ever known.

Jack stared up at the spire of St Bride's. He had walked over here too, as Ashley had done so often. 'You put down your pen and took up your prick.' That's what his wife had said. He'd watched that video of Toni Inglish over and over again. She used her own words. Nobody paid her to write the words *they* wanted. She was burning up her life at high speed, but it was all her life. What was he? He was broken into three: his sex, his job and some tangled deformity called Jack Goodrich. Failed husband, failed father, failed writer. And Phil was right about that too: he was terrified at the fact of his own failure. And the terror had prevented him from doing anything about it. So could he do it again now?

He had studied archaeology because he had wanted to find out what he was standing on, wanted to make his way back to the beginning of things. 'All science is an endless journey backwards,' Percy Hardinge had said in his first lecture. 'Cosmology, biology, geology, psychology – they're all trying to find their way backwards to the original state; to find out where the structures in space, or inside the body, or inside the earth, or inside the mind, had their foundations laid.'

Ashley Simon was archaeologist all through. Time could not be ironed out in him, its helical manoeuvres still twisted and spiralled inside him. All that had happened was that the past was still present, that was all. Sometimes Ashley saw them walking up and down Fleet Street, and he could hear them weeping inside, like a great underground cave where the water had run down the walls for millennia, to collect at the bottom in an enormous pool, where sightless creatures scrabbled about. Blind forces in Darwin's dismal pond. Ishtar spoke as loudly to him as she had in Uruk or Nineveh.

Jack suddenly thought of the first time he had ever seen Phil teach. He had asked if he could sit in on one of her lessons. She arranged her speciality for him: she conducted the whole class without speaking, but by using the phonetic chart on the wall and her repertoire of signs and gestures, she conjured out of them all the words of 'Mary had a little lamb'. He had never forgotten the freak eroticism of her gestures, as she beckoned and tempted them into sound, the choreography of her dumb show as her fingers writhed around the silence.

●

That night at twelve o'clock Dotty was woken by the noises coming from her mother's bedroom. It wasn't her mother's voice that was making them. She took hold of the framed picture of her father carrying her in his arms when she was five years old, and she pulled it under the bedclothes. Then she pulled the bedclothes over her head.

●

'You're going to have to cut those fingernails of yours, you know. I have tiny lacerations fanning out round my nipples.'
  'Marilyn.'

She stopped speaking into the phone and looked over at Dale. He gestured to her to put the phone down.

'I'll talk to you later, my darling. I'm being summoned by my true lord and master.' The telephone was recradled with a plastic clunk. Marilyn blinked slowly several times, for emphasis. 'Is there something you wish me to do, Dale?'

'I'm *paying* for that call.'

'And I'm extremely grateful.'

'Marilyn, there are offices in the Middle East where that conversation would lead to summary execution.'

'*Summery*?'

'*Summary*. A-R-Y. Summary.'

'Struck me as odd it should be so seasonal, that's all.'

'What's-his-cock's coming in a minute.'

'Don't have anyone of that name down in the diary.' She made a great show of staring at the page.

'Baldy.'

'Oh, Jack. Jack Goodrich.'

'Do you think the little one's a poof? The arty one, John Boy?'

'I've really no idea, Dale.'

'I think he's a poof. He's good, though.'

Jack arrived five minutes later. He didn't know what the meeting was for, but Dale had said it was a matter of some importance. He sat looking at Dale from the other side of the table.

'We're moving. Quickly. My printers are doing a lot of work finalising the spec, and Toni Productions are on the phone to me almost every hour. We'll be wanting you guys pretty much full time in a few weeks. I only have one problem, Jack, and I'm hoping you can help me with it. I've actually got to leave in a few minutes – I'll be in a meeting at TP Headquarters in Kingston for the rest of the day, probably the rest of the week.

'Never had much to do with the London direct-mail set-up. I've done it elsewhere, obviously. In Europe and the States – otherwise TP wouldn't be giving me a free run on this one. But here I'd have to do some research. I haven't the time. You know something about it though, don't you?'

'It was one of my jobs at Brewer's,' Jack said, turning uncomfortably in his seat. It had always been his least favourite work. 'And of course I wrote the copy for DMS.'

'That's it, I remember now, it was the DMS stuff that caught my eye. Just remind me again.'

'DMS. Direct Mail Services. The big mailing house and list brokers in Deptford. They wanted a glossy brochure, so I spent some time there and wrote it for them. Not the happiest days of my life, I'm afraid.'

'Just remind me again who owns it. I'm terrible with names.'

'Jim Torrance.'

'Jim, that's right. And you got to know him of course, didn't you?'

'Sort of.'

'Give him a ring would you? Here, use this phone. Explain that you need to scoot across and see him with some of these print samples, so that we can come up with package possibilities and prices.'

'I'm a copywriter, Dale, not a direct-mail agent.'

'I'll be paying you a consultancy fee, Jack, obviously – whatever your top rate for that is. Come on, play the white man, this thing's all about to take off and I need a little high-grade assistance.'

And Jack certainly needed the money, sooner rather than later, however offensive he found the idea of what he was being asked to do. They found the number and dialled. After a long conversation with a sceptical secretary, he was finally put through to Jim.

'No, not the Nobel Prize yet, I'm afraid. No, I don't own my own agency either. Yes, that's right. Listen, Jim, there's something interesting going on, that I think you might like to have a look at. I'm in the middle of a meeting and these people are desperate for the best mailing house in London, so I naturally mentioned your name. What? Oh, all right, the best mailing house in England then. Fine. Europe. What?

56

Well, all this is still under wraps, but it's Toni Productions. You know, Toni Inglish. Exactly. Could I come over with some samples? Well, now will suit me. No more than half an hour – I'm on my bike.'

Dale's face glittered. He handed over the brochures from Dell's and asked for quotes and dummy packages on anything and everything that might be done with them, in whatever combination, in quantities of ten, fifty and one hundred thousand. Jack left.

Marilyn stared at him. Dale avoided her look for as long as he could. Finally he turned towards her.

'Well?' he said.

'Want me to get the bank manager for you again?'

'No.'

'I'll order you a cab, shall I? For your Kingston meeting. Book you down there for the whole week, shall I?'

'I'm going out for the rest of the day, Marilyn, so you can get back on the line to lover boy, and have smutty canoodles all day long. Don't worry – I'll pay the bill.'

Two miles short of Wren's Greenwich College, Jack parked his Honda in front of a vast corrugated biscuit tin. This was DMS. He took off his helmet and looked about him. Waste land. A dead railway rusting slowly in its overgrown cutting. The discarded packaging from several brands of fast food blew up and down the cratered road.

Jim Torrance shook his hand. He sagged a little more than last time, in his expensive grey suit.

'Didn't think I'd see you back. Thought the next time I'd catch sight of you would be one of those book programmes on the telly.'

The accent had a lot more of the East End than Dave David's did.

'Come and see the lovely new mail shot I'm doing for the Fauntleroy Mint.' They walked inside and he gestured at rows of tables piled high with envelopes, printed letterhead, brochures. Twenty or thirty women sat at these tables, inserting pieces of paper and printed card into brochures.

The aural ruins of a song rasped from the speakers of the sound system.

'All this could be done by machine,' Jim said, with undisguised irritation. 'All they've got to do is pay attention to formats and parameters. But some bright spark in an agency, fresh out of art school, makes it an inch wider than my machines can take, and I have to go scouring Deptford for these little darlings, and bring them all here. Can't even leave them at home as outworkers — the company wants access at all times. Still, provides me with a bit of company, doesn't it? And all for the sake of one fucking inch.'

He had stopped behind a woman in her sixties, who was slicking material into envelopes with a machine-like unconsciousness. She looked back over her shoulder towards him. Silver-headed, her eyes haunted.

'I hear voices, Jim.'

'I know you do, darling. You just keep packing, that's a good girl.'

Jack picked up one of the finished pieces. He examined it carefully, pulling the brochure out of its envelope. *The Classic Plates of Royalty*. He flipped through the pages. Plates with artificially enhanced light-spots gleamed out at him, each one a design based on a different royal collection somewhere in the world. With an introduction by Dr Peter Mould of the University of Leeds. *It is with the greatest possible pleasure and excitement that I introduce this superlative . . .* Jack threw the brochure back down on the white Formica table. It landed on its glossy face with a wet slap. He looked at the order form. *I would like to subscribe to this unique limited edition of exquisite . . .* He looked at the letter. *Dear Collector, It is with pride and also a considerable sense of responsibility that we are writing to offer you this magnificent collection. Pride because of the unparalleled craftsmanship that has gone into the making of every single limited and numbered set. Responsibility because all things of real beauty . . .*

'Lovely stuff,' Jim said. 'Real class, eh?'

His hair was entirely white though he couldn't have been much older than forty-five, his face already wrinkled with calculation and responsibility. They said he was a millionaire many times over. It was his Corniche parked outside. They said his father had been a small-time crook in Leytonstone. Jim had done well for himself.

'So, you're working with rock stars now?'

'Not exactly,' Jack said. They were walking through another section, another aircraft hangar of a space. Women in cheap clothes with cheap hair-dos, some white, some black, some Filipino, tended machines and stacked material. Some of them moved their lips, but he couldn't work out whether they were singing along, or only talking to themselves. They came out finally, into the relative silence of the reception area.

'Free for lunch?' Jim asked.

'Yes,' Jack said. He wasn't expecting that.

'Where is it you come from again?'

'Oldham,' Jack said.

'Still got the north in your voice.'

Jim said they'd use his little four-wheel drive. When he went in the Corniche, he had to leave bigger tips.

'I'll take you to the Captain's Tower on the Isle of Dogs. Get a nice view from it. Amazing what's gone on down there. Know it at all?'

'No,' Jack said. 'Be my first time.'

He watched through the window in silence as buildings loomed up before him. Giant polychrome exteriors. Clouds swept across their mirrored skins. Twice he saw the car appear briefly and then flick off the wall again. The buildings kept changing focus as they sped across the surfaces. As they approached it, Jim slowed up and squinted upwards through the windscreen.

'Just *look* at that fucker.' His voice was hushed for the first time.

Rearing up out of the heart of the Docklands Redevelopment Scheme was the Captain's Tower. The frame was primarily orange, though there were strands of green for the window-cleaning platforms. Most of the windows were a dark grey polarizing filter. At the top was an enormous broken pediment in synthetic white marble, with a dollop of cream baroque for its quiff. And immediately underneath that was the Captain's Tower Restaurant.

As the lift breezed through twenty floors, Jim pointed quizzically to the top of Jack's head.

'It's neater,' Jack said.

Jim was obviously well acquainted with the menu. Jack accepted his recommendations. Terrine for starters, followed by wild boar. And a Margaux.

'I thought you'd be famous by now,' Jim said, sipping his wine.

'So did I.'

'So, what happened?'

'I don't know, Jim, I'm still trying to work it out. My wife says it's because I stopped sleeping with her. Never wrote anything decent after that.'

'Probably put a curse on you. Mine did. Just trying to sort out the settlement with her now. I should have divorced her when I was still a warehouseman, I could have afforded it then.'

'You don't seem to be doing too badly, Jim.'

'Not complaining. But then I'm not encumbered with your educational qualifications.'

'What happened to Harry, by the way?'

When Jack had done his work for DMS, Harry had been the one who was called on to explain all the different areas of production. He had also been head-warehouseman. And, more importantly, he was Jim Torrance's permanent whipping-boy. Whenever anything went wrong, Jim's dark cry would go out over the PA system, 'Harry, get in here would you?' He had resigned twice during the one week Jack was there.

'When his daughter left home', Jim said, breaking a bread roll, 'he resigned for the last time. By that stage his wife was already living with some plumber in Croydon, so I suppose he reckoned he'd had enough. I told him to get in there one day, and he walked through the door and told me to take my Rolls-Royce and my house in Kent and stick them both up my arse. I hear he now lives in a nursing home on the coast. Never says a word, just stares out to sea all day, watching the splishy-splashy. Just think of that – he's got a better life than I have. Free of care. Mine isn't.

'So, come on then, what's the story? You giving Toni Inglish one, are you? You both go to the same barbers.'

As the food was served, Jack explained as best he could all he knew of the project.

'And Dale Freeman, who's he in all this?'

'Seems to be operating as the agent for TP. He did show me an agreement they'd signed with him.'

Jim thought for a minute.

'Well, I'm interested obviously. Tell him, or them, by the way, that I can also provide a fulfilment service, send all the goods out for them when the orders come in. Just opened a new place down in Reading.'

Jack handed him the samples.

'So he wants me to give him fifty-seven varieties on this lot, does he? All right, I'll get one of my boys on it. How was lunch, sir?'

'Best I've had for some time.'

'I'll drive you back then, and you can pick up your two-wheeler.'

•

The sound engineer leaned forward and threw the switch. He simply couldn't listen to it any more. He stared out of his glass booth as Toni's bagman argued. The piece of leather-decorated lowlife with whom he was doing the arguing shrugged and started to walk away, and he was already after him, tugging at his arm. Lowlife smiled, the sort of smile that deserved a broken bottle in the middle of it, because he knew that what he was supplying was needed, whatever his prices. The sound engineer knew what the man had said, he'd heard him say it before: if you don't like my prices, go down there on the street yourself and pick up everything you need for the night. Just tell them it's all for Toni Inglish and you shouldn't have any trouble getting what you want.

So he handed over the money, and lowlife handed over the stuff. He pocketed twice its street value and didn't even bother to offer any change. Then there was some shuffling and whispering over in the corner till Toni went off to her little bathroom, the one they had to reserve especially for her while she was recording, in case any telltale flecks of blood anywhere might upset a bass player, or interest someone whose brother worked on one of the smaller-format newspapers.

She was back five minutes later, with her sleeves rolled down. He could see by her face that her body had stopped screaming, that the junk was filling her veins and quelling whatever creature it was lived inside those track-lines. He didn't know: the more he worked with her, the more of a puzzle she became. He switched on again. She had picked up the guitar.

'We'll do "Café in Amsterdam",' she said, already strumming. The three musicians lolling on the big couch in the corner started to stumble up.

'Do we know that one, Toni?' the bass-player asked, gently.

'It's in E,' she said. 'You'll pick it up.'

Oh Christ, thought the sound engineer, it's going to be one of *those* sessions.

●

Tim Tasker sat in the perfect underground silence of his workshop. Around him the castings incubated in their little white pods, row upon row of them stretching over the cellar space like foetal extras in a sci-fi movie, brooding silently inside their rubber. He hated reproduction work, but it brought in some regular money, though not much: something anyway to pay his side of things. Sal was going to love what he was working on now, he knew that. This was where his skills really came into play, as he fashioned little fetishes to decorate the head of Toni Inglish. His sharp metal graver cut through the skin of the turquoise, and a moment later there appeared the hieroglyph of a phoenix swallowed by its own flames.

•

Jack turned the coloured pages. Bras slipped over breasts, G-strings tugged away from pubic tufts, soap bubbled over flesh as though Venus had just stepped from the boiling waves. Some turned inside-out as though a snail had emerged, blind and vulnerable, into the daylight, surrounded by a tangle of delicate undergrowth. Women tricked out in white stockings clutched other women, without much conviction. Some held up their breasts like holy offerings, as though auditioning for a part in the *Song of Solomon*. One had a pair that rose from her fingers like helium balloons. Nurse's uniforms, police uniforms, school uniforms. Then pages of advertisements: dildos of various sizes, like ancient ossified fingers, wrinkled and bent, canvas straps lying dead about them. Toll numbers made large promises: let your ghost milk fly into the telephone's mouth. Women's faces lurid around their own finger-sucking smiles. One fellated, in delirious ecstasy, a plastic banana.

He closed the magazine and carried it through to the kitchen, where he threw it in the bin. Didn't even know why he'd bought it. A sudden impulse at the paper shop. What was the use? Mannikins. Baboonery. Bodies merely gesturing desire. He remembered Pelikan's tribute to his true master, Rouault. He'd studied with the old man in the days when he used a brush instead of a camera. The whores in that film were at least real. They had all the artist's sympathy – women engaged in parodies of love for cash. But it was Pelikan himself who had said if time is only money, then film will degenerate to cinema. *Cinema* was his term of ultimate abuse – it applied to any representation where dazzle took precedence over truthfulness, applied in his view even to the way people took to showing themselves to each other.

•

Toni stopped half-way through the middle eight, and stared at the sound engineer in his booth. He threw his switch again.

'Get them out, Finegan.'

'All right, boys, let's leave Toni in here by herself for a while, shall we?'

With shrugs of exasperation, the musicians unstrapped accordions and bass guitars and filed out of the door.

'Now, put the recording light back on,' she said.

'It's on.'

'I'm doing this in one take, so don't fuck up in there, Finegan.'

'Solo on guitar?'

'Can't see anyone else round here.'

'Whenever you're ready.'

He watched her closely as she concentrated on putting some drift between herself and all those previous fouled tracks. He had seen her grow more and more frustrated as the session men sloped along behind her, dragging the tempo. They were actually good, but she intimidated them. He'd seen her do it before. It didn't help that she could never play a song the same twice over. He had both hands on the sound-level buttons as she started up. There were two bars of her guitar intro and then she hit it. Suddenly her voice was there, she was inside the song. He checked swiftly to make sure everything was moving. Thank God, there was still enough tape on the spool.

> Sitting in a café in Amsterdam watching the rain
> Pouring on down the dark side of the cold window-pane
> Drinking and thinking, another whole evening to kill
> Got a hole in my heart an ocean of wine couldn't fill

The other musicians were watching her through the glass, but they couldn't hear anything as she sang with her eyes closed. They could see that she was doing it though, whatever it was she hadn't managed to do with them.

> Berlin and Rome
> Seem a long way from home
> New York and Jerusalem too
> But no journey goes far enough when I'm thinking of you
> And I'm constantly thinking of you

As I sit here in a café in Amsterdam watching the rain . . .

'You got that?'

'Got it all.'

'Do your magic, Finegan.'

'You're going.'

'I'm going.'

'Berlin? Rome? New York? Jerusalem?'

'None of your business.'

'And you'll be back?'

'When I return.'

He watched her put the guitar into its case and she was gone. He played the song over to himself through the headphones. They had a take. 'Right,' he said through the microphone, 'I want the accordionist in first. Pick it up at the end of the first eight bars, and give me light touches, little tricks over the tune, until I signal you to really go for it. It helps me to signal, by the way, if you don't have your eyes closed, Sam. Anyway, you can all relax now, boys: she's gone. The little lady's hit the night again.'

She went to Victoria and looked at the departures panel. Brighton. Well, why not? There was nothing you couldn't buy at a few moments' notice there.

She found a ramshackle hotel along the sea-front by the pier and checked in. The receptionist studied her in her black-leather jacket and white T-shirt and jeans. The shaved head. The phoenix on the neck. The milky blue unworldliness of her eyes and her skin: parched paper, tearable. As Toni walked upstairs with her guitar the receptionist prodded the barman. 'That's what's-her-name, isn't it?'

'Nah. They've all started dressing up like that now. Leather jackets. Tattoos. Guitar cases. Toni Inglish would never stay in a dump like this.'

Maybe it was the way she had been brought up, but she gravitated back to these seaside resorts. It was on these rusting piers that her father had told his terrible jokes and sung his vaudeville tunes. What do you call a man with a rabbit up each nostril? Warren. All the nice girls love a sailor.

Southend. Brighton. Morecambe. Blackpool. Herne Bay. Folkestone. She remembered those crowds of working-class faces. How badly they wanted to like the people up there on stage; how determined they were to enjoy themselves. It was too expensive to be gloomy. Back to work next week.

Sometimes her mother had joined him in the act, playing piano or viola and staring at her father with unrelieved displeasure, as his manic cavortings went more and more out of control. Toni remembered how the stage act and the home life had become steadily indistinguishable, until she never knew any more whether the theatrical disapproval was real, or the home displeasure a sham. There was always the distraction of moving on to the next venue. Fish-and-chip smells and boozy breath, and gusts of late-night laughter rolling up and down the streets.

She sat by the window and stared at the waves breaking on the pier. The wind was getting up. A solitary girl in a long raincoat walked grimly and slowly along the promenade. How big were the holes inside her? Who had drilled them?

She went downstairs to the little bar. He saw her in the mirror as he counted change into the till.

'A whisky please, with ice.'

He poured her the drink, eyeing her again in the mirror.

'Storm coming over,' he said. 'Weather forecast said it's headed all the way from Newfoundland. A nasty one. It'll be banging a lot out there later.'

'Good,' she said. 'I like storms.'

'You know you look just like Toni English.'

'No,' she said, downing her drink, 'that's a lie. She looks just like me. I know because I used to sleep with her husband, and he told me. See you later.'

On the pier the waves were beginning to lift. She liked the way the wind slapped her in the face. All the way from Newfoundland. Later, as she made her way through the streets, she peered into the various bars – she could smell the ones where they were dealing. Sitting in a dark corner she passed over the notes and took the little bags in exchange. No telling if that white stuff inside them was what the boy claimed. It wasn't as if either of them would be referring the matter to the Trading Standards officers.

Back in the hotel room, her head suddenly as clear as ten miles of Arctic sky, she started to write at the table by the window.

> Out-of-season winds have hit the heart of this town
> Blowing from the clifftops to the pier
> There's a black storm combing the Atlantic tonight
> And the barman said he thinks it's heading over here
> The small hotels look empty and the wind's running wild
> Swept here from those bad Newfoundland skies
> Gulls have lost their voices at the edge of the sand
> Buoys are warning sailors with their strange mourning cries
>
> Down the promenade walks a sad girl in a raincoat
> Rooting through her pockets for the riddles in her life
> Lashed at by the waves and stared down by the lamplight
> She looks half-ready to become the sea's latest wife
> She's come out to escape from the sadness of hotel rooms
> The creaking of the bedsprings and the moaning of the
> > storm
> The solitary drinker trapped inside the bar-room mirrors
> Smiles as if to say, Oh my love, tonight I'll keep you warm
>
> England all your broken heroes
> Gathered round your ragged shores
> Homeless kids and desperadoes
> Bottled tears behind locked doors
> And more
> And more

She swung the guitar up on to her knee, and started to pick out some gentle chords and hum. If she got the words right, the music always found itself. What was this? One of those old tunes that fell out of the sky, as though it had always been there, waiting.

Downstairs the young barman was looking at the photograph in the paper which the receptionist had handed to him. He studied it closely. There was no doubt it was her. He tried to remember all the things he'd read. After she separated from Kurt Illen with what amounted to a public abortion, she had made (or more often shouted) statements on her way in and out of hospitals. The famous one, the one the press had so delighted in, was spat out at a reporter from the *Sun*: 'I can't actually fuck people I like, you see. That's the real problem. So, you're certainly in with a chance, given the way I feel about you.'

He peered into the mirror and pressed his hair carefully against the side of his head. He looked all right: his spots had held off the whole week. See you later, she had said. When she had come back into the hotel, she had stared at him, hard. He switched off the main light and locked the outside door to the bar. Then he poured out two glasses of whisky (one with ice).

Upstairs in her room the pen moved across the page. She didn't need to think about it at all. Sometimes it was like that. The wind was growing louder all the time. There was a knock. She had picked the chords out delicately enough with her fingers, she hadn't even used a plectrum. Surely they couldn't complain about that? Or was she about to get busted again? She went quickly into the bathroom and taped the various little packets and her gear behind the toilet. Not that any of *that* would delay them long, if they really had a mind to put her away. But they were surely too quiet to be the filth. They'd have been shouting by now.

He stood there, holding both glasses and smiling as if he'd just inherited the whole of the south coast.

'Wondered if you might like a nightcap,' he said.

'Thought you might join me in one too, I see.' He nodded.

She opened the door wide and let him in.

'Nice guitar,' he said, as he sipped his drink. He didn't really like whisky.

'That's my famous Martin.'

'Is that the one . . .'

'Yes, that's the one I broke my husband's jaw with. Didn't damage it at all, the guitar I mean. In fact I think it's probably improved the tone. If anything, Kurt's singing's been better since then too.

'So. Did you simply want to chat about my musical equipment? Or had you something else in mind?'

It had always seemed an act of violence to her. Maybe that was because her first one had been. But if it was going to be an act of violence, she had decided she wasn't going to be its victim. Or not the only one anyway.

He didn't know what was happening, but he was excited enough. She'd always been able to do that. She pumped harder than he did, but he was the one who cried out, and as he did, she whispered in his ear, 'When you die, it'll be just like coming inside me.'

Afterwards, for the first time, he felt like no one at all. He climbed out of the bed without saying anything and put his pants back on. At the door he turned round.

'Do you always do that?'

She was smoking a cigarette with her eyes closed.

'Why don't you drop Kurt a line and ask him? Strange thing about men: what attracts them to women in the first place is the selfsame thing they come to hate. It can take some men a whole lifetime to discover that. You've learnt it in twenty minutes. You should pay me.'

'I've only got a couple of pounds,' he said, fumbling in his pockets.

'Oh that's too much,' she said. 'I've never been paid *that* much. It did you no harm at all, you know. That was honesty you just bought and it cost you nothing. It's the next one, the one who tells you over and over again how much she loves you, that's the one you should watch. She might destroy you. She could mortgage your immortal soul.'

He was gone. She put the bolt on the door and sat back down at the table.

> Morning brings the shellfish smells, the rusting coins in
> wishing wells
> The hangover apologies, the bottles on the sand
> Gulls with their sarcastic screams, hamburgers and plastic

The gypsy with her promise to trace fear inside your hand

She had a song, but she was going to feel bad in the
morning. She might even feel bad long before the morning.
Maybe that was just the price of the job she did. Outside
the wind was hammering at window boards as its rage
increased. All the way from Newfoundland, and all you find
at the end of the journey is Brighton.

# 2

# Secunda Scriptura

*Elamite*

JACK GOODRICH BRAKED AT THE TRAFFIC LIGHTS ON THE Fulham Road. As his foot clunked the pedal down into neutral, his helmeted head turned to look in the television-shop window. She was there on one of the screens, her eyes alien with intensity. It was impossible to make out what she was singing. The lights changed and he accelerated away.

Back at the flat he played the video as he pulled himself out of his clothes. For one moment he stood naked in front of the screen as she sang 'A white face in among the poppies/ You're a clown in the valley of death'. He'd only realised the week before that the song was about Sylvia Plath. He pulled his running shorts on.

Down on the tow-path he did twenty press-ups, before sidling into his run. How long ago had it all started? He couldn't even remember. Beatles. Stones. Exciting days up there in Oldham. There seemed to be a new song you wanted to learn each week. One day he heard Dylan, and after that nothing was ever the same again. He switched from his leather hat and Cuban-heel boots to baggy Levis and a work shirt. Took his guitar with him everywhere. At the local folk club they banned anyone from singing Dylan songs, while they droned on about wild rovers and dancing for your daddy. That was authenticity, apparently. For a while he'd convinced himself he might actually be a song-writer, then he heard 'Mr Tambourine Man' and he knew he was wasting his time. No one else was ever going to write like *that*. Maybe it was Dylan who'd pushed him into archae-ology: he didn't want to have to compete with the boy from

Minnesota, in any sphere at all. But he could still be a writer, couldn't he?

He'd never much liked women singers, and particularly not Joan Baez with her perfected frigidities. He'd gone to a Joni Mitchell concert once, but found her live voice a lot shriller than the records had led him to believe. He liked Edith Piaf, but that was because her whole life seemed to turn inside out and disappear into what she was singing. It was something that happened with John Martyn on a good night, or Joe Cocker or Tom Waits. But it didn't happen all that often with women. Women seemed to be too often smiling through their voices. But not Toni: she never smiled through her voice at all. If it came to that, she never smiled through her face either.

When he stepped back into the flat he saw the answering-machine light flashing. It was his father.

'Your mother's not been too good again this week, lad. It'd be nice for her to see you. And Dorothy of course. It's been over six months now. We know you're busy, but give us a ring anyway. By the way, the good news is, they've found out what's wrong with her. A tumour. Inside her head.'

Guilt. The ghostly nausea of guilt.

He hated sickness so much that Phil had once said he hated the sick too. He could hardly go into the rooms where they lay. It was as though a tiny splinter of death pricked his skin each time. All sickness was a premonition of the grave, hallucinatory in its intensity.

*Ashley Simon drove along Clapham Common South Side. He had pulled the car over and parked before he knew why. As he climbed out he saw the building, vacant and decaying, festooned with security signs, though they were starting to decay too. The South London Women's Hospital. Without even looking about him he made his way around the back, spotted the broken window on the first floor and climbed quickly up the main drainpipe. Once inside he was pinned back against the leprous wall by it: a palimpsest of pain and dereliction. He was transfixed, corroded with the splayed*

*agonies and griefs laid one over the other, in a ply no thicker*
*than X-ray celluloid. Cancers, bacteria, viruses. The grey,*
*riddled, supine creatures had shed their shadows here like linen*
*shifts. Dead wombs triggered out of chloroformed bodies and*
*incinerated. The air was dense with screams that only he could*
*hear. His mind punctured as a thousand needles entered its*
*skin and the morphine squirted. He was smudged with disease.*
*He felt male instruments sharpening inside his flesh. Foetuses*
*who'd swerved away from life stepped through him silently,*
*their shrunk heads hardening to gargoyles in this vacant building.*
*The air had turned inside out. When he stumbled out again*
*into the street, he could barely breathe. He leaned against the*
*wall for three minutes before he could walk. The world of*
*healing.*

*When he'd finally made it back to Cloth Fair, he lay flat*
*out on the bed and waited as his mind slowed up. Too much*
*information. What would be would be.*

It had started on a little dig in Dorset. They'd found what
seemed to be a temple to Mithras on a hill beyond Dorch-
ester. Jack was on his knees when he picked up the nail,
about nine inches long. It was a nail, that was all, a black
twisted Roman nail, from a cross-beam most likely, and
probably the same size as the ones they'd used to hammer
Jesus to the cross. He'd dropped it and stared.

The next day they all went (with jaunty cynicism) down
to the Victorian reconstruction. It was a heritage centre: a
nineteenth-century village. You paid for a ticket at the
gleamingly restored chrome cash-till and went inside. And
there before you was the place one hundred and thirty
years before, all fastidiously recreated. A waxwork man in
muttonchop whiskers wearing a leather apron had frozen
in a moment of labouring nostalgia, as he heaved his laden
tray over the cobblestones. Jack had climbed the narrow stairs
and peered in at the small bedroom with its drapes of laced
garments; a petticoat lay waiting on the sagging double bed.
Bless this house, O Lord, was embroidered over the mirror.
Something there, between the big inarticulate boots on the
floor with their rough tongues hanging out, and those moth-

delighting underclothes, some shudder that still shrouded them went through him like an antique bullet, and he was out, out through the rows of tin hoardings, advertising remedies and pleasures, and into the nearest pub. He had heard some echo of a cry, whether of orgasm or birth or death, he didn't know. What he did know instantly was that time did not move on at all, that it was all around him, and beneath him, but he could only ever bear to focus on one tiny fragment of it. To see and feel all of it would have been to go insane. And that was precisely what Ashley Simon was, for the purposes of the world: criminally insane. How else could you describe someone whom time made such delinquent inroads through, someone for whom the oneiric thrived even among surgical instruments? A shaman in the asylum of clocks, a madman who would not even identify death itself as an enemy.

Jack avoided them, but they still caught up with him from time to time, these fluke chronologies. In his father's words on the answering machine, he could already touch the cold sheets wrapped round his mother's body.

•

Jack's mother died at three in the morning the following day. The tumour had been a hungry one and it had finally bitten right through her brain. Jack had still not phoned by the time his father called him at nine a.m.

'She's gone, lad.' Jack took his breath in slowly.

'I'm sorry, Dad, I only got back in the early hours. Been on a job in the west. I was just about to phone you.'

'Anyway, makes no difference now. She's gone.'

'I'll come up then. I'll get the train this morning.'

'Ay, well I'd appreciate that, anyway.'

He sat on the train and stared through the window. His mother dead. He tried to find some meaning for that, but there was no meaning for it at all. She'd been alive and she was dead. Once he'd crouched in her womb and fed from what her body gave him. And he'd not seen her for over six months. Indeed he'd thought about her as little as he could.

The personality disorders. The infection of the urinary tract. The incessant pissing into a commode on the living-room floor before they took her into hospital. The yelling at his father. The obscenities he had no conception she'd held inside her mind. 'She's not herself, lad. That's not your mother talking.' Twenty miles south of Manchester it started to rain.

He walked from the station, though it took him thirty minutes and he got soaking wet. He always forgot how red the place looked, with those bricks. In the rain that cardinal rouge was the most melancholy colour in the world. The colour of faded Victorian drawing-rooms, or the splatters on the operating-theatre floor. So many shop windows were boarded up.

Just before he turned into the estate, he stared up the road towards Saddleworth.

The curtains were pulled to in all the windows: the house had closed its glass eyes in grief. The side door was open. He walked in. His father sat in silence on the couch in the darkened room. He stood up when he saw Jack.

'The undertaker'll bring her over tomorrow, when they've sorted her out and everything. That's what I arranged. She would have wanted to have come back here, rather than be laid out in one of those parlours for days at a time. She never liked them.' His voice close to tears. 'You can stay in your room. We always kept it ready, just in case, so I don't think the sheets have been on all that long. She'd have aired them, if she'd known you'd be coming.'

'Can I make you some tea, Dad?'

'Well, that'd be nice, yes.'

Jack stared at the kitchen walls as the kettle boiled and steam scrolled up the window. Nothing had changed in fifteen years, except that the oily texture of the wallpaper had grown a little more dried and dim. A mural design: pictures of the sea breaking against the friable cliffs of Normandy, little arched limestone chunks with the waves passing through them. That had once been his image of escape and freedom. Life away from Oldham.

They sat with their tea. Jack wanted to go over and touch the old man, but he couldn't: they'd hardly ever touched since he'd been six or seven. Small with grey, slicked-back hair, and wearing his woollen suit, with a tie, he kept turning towards the window with the curtains drawn across it and breathing in a little more deeply than normal.

'Shame you couldn't have seen her before she went.'

'I didn't know she was going, Dad.'

'How was it in the west?'

'The west?'

'Aye, the west. How was it?' Those eyes, shrewd as ever and precise in their focus, turned towards him.

'Oh fine. A job, you know.'

'Where?'

Suddenly his mind was blank. He couldn't think of anywhere at all in the west. Or the east. Not even in the south or the north.

'I was at home, Dad. I'm sorry. I would have come, you know that. I didn't know it was all that serious. Phil's asked for a divorce.'

'About time.'

That night he took his father out to Mistress Shipley's Fish Parlour. They had haddock and chips with mushy peas and a pint of beer each. The bill was so much smaller than any equivalent in London that he left a tip which amounted to twenty per cent. The waitress simply looked at him in silence.

On the way back they went into the local. They had another pint. They drank without speaking as machines blipped and bleeped around them, and some distant recording of Elvis folded back the years. The seat his father sat in had a gaping hole where the grey rotting sponge showed through the red plastic. When they arrived at the house, his father announced he was going to bed. 'Didn't get much sleep last night. Help yourself to whatever,' he said.

Jack put the kettle on, but poured himself a whisky while he waited. Christmas whisky – the bottle was only ever opened once a year. He picked up the photograph of Jack Goodrich twenty-odd years ago in his gown receiving his

B.Sc. at Lancaster. How he had smiled into his future, as though he already recognised it in the camera lens, smiling back at him. His undergraduate thesis on the cult of Inanna-Ishtar had been the deciding factor in winning him a first. Percy Hardinge wanted him to do research and had said he would personally supervise his doctorate, but Jack had wanted to be out of academia, and soon: he didn't like it, he thought it stank. Quarrelsome as politics, but less accountable in its murderous manoeuvres. He would make it elsewhere, on his own terms.

Some Marxists and feminists had already attacked his short article about Ishtar in the university magazine. They were insisting that Ishtar, as a goddess of war, was a later Bronze Age accretion to the Neolithic fertility figure, but Jack couldn't buy this any more than Percy Hardinge did. There was no evidence for it: she had always been portrayed as both fecund and murderous, Queen of Heaven and Queen of Hell, patroness of mercy and tutelary deity of slaughter. She both gave birth to Tammuz and put him into the underworld. She was also his devoted lover. Ishtar, he knew, was lethally irresistible. She could not have been so irresistible had she been less lethal. She moved imperiously through the gates of hell. Her own sister laid death's eye upon her and she hung from a hook for three days, turning gently in the silence underground. The fertility goddess, worshipped by temple prostitutes.

Later, he pulled the curtains back from the front window and stared out. That window opposite. He remembered the afternoon he had looked out and seen Mr Crosby naked behind the half-closed curtains, his whole body covered with chancres, like an enormous white reptile that had learnt how to stand on its hind legs. He remembered the zigzag blade of the whispered word as it entered his ear: syphilis. Mr Crosby had had a job sweeping up at Woolworth's, and one afternoon he had come back from the store to find Mrs Crosby sprawled out on the kitchen floor, her head inside the oven. Jack remembered the smell of gas, how it used to sweeten oddly at the top of your mouth, before it turned sour again. Police cars and ambulances had blocked the road.

Then there was the moor. They had cycled to Saddleworth while it was all going on, and had watched policemen, dressed head-to-toe in plastic suits, scraping with their instruments at the rough pelt of furze to make the moor yield up what was left of those little bodies in their shallow graves. He and Tommy Meadows had leaned their bikes against the old tenter posts and stared down at it all, up there at the top of the world. Lesley Ann Downey. John Kilbride.

The next morning he rose early and put on his running gear. He stopped now and then and looked at different distant items from his life. He halted before John Tilney's father's garage, on the edge of the ruined tarmac that had once been a playground. They had sat in the back of that corrugated shed, with the lights off, listening to the record player, groping for whatever their girlfriends allowed them to touch. Denise. Fourteen years old. He had kissed her where her breasts sloped up towards her neck. He could still smell that soap.

His mother was brought back to the house inside her coffin. He and his father made their way around her with trepidation. Jack soon avoided going into the room altogether, though he noticed how her lips had tightened into a kind of severe smile, and how the flesh colour had moved from pink to a sort of white rinsed through with blue. There was a curious menace to her closed eyes, as though they might snap open any minute. She might still be in one of her crocodile moods.

The next morning he woke to the sound of voices, or one voice anyway. He padded downstairs quietly. His father was talking to her, matter-of-factly, about the funeral arrangements.

The funeral was on Friday. At the same church where Jack had been baptised and confirmed, taken his first communion, and gone for many years each week to confess. Forgive me, Father, for I have sinned. It has been one week since my last confession. I told lies, Father. I was disobedient,

Father. I said bad words, Father. And anything else, my son? (Pull the air in through your teeth.) I was impure, Father. And was this act of impurity committed with yourself or with another? There was more than one act, Father.

Sundry relatives arrived. Jack couldn't even remember who some of them were. And a few of his father's companions from his forty years at the local mill. He fingered the carved initials in the wood's grain on the pew in front of him. I.S. and J.B. He tried to remember the names of the boys in his class.

The Canon took the service. Jack could still remember him, but in those days he'd been a humble priest. He had that gravitas, though. Jack thought ceremonies should have some weight, even the ones he didn't believe in.

'Rosemary has gone ahead of us into God's kingdom and may intercede for us now with the Almighty. As we pray for her soul today, we should also pray for her husband Michael, whom she has left behind in this vale of tears, until such time as he too goes to join her, to give praise with the angels and saints.'

His father's shoulders started to heave, and as Jack put his arm around him his own tears came too, scalding his cheeks. He wasn't sure who he was crying for, though. He doubted it was his mother.

The cortège moved blackly up the road to the graveyard and they all threw their pieces of earth on to the echoing pinewood, then left her there in the ground. His father started to cry again and Jack's feet moved edgily back and forth on the hard ground, as though he were scared of standing on someone's fingers. He noticed the coffin-bearers, thirty feet away in their dark suits, smoking and talking easily among themselves.

Back at the house, Jack helped people to the sandwiches the local delicatessen had prepared, and looked intermittently at his watch. People talked and, once in a while, started laughing, then looked guiltily at one another, wondering if they were supposed to laugh. His Auntie May, who seemed to have become entirely spherical in the years since he had last seen her, came over to him.

'You still down in London are you, Jack?'

'That's right, Auntie.'

'Still married?'

'Not for long.'

'Seems to be more and more the way these days, doesn't it? Why is it all your generation get divorced?'

'What we can't understand is how all your generation stayed married.'

'No choice,' she said, shaking her candyflossed head slowly. 'We couldn't afford otherwise, lad.'

'Not sure I can either.'

He was staring over Auntie May's shoulder at the picture of him as a little boy standing on the Central Pier in Blackpool, holding his mother's hand. It was on that trip that she had stumbled by mistake into the men's urinal in the subway under the road. Fifty men all facing the wall: it was England's most extensive facility.

'It were like the St Valentine's Day Massacre,' she had said when she came out again. Mrs Brown's lodging house was only three streets down from the pier. The glinting metal in the toilets. The shiny banisters you weren't meant to slide down. The smell of polish mingling with the smell of egg and bacon every morning.

Jack found himself studying the old radio on the sideboard: it must have been forty years now that it had sat there. He peered into its open back. They were still inside, those big valves, smitten with fluff. He remembered how, as a child, he had stared into it and wondered how such great dirty bulbs could summon sounds from the air.

Finally, after two hours, he told his father that he'd have to go.

'I've some work down in London won't wait any longer, Dad.'

'Well, you've been here a few days now.'

'I'll phone you tomorrow.'

'If you've got time then. Something your mother wanted

you to have.' He went over to one of the drawers and took out a small paper bag. He handed it to Jack. 'One other thing, lad. For the headstone – your mother's headstone – you'll do the words, won't you? She'd have appreciated that. Something that rhymes. I've ordered black polished granite. It's the most expensive one, but it does look nice.'

On the way back down on the train he opened the bag and turned the contents over and over in his hands. Her rosary beads, their wooden spheres stained with the sweat of her fingers from all those years of petition and beseeching. He counted them out and remembered the translucent amber of those prayer beads in Bodrum. The men had clicked away at them all day. It had been Halicarnassus once, one of the wonders of the ancient world, and each day he walked round the crusader castle. Fragments of statues, whole stone heads lying on the floor. Rulers gone to ground. He could actually feel the criminal fingers lifting the stones up in the darkness and covering them with dirty sacks. A truck with its engine running twenty yards away. But he didn't know whether the hands were his or someone else's. Then the sun dropped from the sky as though it had simply lost interest in staying up there. A man led a camel down the dusty street. The camel's face said that it knew everything, had seen it all before, was bored with men and their conniving ways.

You're praying to Ishtar, but without her weapons, Mum, he'd once told her. It's just Ishtar minus the sex. Numen of the storehouse, forgiveness of sins, amazement of the land. His mother had simply looked at him sadly and walked away without a word.

He took out the copy of *About Time* he'd brought with him, and looked at the cover. 'This brilliant debut novel . . .' Just how brilliant had his script been though? Maybe Pelikan had never contacted him because it simply wasn't good enough. If he could only find it, he'd know. When he had given the final typescript to Phil and she had read it, she had astonished him by what she said.

'Real bundle of trouble aren't you, Jack? It's a powerful book, but you really are a sucker to yourself.'

•

Jonathan Hamble called in at the Coach and Horses. He had his big art bag with him. He ordered a pint and sat down near the window where he could look out over the green at St Anne's. An oddly unlovable church, he always thought, stuck there in red-brick incongruity in the centre of all that grass. His eyes wandered. He was smiling vaguely at the tall young black man, who strode over from the bar and put his glass on the table.

'Mind if I sit down?'

'Feel free,' said Jonathan. He loved the shape of that head, and the hair cropped so close to it. A perfect profile with its strong, long nose. Jonathan itched to draw it. The smile flashed out, white from the eyes and teeth against the rest of his face. It was a smile that might never have walked through the valley of the shadow of death. Maybe it hadn't.

'Artist?' the man said, nodding at Jonathan's bag.

'Designer. For a living anyway.'

'And you?'

'Writer. No, you won't have heard of me, before you ask. So an artist's model at the moment. Among other things. For a living, anyway.'

Half an hour later, they were back at Jonathan's house. Terry looked about him at the paintings and sculptures and whistled. 'Must be a few bob here.'

'Must be, I suppose. Seven pounds an hour. That all right?'

'My evening rates are usually steeper than that. Certainly for the Putney School of Art Life Class, where I'm very popular. But so that you can get a taste of what I offer, we'll start with seven. Cash in hand.'

'Let's go down into the cellar – that's where I draw.'

'Not too cold, I hope, if I'm taking all my kit off.'

It wasn't cold. Jonathan had extended the central heating with a couple of radiators, and had placed a thick rug and plenty of cushions on the floor. Gymnastic contortions he approved of, but he had no use for hypothermia. Left that to the Pre-Raphaelites: Ophelia turning blue under the bathwater. Terry slipped out of his clothes with practised fluency, and stood with his hand on his hip, confident of poise and muscle-tone. He knew well enough what he offered, and its price.

'Michaelangelo's done that one,' Jonathan said, dipping a twig into black ink.

'Not in these flesh tints he hasn't.'

'Try to swallow your prick, if you wouldn't mind. You can come at it from any direction you like. Standing, kneeling, or flat on your back. Hang from the ceiling if that helps. But try to close the gap.'

Half-way through, eyeing Jonathan intently, Terry started to make it rise. Various Mapplethorpe photographs flicked through Jonathan's mind.

'No. But thanks anyway,' he said casually, continuing his rapid movements across the fifth of the large sheets he'd covered.

'You sure?'

'Yes.'

He wasn't though, and Terry knew it. He had a face and a smile people couldn't keep away from, as though they'd found an unexpected cave, and simply had to discover what treasures lay hidden inside.

●

'You should have called,' Jonathan said. The only time Jack had ever known him to look that way. As though he wished that Jack weren't there. His lips tightened into a smile that wasn't a smile at all. He was still in his white dressing gown.

'Sorry. I just thought, with me being away all week, I'd drop by to see if there was any news from our Mr Freeman.' He had pulled off his crash helmet and was following Jonathan through to the kitchen.

'Have a quick coffee, Jack. Then I really must get on. I was up half the night on a project.

'Freeman. No, not a murmur. Think you'd better accept the fact that we may well not hear any more from that direction. Though we may live to see our fine work resurface, fractionally modified of course, in about six months' time. Where were you by the way?'

'My mother died. I was up in Oldham for the funeral.'

'Fuck. I mean I'm sorry, Jack. Didn't realise.'

He walked through the hall towards them in a long white towelling gown, identical to Jonathan's. Jonathan looked up briefly to the ceiling. Then he clapped his hands.

'Jack, this is Terry. He stayed over.'

'To help with your project?'

'Exactly.'

'Hello, Terry.'

'Hello.' Terry looked as imposing in a dressing gown as he had in his clothes, or without them for that matter. It was hard for Jack to take his eyes from that close-cropped head. That was obviously the way to look, if you could manage it.

'Right, well thanks for the coffee. I only dropped in on my way to town. Just to see if there was any news. Can't stay — I've got a meeting to get to. So I'll be in touch obviously.'

In the garden, he turned back and looked briefly at Jonathan, who shrugged and then pushed the door closed.

'I suppose you kept your meter running,' he said to Terry, back in the kitchen. 'How much do I owe you? Will I have to sell a painting?'

'Oh, breakfast will do. Does your friend pose as well?'

'Not for me he doesn't.'

On his bike, heading back towards Putney, Jack kicked the machine through its gears. A handsome black bastard, that was for sure. He only hoped the son of a bitch wasn't a writer, otherwise he might be out of business altogether.

When he arrived back, he put Thelonious Monk on the record player. It always startled him, how Monk seemed to find a thousand fragments of a song on the floor, smashed down even into the tiniest shards of discordant notes, and then wondrously reassembled them into feasible architecture. Heart-scarring, laconic elegies. Crazy-paving ballads. Surreal birds swooping at the demented concert of creation. Nice work if you can get it. Memories of you.

He wasn't even gay and he was jealous. How could that be? Or maybe he was simply getting lonely. If you could only be lonely, Jack, Phil used to say to him, you might find some redemption in life. You might find love. But people like you screw their way out of loneliness. Pumping away out there, in and out and up and down. Loneliness is simply one more hole you have to fill up, isn't it? Just one more opportunity for your expansion. You can't see anything with a gap in it without getting in there and shafting.

Once a month he promised himself he'd give up sex for ever. Forget there was anything for anyone even to contemplate touching. An ancient site now abandoned. A worked-out quarry of tumescent flesh. This erection condemned by the district surveyor. Just spend his time working and reading. And writing maybe? It was about time, surely. Describe the passing years, Jack. You can do that, can't you? I thought that's what you were for. Abjure the insanity of all these tangled couplings, which bring nothing but grief and regret the morning after. To you and others. Then he would creep out on himself, when he wasn't really looking, creep out furtively, while all his resolutions were asleep. By the end of the night anything would do. Anyone from anywhere, even refugees from their own minds like him. Vagrants in the metropolis of meaningful relationships, sleeping rough under brutalist concrete. Somewhere to put himself inside, that was all, however briefly. Somewhere he might get lost in the darkness and the warmth.

Once he had gone to a traditional Chinese herbalist over in Clapham, after he read in a magazine that there were age-old oriental methods for alleviating male desire. He had been led into a tiny room by the man's son, then the ancient Chinese had himself been led in. He was almost blind and largely deaf too. This had depressed Jack to begin with: it was like being offered cures for baldness by men in barbers' shops, who invariably had not a single hair on their heads. The son left, and it became rapidly apparent that the old man knew only two or three words of English. After much gesturing at his crotch by Jack, and pointing to one of the life-size charts of the human body, cratered with regions of yin and zones of yang, the old man had suddenly nodded vigorously with understanding. He had gone to a cabinet and extracted a number of small boxes, multicoloured like firework wrappers. These he had handed to Jack, and the son had returned and charged him thirty pounds.

Back at the flat Jack tried to read the instructions, but they were all in Mandarin, so he had simply taken one of the grey blocks from one box and another from the second, and swallowed them with water. Twenty minutes later, he had stiffened unassuageably. Even his usual remedy of a hard, swift run didn't work, and he had limped back to the flat after half a mile, pulling his sweatshirt down over his shorts as best he could. Evidently the old fellow had got hold of the wrong end of the stick.

But now his hair was all gone. He looked in the mirror. He didn't know. Maybe he could find a bald woman, like those mannekins naked in shop windows he always found so oddly arousing. The smooth alabaster of their skulls and breasts and mons. Pygmalion's lady, warming up inside her marble. Hairless perfection like David Bowie in *The Man Who Fell to Earth*. He had a feeling, if anything, that he probably looked better than he had for a while. Jonathan had said so, hadn't he? But maybe that was one of his fetishes: Terry looked like a slap-head too.

He phoned Phil.

'How was it?'

'It was a funeral.'

'Are you all right?'

'Radiant.'

'Do you want to come round?'

'What's the matter? Jeremy at home washing his hair tonight?'

'Fuck off, Jack.'

'Dotty?'

'Fine. Just fine. Looking forward to seeing you.'

'Sure she hasn't mixed me up with the other one?'

She hung up.

He drank some whisky before he went out. He dipped in and out of a miscellany of bars. There was a new one with an Irish name in the middle of the High Street. The inside of it had been carefully contrived to make it look as old as possible, no expense spared. There was a scumble of ochre colours everywhere, and the drinks list and the menu had been printed in sepia on pre-blotched parchment. The stools had all been carefully scooped out prior to varnishing, to give them the feeling of thirty years' use. Ceaseless tremulous laments issued from the sound system. American country dirges. Wailing peroxide women. He couldn't stand it.

He ended up in the big one by the river, as he always did. Here women came in with other women or alone, and often left with men. Enough of them had left with him over the years for him to know. The place was rigged out with cartwheels, barrels, empty jeroboams, rotted parrots' cages with dusty Victorian dolls crammed inside them. On the ceiling, pin-ups from the 1940s stared down at him. Stocking-tops. High heels. Diaphanous negligées.

The music was quieter, though he didn't recognise it: new wave, downbeat and demotic. Self-deprecatory love talk over a hammered acoustic guitar. It was still just light enough outside for him to see the flow of the river. The tide was going out. Suddenly, wind came yelling out of nowhere, and the sky became a commotion of leaves and gulls. Why so many gulls in Putney? He'd noticed them many times before. What would Noah have made of it? Seconds later, sheets of rain whipped down the river. He hit the back of his throat with a slug of scotch. It burnt. A good strong fire. Let it burn brightly tonight.

He had been keeping his eyes open for any unaccompanied women. She was dressed in tight blue jeans and a black velvet jacket. Her face was parched with make-up, except for the vivid slash of her lipsticked mouth. Her red hair was a great ragged flame, all the way down to her shoulders. She looked about her, trying to take a fix on the place. A newcomer, evidently. Sat down at the table opposite him. It was the only table still left vacant, but she smiled at him. After he'd finished his scotch, he walked over.

'Would you let me buy you a drink?'

'Yes. Thank you. A gin and tonic.' That accent.

He ordered a large one and another whisky for himself.

'You from the north?' he asked, when he came back.

'Yes. You too, from the sound of it.'

'Oldham.'

'Leeds.'

'Small world. Come down to make your fortune, then?'

'Something like that.'

An hour later, she accepted his invitation to go back to the flat.

'This is a nice place,' she said as they went in. 'You own it?'

'Yes. What'll you have?'

'Another gin, I think.'

He went into the kitchen and poured out a substantial gin and tonic with ice, and a whisky for himself. Two, maybe three measures each. Then, before he took them back in, he slipped down to the bedroom at the bottom of the corridor and made his bed. When he arrived back with the glasses she was standing by his desk, still with her jacket on and with her big leather bag hanging over her shoulder. He put both glasses on the table. Then he put Ry Cooder's version of 'He'll Have to Go' on the record player. Flaco Jimenez's accordion was enough to make even the wind dance. Face. Breasts. Haunch. She was very slim. He could feel her bones. Anything but the shape of your own wife, that therapist had said. She rubbed her hand against him gently. How quickly he had risen from the dead.

'What's that picture?' she said. He had his face buried in her hair where it swerved out from her neck. The cocktail of a woman's smells never ceased to astonish and delight him. Lacquers and perfumes.

'A place in Galilee called Safed,' he said.

'Where's that, then?'

'Israel. It was the centre of Kabbalah studies. That's where Isaac Luria lived.' He let his hands squeeze her for a moment. 'Just before I took that photograph, I walked into a tiny synagogue. It was dusty, midday, and I walked in there and stood for, oh it must have been five minutes, looking at the place in silence. Then this tiny old man appeared from the corner. I could have sworn I'd looked everywhere and never seen him. And suddenly he was there, with his skull cap on. Stared at me. Said nothing. Walked out of the door.'

'That's interesting. You'll have to give me the money first, you know.'

He lifted his hands away.

'What?'

'You'll have to give me the money first. Before I do anything. Twenty-five pounds.'

'This is Putney, love, not Soho, or King's Cross. I don't pay for it. I've never paid for it. You need an *A to Z*.'

'You've never paid for it?'

'Never.'

'You might have to start thinking about it before long.'

'I don't have any cash anyway,' he said, as he picked up that glass of whisky and took a hard slug.

'Well, don't mention cheques to me.'

'I'll tell you what I'll do,' he said. He walked over to the drawer of his table and he took out four misshapen silver coins.

'Know what these are, do you? Denarii from the reign of Pius Antoninus. Second century, common era. Minted in Europe, but accepted as currency in Britain at the time. It's a sort of very dated ecu. I stole them on a dig, can you believe that? What a twat, eh? But then, you've already worked that one out, haven't you? I just couldn't help myself, you see, then or now. They stuck to my fingers. Any numismatic dealer worth his salt will give you at least fifty pounds for them. At least.'

She stared at him. Her breasts had been fuller than he'd expected when he'd brushed his hand against them. He still looked at the curve of her silk blouse as he spoke.

'You're really weird,' she said. 'I thought you were weird to begin with.' She let herself out, banging the door as she went.

He drained the whisky in his glass. It must have been ten minutes later he first noticed his Leica had gone. It had been sitting there at the back of his desk. His beautiful black-bodied M6. All two thousand quids' worth. That big leather bag on her shoulder. Not much point phoning the police, was there? It could get tricky trying to explain. That's the most expensive sex I never had, he thought, and went to pour himself another glass of liquor. There was a knock on the door. She had come back. She was going to pull his beloved camera out of that leather bag of hers and hand it to him. I couldn't do it, she was going to say. Maybe if you'd been a southerner, it would have been different. Forget about the money. Let's go to bed.

He opened the door. It was Martine from the flat opposite.

'Could you lend me some tea, Jack? I've run out and I don't want to leave Louise by herself.'

She came inside and he offered her the gin, still frothing over its ice-cubes. To his surprise, she took it. She was nearly as tall as he was, with long curly dark hair that she frizzed up once a fortnight. It was looking singularly unfrizzed right now. What a sad face Martine had, with those little crescents of dark blue flesh beneath her eyes. She was Swiss, from Geneva. Her husband, an architect, had started a successful practice in London some years back. He seemed to leave her once a year. She had a six-year-old, called Louise.

'Hard I think, Jack, starting again.'

'You talking about me, or you, Martine?'

'Both of us, maybe.'

'I left my wife the better part of eight years ago.' He couldn't help wondering what she might feel like underneath her clothes all the same. Now wasn't the time to try to find out. Not now, and not any other time either.

'Left her *house* eight years ago, maybe. Would you like to come to dinner next Friday? I'm a good cook. It's not the food that makes Charles keep leaving me.'

'If you agree to smile.'

She smiled. He couldn't remember ever seeing her doing that before. An odd girlish smile, crooked, something untouched by all the years between.

'He'll be back, Martine. He always comes back.'

'Not this time. The divorce proceedings have already started. On the basis of his adultery. Chivalry, I suppose.' Her accent was still French about the English *sh* sounds. One week at International House with Phil would have sorted Martine out.

'But you were his secretary.'

'I'm still his secretary. He just doesn't want me to be his wife any more, that's all.'

'Does your daughter collect coins, Martine?'

'Louise. No.'

'Give her these anyway,' he said, walking over to the table and picking up the four denarii. He put them into Martine's hand. 'A girl can't start too soon, you know, collecting coins.'

●

She always tried to clean up before a tour. Otherwise she grew so wasted her intake doubled. It started to get even more dangerous, and it was dangerous enough already.

She sat on the bed in the clinic and sang gently to herself.

> He took three stars from the evening sky
> Drained the sea of salt water
> Now he's eating flames like a lizard in the sun
> He's been with the devil's daughter . . .

He was there suddenly in the room beside her, his white coat unbuttoned, his notes in his hand. Solicitous smile. Professional. He seemed to have been talking for a minute or more before she registered that he was talking about her music. That was a new tack since the last time. Now they really were after her soul.

'It intrigues me how so much of your work is about reconciliation, Toni. And God. In that interview in *Rolling Stone* you were asked what made you an artist, and you said,

"Watching my father dance so badly on English piers in the pouring rain." What sort of relationship did you have with your father?'

A firm face, serious jaw. Brown eyes. Six foot and more. Could have been an officer. Her substitute drugs weren't the same: methadone, various tranquillising cocktails. They didn't fill the hole, but she had to have something. She could think straight enough. She'd had inquirers before, with the little guns in their minds, trained resolutely on this particular rabbit.

'You mean how did he wound me?' she said. She didn't look at him. She hardly ever looked at anyone when she spoke, it distracted her. She looked instead at her guitar propped up in the corner. She couldn't see it now without seeing Kurt's broken jaw too. 'Well, he went to the shop one evening, for some cigarettes, when I was twelve years old, and he never came back. We were in Scarborough. He was doing a disastrous show, but then he'd done plenty of those before. We went to the performance the next evening, thinking he'd have to be there, but he wasn't. He was gone. We never heard from him again. My mother's hatred became a perfect circle: the snake's mouth swallowed its own tail. There's no pier in Scarborough, you know. That's because it's got a harbour, and you don't need both. I can still remember standing on the harbour wall with my hand in his. Little hand and big hand. Sweet, isn't it?

'You mustn't believe everything you read about me, Doctor. I'm a devout person: I believe in God, and it's a God who, just like my father, looked at his creation one day and then cleared off for ever. I don't blame him for that. He left a fragment of himself inside me, they both did, so what could the word *blame* possibly mean?

'But that's only one of the holes I'm filling up. There's a much bigger hole behind the little ones. Keep pressing on, Doctor, don't get distracted by the details of biography.'

'Why needles? Why not smoke it? Most of the people coming in here these days smoke it.'

'Not the same hit.'

94

'You'll run out of veins in your arms. They'll all collapse.'

'I've got plenty of veins in my legs. Miles Davis shot up through his ankle. If Sylvia Plath had taken a shot instead of putting her head in the oven, she'd probably still be here. The first time, it's like dying and being resurrected. But then I suppose you've never tried?'

'Would I have to develop cancer to become an oncologist? Why keep coming to these places, if you've set your heart on dying a junkie?'

'I'm not a junkie.'

'Loose bowels. Cold sweats. A relentless craving for . . .'

'If I were just a junkie, I wouldn't be here talking to you, would I? You know that. I'd be back out on the street. And I don't want to die either. Not while there's still work to do. William Burroughs was on this shit for forty years.'

'Would you like to sing me one of your songs, Toni?' His voice was already quieter.

'No. No, I wouldn't. Anyway, you can't afford it. My fees are even higher than yours.'

'Why do you shave your head?'

'There was a regiment of women during the First War in Russia. All women. All had their heads shaved. I'm not sure they ever fought, but they walked round Petersburg with their uniforms on, and their shaved heads, to shame all the men who were deserting. Or maybe it was those women in Paris in 1944, remember, the ones they said had screwed Nazis. What difference does it make, Doctor, I mean give me a clue, what fucking difference does any of it make?'

She was rocking back and forth on the bed, her arms wrapped round her knees. How she detested all the speculations of belief, inside their churches, inside their hospitals, inside their minds. She studied the anarchic sparks inside herself with great delight: this was her gnosis. It didn't matter how dark it grew outside.

'Why the phoenix?'

'Considering I'm paying you, I seem to be doing all the work here. Live for five hundred years, then instead of checking into the old folks' home to watch *Neighbours* and

*Blind Date* you build yourself a funeral pyre, and flap your wings at the sun until the flames get going. Nine days later you'll find you're just the way you've always been, ready to cut your next album. They used to say that it was Christ. After five hundred years it makes itself a coffin out of frankincense and myrrh. And a worm wriggles out of this dying mess, and soon enough the worm grows wings. Sound familiar at all?'

'Underneath all the violence in your work, Toni, I always sense an ultimate commitment to reconciliation . . .'

'I hate Woodstock you know,' she said quickly, rocking harder back and forth. 'I hate the soft millennium. Children of Aquarius and their winsome smiles. I don't want to float off in some astral body. I want to stay here and work, however blasted I sometimes need to get before I can do it. You mustn't make out the soul's as shallow as a kidney dish. It's got to be at least deep enough to drown in.'

'I greatly admire your work, Toni,' (there was only weariness in his voice now) 'but if you carry on like this you'll be dead soon, don't try to convince yourself otherwise. It used to be all the different drugs when you first came. A little rainbow of intoxicants. Now you seem to have settled down more and more to just one. Burroughs is the exception, Charlie Parker's the rule.' He had put down his notes. He was stroking his knee with the flat of his hand, back and forth, and looking across towards the window, and the dervish leaves in the wind outside.

'And with the last fix, Doc, I'll fly into God's arms. It'll be my father's arms though, not my mother's. My mother can't sing, you see.'

That night she released herself from the clinic.

•

The telephone rang. Jack let the answering machine engage, and only picked it up when he heard who was speaking.

'Josh?'

'That's right. Fresh into Heathrow from Tel Aviv. You free this evening?'

'I am now.'

Joshua Segal: how many years since he had seen him? They had been undergraduates together at Lancaster. It was Josh who had taken him to Israel, Josh who was so smart he had discovered an underground inscription in Jerusalem and translated it. Jack stared at the Quittol bottle on the table and his notes at the side of it. He'd better get this finished now, before the wild man from the Levant arrived.

Jonathan had been asked for some surface graphics for a new type of bottle. They wanted something sexier, they were repositioning the disinfectant gathering dust on the top of the toilet. The old marketing strategy wasn't aggressive enough. Jack read the brief again and pondered the fact that they were changing the colour of the disinfectant itself. It was no longer to be hospital amber, but blue, aqua blue. *Blue Wave from Quittol* – that was it, wasn't it? Seascapes, nice clean beaches, pebbles scrubbed clean. The freshness of the ocean in your lavatory every morning. Nature's great salt scourer. He started hammering his word processor. He printed it all out ten minutes before the doorbell rang.

Jack pressed the door-release and stepped out into the stairwell. Josh stood above him at the top of the steps with the light behind him, clutching a tall frowzy blonde who, by the way he was hanging on to her, must presumably be drunk. You might have mentioned it, Josh, he thought. It was only as he swept her down the stairs laughing, and they tumbled into his flat, that Jack realised she was a life-size inflatable doll. Josh thrust her into his arms.

'Nadia. All the way from Petersburg. She's yours now, and I've told her to be gentle with you.'

Jack placed the de Kooning woman in the chair by the window, and looked at her inquisitively.

'You didn't bring her on the plane from Tel Aviv like this, Josh?'

'No, she's grown a lot in the last half-hour. I gave her a blow job in the back of the taxi, and slipped on those flimsy items of clothing – you should have seen the driver's face. Never realised how difficult it was to get suspenders on; only ever had to worry about getting them off before. Get the glasses out, why don't you, there's duty free to open.'

As Jack came back in from the kitchen with the glasses, Josh was explaining things to Nadia.

'So if you're very good, Jack will give you a ride in his time machine.'

Her hair was unnervingly convincing, and so were the legs with the black tops of her stockings showing, though she had a way of sitting unexpectedly akimbo. There was some fatal asymmetry about her, but Nadia looked as though she was already settling in all the same. Her expression was demented, yet at the same time oddly tranquil.

'Still have it, Jack, the time machine?'

There was mischief in his eyes. Jack poured out the whiskies.

'As I remember, we've done this number before. We both agreed that, whatever else time is, it's not a straight line.'

'So what is it then?'

'A vortex. Maybe even a helix.' Jack drank some more whisky.

'A double helix maybe?'

'Could be. If you want to place your bet both ways.'

'Going up and down, forwards and backwards at the same time.'

'Like a film that keeps replaying the past.'

'Did you ever seen the ones of the camps?' Josh said, his voice growing suddenly quieter and his smile disappearing as he turned to look at him. Josh's eyes seemed to have grown browner, as his hair had greyed. His forehead looked even taller than before. It was engraved with wrinkles now. He'd inherited the traditional electric mop of the Jewish intellectual. Einstein's coiffure lived on.

'Some,' Jack said.

'They show them all the time at Yad Vashem, you know. I can't go there any more. How the fuck did you end up writing the copy for Quittol's global relaunch, Jack? Forgive me, but I glanced at your brief while you were in the kitchen. I don't remember you this way.'

Jack shrugged and stared out of the window at the pavement above him.

'I blame my early Trotskyism. Taught me there was nothing much to choose between the varieties of capitalism. You have to sweep it all away, it's all oppression. There's the same total condemnation – the same requirement for apocalyptic hygiene. So why should I be out on the streets of Calcutta helping to educate the poor, when I could be here in the comfort of my own home, writing copy for Quittol's global relaunch? It'll all come crashing down anyway.'

'You don't believe in the revolution now.'

'Not any more, no. Do you? That's not the way it's going to come crashing down, is it?'

'Why *did* you stop being a Trot, out of interest? You were a Trot when I first met you, the most articulate one in Lancaster. By your third year, you'd packed it all in.'

'If you could believe in a rationale of history, then in one sense you had to believe that history was rational, accountable. And I stopped believing that. My experience of time was different.'

'As I remember it,' Josh said, smiling again, 'Marxism was brilliant at diagnosing what was wrong, and completely hopeless at ever putting it right. Which is why Marxist teachers were so engaging, and Marxist leaders all turned into mass-murderers. It was a good essay you wrote though, about the pyramids being the ultimate form of surplus labour, the margin of death on the horizon. Do you still have your little glitches on the timescale?'

'Less and less, thank God. You know my Church's teaching on that, do you? Classic form of demonic possession, being able to shift back and forth through the years. Did you think I was nuts? I never could work it out.'

'There's a lot worse things to be than nuts, in my book. But no, I didn't, as a matter of fact. It sounded plausible enough to me. Why *should* time just keep moving forward? Whoever proved that one, to anyone's satisfaction? I'd thought Einstein proved at least the possibility of the opposite. Percy Hardinge was most intrigued, you know.'

'You told him?'

'I told him. I said you were ashamed of it, swore him to secrecy. That impressed him. I think if you'd gone round boasting about it, he'd have thought you were a charlatan. He had a theory, you see, that all great archaeologists had something uncanny working for them. He said to me, Look at Schliemann with Troy, or Layard with Nineveh. It simply didn't make sense that these guys stumbled on those sites. They turn up sweating, and a few days later, history's theirs. It *is* pretty improbable, when you examine the evidence; in fact, logically, it's almost absurd. So old Hardinge reckoned some people still heard the past, maybe even saw it. Voices from underground. Hardinge even thought there was still something uncanny in poetry. He said that's what led Schliemann to Troy: his absolute trust in the text of the *Iliad* as he rooted about up there in Hissarlik, ignoring every single scientist and philologist of the day. He reckoned the writings had summoned him over a couple of thousand years. So what with you being a writer . . .'

'Trouble is, that it was also trusting the ancient texts so much that made Schliemann misconstrue Mycenae. The Troy he found wasn't Homer's Troy at all. He was at the wrong level.'

'Ah, Jack, why do you always make things so hard for yourself? Even when you're offered a gift, all you can do is to question its provenance. Anyway, that's why old Percy was so disappointed when you went off to become an adman. He thought you might rediscover Atlantis.'

'I'm a weak swimmer, Josh.'

'Were you really scared of turning psychotic? Or was all that Ashley Simon stuff just good copy?'

'I'd still say it's the past that drives you crazy, the past buried inside.'

'The bit you can't excavate that keeps on talking, you

mean? Gibbering away down there in the tomb? So the old Viennese quack had it – it really is all down to your mummy. And now you allay the spirits by writing about the blue wave, I see. The tide's freshness through your lavatory bowl each morning. Let the dead bury their dead, but help them where necessary with a pyramid-load of banality. Sorry, Jack, I've only been back in the country an hour and I'm already insulting you.'

'Insult away,' Jack said, pouring himself more of the whisky, and feeling mildly drunk already. 'I've missed your insults. Maybe they kept me honest. I'd better take you to a restaurant and feed you, before I forget.'

'If I forget thee, O Jerusalem . . . Ah, don't get me on to Jerusalem. Not yet anyway. Hey, I nearly forgot.' He hunted in one of his bags and pulled out a book. 'There you go, comrade, my latest.'

Jack took the book from his hand. *In the Temple's Shadow*, by Joshua Segal.

Just before they left the flat, Josh turned to him with sudden urgency.

'Jack, I know this isn't very English of me, but I don't suppose there's any chance you could get me laid is there? Some English girl with a candle in her window just waiting for the phone to ring, and then you say, Come and meet my brilliant intellectual friend, fresh from Jerusalem. Enjoy. I'll happily pay for a meal for her, and a friend of hers, come to that, if you yourself . . .'

'Can't even get myself laid these days,' Jack said laughing. 'Sorry, Josh.'

As they walked up the road together, he told him the story of the lady from Leeds.

'And she said you'd have to start paying for it soon?'
'She said that.'
'Bitch.'
'Maybe she had a point.'
'What are we eating?'
'Afghan.'

'Not much chance of any fillies frolicking there then, is there? Ever tried to fight your way inside a *burqa*, Jack?'

'No.'

'Only did it once. I've still not recovered the full use of my index fingers. I think their mothers sew them in. Like cushions. Impenetrable cushions. Do you mind if I sleep with Nadia tonight? She'll be yours forever after, remember. Just the one night, Jack, I'm a desperate man. And it's not true what they say, by the way: that women are spoiled for you guys after they've been with us. It's a bit of a come-down for them, obviously, but with care and nourishment, they can still be reconciled to a Gentile fate.'

'You haven't changed, Josh.'

'You have, though. That's one serious haircut, boy.'

As they sat down inside the restaurant, images from their time together at Lancaster were filling Jack's mind.

'Is Percy Hardinge still alive?' Jack asked.

'Alive and digging, until last year anyway. And he's Sir Percy Hardinge now, if you don't mind. I was planning doing an interview with him. Want to come?'

'Not just at the moment,' Jack said, wondering how he could explain the last ten years of his life to the man he'd so respected.

'He was excavating the ruins of Carlton Abbey in Yorkshire,' Josh said. 'Pieces keep appearing in *Archaeologia*. The Carlton Shield, showing the Virgin and child. Early thirteenth century. Some pilgrim badges. Lots of coins, some as early as Edward III. He was trowelling the infirmary last October. Some interesting medieval surgical instruments. Did you ever send him *About Time*, Jack?'

'No.'

'Why not?'

'I'd hoped I'd be able to invite him to the film.'

'Ah. You should, you know – send it to him, I mean. He understood mania.'

Jack tried to explain the intricacies of the menu to Josh, who finally shrugged his shoulders and said, 'It's not kosher,

whatever else it is, so why don't you order for both of us?'
Jack did.

'So what are you on to, Josh?'

His face darkened momentarily.

'Yesodot Mikdash.'

'Which means?'

'The foundations of the temple. A secretive group operating in Jerusalem. Funded by a Yank millionaire.'

'And?'

'These guys are real fucking whacks. Recovering Jerusalem for the Jews from underground, and each time they locate another Jewish foundation, they turf out anyone above who's not one of the chosen. Palestinians, Christians, Armenians. They make offers that can't be refused. If they *are* refused, then they find some little irregularity about planning permission, safety, hygiene, anything. If they can't find that, they use their paid security men to intimidate. And these are real thugs, believe me. They don't care whether it's women or children they're frightening. These guys are out to rebuild the Holy City. Anyone who gets in their way is asking for serious trouble. They can even show you the very rock the Shekinah rested on, before she took off. They've got a complete topography of everything since Moses. When there's no real evidence, they speculate from old, unreliable accounts. When there isn't even that to go on, they make do with some kind of spurious kabbalistic numerology. At least that's what I *think* they do. Then someone else loses a home or a school or a hospital. It's making me ashamed to be Jewish. You could say it's no more than the government itself has been doing for the better part of thirty years. You could say that, and in fact you'd be largely right. But the Mayor of Jerusalem has dinner with these characters, and then comes out the next day and tells us all they don't exist, that we're imagining it. I won't be told something doesn't exist when I know that it does.

'You remember Edward Haresh? I took you to see his shop near Jaffa Gate. His father had that shop before him and *his* father before that. They found some stones in a

103

tunnel that ran parallel with the shop. And they've decided they're important foundations, these stones. I don't know what evidence they've based this on, I don't see how anyone could possibly know, not yet anyhow. Two weeks ago, Edward's shop was knocked down. The top floor, built thirty years ago, was in breach of the regulations. It stuck out two feet more than it should have done over the passageway.'

'Can't the government do anything?'

'Ah, Jack, what an innocent you are. You're not listening closely to what I'm saying, are you? Eat your food and pay attention. In the first place Yesodot Mikdash doesn't exist. It's the fantasy of paranoid investigative journalists like me. There's just this group of pious Jews, with the dust from ancient masonry dropping on to their yarmulkas, prodding away down in time's cellars. What could be wrong with that? This has been our journey through time, to return to Jerusalem. And they need a bit of protection, I mean who doesn't these days in the Middle East? So they have armed guards. The government subsidises those guards, as a matter of fact. The Palestinians know this, and say it, and the Prime Minister shrugs the well-tailored shoulders of his Armani suit and says, Where do all these calumnies appear from? I tell you, Jack, these sons of bitches are frightening, they're like a single crazy image of all that is craziest in Israel today. And I'm about to establish who the American with the greenbacks is. What's this, then?'

'This is your next course. Don't look at it like that. You're not going to have any sex tonight, Josh, so eat. Enjoy.'

'You said that well. My mother always reckoned you were Jewish somewhere in the backyard of your genealogy.'

'How is she?'

'She's dead, Jack. She's down there in the dust too.'

'I'm sorry.'

'She wasn't, by the end.'

'Surely all excavation work in Jerusalem is controlled by the authorities?'

'Indeed it is. But look here, Mr Goodrich, the state of Israel would not exist at all without goodwill and subscription from the USA. Everyone knows that, particularly the Arabs. So if a wealthy donor, who wishes (for understandable reasons of security) to remain anonymous, gives substantial funding to help excavation work in the Holy City, and a group of dedicated amateurs offer their work *gratis* in areas not concerned with major sites, do you seriously expect us to turn such offers down? This isn't an archaeological critique that you in the West are engaged upon, sir, it is straight-forward anti-Semitism. That's the response, should you ask.

'Yesodot Mikdash. I've traced their American funding to two groups, one called Cherith Brook International and another called Ravens Inc. Any bells?'

'Ravens. Cherith Brook. Sorry, Josh, you'll have to help me out, I spend too much time thinking about lavatory bowls these days. Have some of this one, it's delicious.'

'It looks like a poached egg that's lost its yolk. This is good food. You must understand I'm only piecing things together here, bit by bit. But a number of statements make it obvious that these guys are twenty-two carat gold messian-ists. And you'll remember the tradition that has Elijah returning shortly before the coming of the Messiah himself. You pale Galileans reckon he was John the Baptist. So how do you feed Elijah, while he's still in the political wilderness? Come on, Jack, you don't have to actually put your head *down* the toilet bowl to earn a living, do you? *And the word of the Lord came unto him, saying, Get thee hence, and turn thee eastward, and hide thyself by the brook Cherith, that is before Jordan. And it shall be, that thou shalt drink of the brook; and I have commanded . . .*'

' . . . *the ravens to feed thee there,*' Jack said at last, with a smile.

'Welcome back to the world of intellectual inquiry.'

'So where are they based, this messianic group of yours?'

'There's a building on a reclaimed site in East Jerusalem. Very secret, very heavily guarded. But the real headquarters, I reckon, is on the Upper West Side, New York, which is where I'm headed next. After I've seen a few editors in

London. I don't always receive a very warm welcome from some of the editors back in Jerusalem these days.'

Josh suddenly went into a reverie, and Jack saw something he'd never seen before in his face. Just a passing cloud for an instant.

'You scared, Josh?'

'I'm scared, believe me. I've seen those fuckers in operation. But I can still see that look on the face of old Edward Haresh as he stared at me. He didn't say anything. He didn't need to. But I think the expression on his face would have translated into Hebrew as, So are you just going to stand there, big boy, while they bulldoze my father's shop?'

Walking back to the flat afterwards, Josh finally asked, gently, 'Phil?'

'She wants a divorce.'

'Ah. Always liked Phil. What was it with you guys?'

'Don't ask me. The shrink I went to tried to convince me that she'd made me lose confidence in myself as a lover.'

'Run that one by me again.'

'You know, Phil was really very capable. I suppose that was part of the attraction. Never met a girl like her – they didn't make them in Oldham. Part of that upper-middle-class tradition. Pilot's licence, competent sailor, mountain climbing, interior decoration, riding. She once fixed the car, for Christ's sake. She was always so *busy*. Maybe she just didn't have time to have an orgasm.'

'Maybe she didn't have time to let you know she'd had one.'

'Does that strike you as likely, Josh?'

'No, but I'm not a woman. I don't know what goes on inside. I had one girlfriend who just moaned very quietly and moved her head gently from side to side. Always exactly the same volume of moan, always the same slow rate of head movement. I asked her once if she ever came. She said I didn't understand. She said men didn't understand, but she didn't blame us, because of all the twaddle written on the subject this century, all the films, all the tapes, all the videos. She said she could achieve orgasm, but she had to concentrate for that, and it made too much of a meal of it usually, given as how we didn't have all the time in the world for our trysts as it was. It was a lunchtime arrangement, above the bank where she worked. She said it was the difference between going to a concert and just switching on the radio and relaxing. She didn't feel like listening to anything orchestral with me, particularly as she had a feeling it would be Schönberg rather than Mozart, so I suppose I was the Country and Western channel. Maybe that's the way Phil liked it too. Maybe we're the only ones who *have* to keep going till we spill over.'

'What happened to Mira, Josh?'

'She left me.'

'Why?'

'Give us a break, will you? And not a word of this in front of Nadia, understand? Mira and I decided on an open marriage, that's all. It's just that her side opened up a little more than I'd expected. Opened up so much that she went and married someone else. She's got a closed marriage this time, certainly closed to me, anyway.'

Back in the flat they drank coffee.

'Nadia's quiet tonight, Jack, but don't be misled. When the mood takes her, she's Mata Hari crossed with Salomé. Do you remember Sandra Diskey at Lancaster?'

'How could I forget?'

'You remember that time she borrowed the projector and screen?'

'She just wouldn't let up. I finally gave in. I was terrified I'd never see the stuff again. I was responsible for it all.'

'I never did tell you what happened, did I?'

'Didn't realise you knew.'

'She invited me to a private screening. In that big house she lived in, outside town. I began to realise as she loaded the reel, there were only going to be the two of us there. Then she showed me this compilation. All films about Hitler, one after another. Documentary footage. Hitler ranting at Nuremberg, Hitler silent with his arm raised as the troops marched past, Hitler striding up an aisle in Strasbourg

Cathedral with this hushed and reverential look on his face, Hitler on the balcony up in the hills with Eva Braun, Hitler entering Vienna, Hitler laughing with Mussolini. No sound-track. No subtitles. One reel and that was all.'

'And?'

'Afterwards she took me to bed. Don't ask me what it meant, Jack, because I don't know. Didn't then, don't now. After she'd taken her clothes off, she said to me, "I've just had a cap fitted." That was a new one for me. I felt as though I'd been forced into a lay-by, instead of driving through to the centre of town. Strange isn't it, the way women can never know the size of themselves inside? Only men can know that. Strange. Do you think they ever think about it?'

By the time Jack woke the following morning, Josh had already left. There was a note on the table.

> Thanks for the hospitality, comrade. I'll repay it on my
> way back through. Take it slowly with Nadia. Don't
> be fooled by her flirting. I've a terrible feeling last night
> was her first time.

When Jack was washed and dressed, he phoned Jonathan to make sure it was all right for him to come over. He always phoned now. When he arrived at the house in Kew, it was Terry who let him in.

'Hello, Terry, how are you?'

'Fine, Jack. Yourself?'

'Been worse. How's the play going?'

'Coming on. I've got the title now.'

'What is it?'

'*Don't Cross Your Legs Till You Die.*'

'Just remind me.'

'The Crusades.'

'With you now. The figures on the tombs?'

'That's it. I read Jonathan's copy of *About Time*, by the way. You shouldn't have stopped writing, do you know that?' Jack looked at the brave young fellow, so open-faced. Was he being condescended to?

'I didn't. And I have *The Blue Wave* here in my bag to prove it.'

●

The concert hall in Dublin was accruing all the sound and commotion that always ushers in a major gig, all the clatter and the shouts. She sat in the dressing room, strumming her guitar and humming. Her manager, Seth Waterhouse, had been walking around, pointing his all-purpose smile downwards at everyone, like an usherette's torch.

He peered in at Toni again. He was nervous.

'How are we doing, Toni?'

She didn't need to open her eyes. His voice smiled enough. She'd liked him once, thought he was a genuine bloke. Even slept with him that one night in Chicago. That was in the days when she still imagined she was searching for a genuine bloke. The more genuine they were, the more they bored her, the more she detested everything they were genuine about. But in those days he played the bass guitar for her band. Badly. Now she called him Onion: under each layer of skin was just another layer of skin. It could make you weep.

'How are *we* doing, Onion?' she said. 'You planning on coming out there with me, are you? Remember, there's all those people who turn up empty and expect to be full by the interval. Sure you've got enough inside there to start handing it out?'

'I just wanted to make sure everything was all right with you, that's all.' Onion's wounded tone.

'You just wanted to make sure I'm not so full of smack that I can't even be bothered strumming my guitar, but stand there giggling into the mike, like that night in Illinois. You just wanted to make sure your twenty per cent is safe. How *is* the red Ferrari, Onion?

'Anyway, your interest is secure this evening. I've had two glasses of wine and a joint, and I think we could agree to call that abstinence, in terms of little Toni Inglish. I'll be making up for it later. Tell the band not to come on until I've done the first number.'

'I thought you were starting with "Devil's Daughter".'

'Girl's got a right to change her mind, hasn't she? Now tell the man in the shiny suit to announce me. One spot, on the mike, and that's all.'

Seth stood in the wings and chewed the back of his left index finger as she walked on. The audience couldn't work out what was happening, and neither could he.

In her black dress she was almost invisible as she stepped swiftly across the stage. The white moon-disc of her face slid into the spotlight. Applause started but she was already singing, and the applause died out again as they tried to make out the words. He'd never heard the song before; she must have just written it. And she was singing *a cappella*. Thank God we've started this tour in Dublin, not New York, he thought.

> There's an English soldier face down in a muddy field
> And an English soldier's kneeling at his head
> One soldier killed the other
> He killed his English brother
> All around are English soldiers lying dead
> And the snowstorm blows and rages over Towton
> Palm Sunday back in 1461
> The red rose and the white rose
> How the English blood flows
> Now the killing in the killing-field's begun
>
> Soldiers of the islands in their graves
> Lying underground or under waves
> Soldiers that the battle couldn't save
> Soldiers of the islands in their graves

As the chorus about those English soldiers started to sink in, a few boos brayed at the back of the hall, but Toni just carried on singing with her eyes closed, clenching her hands in front of her.

> There's an Irish soldier lying in the trenches
> In the mud of Flanders as the rockets fly

He's here to save the valley
In his corpse-strewn little alley
Hasn't even bothered to ask why
But he'd rather be back home in County Sligo
Where daisies' heads peer up above the grass
If you stick your head up here
Your face will disappear
As your eyes get closed for ever in the blast

This time as she started into the chorus, the boos had grown louder. She didn't pause, didn't hesitate and didn't even open her eyes, but went straight into the last verse.

Now there's a Scottish soldier crouching in an alley
It's Londonderry 1985
Spins up towards the windows
Every time the wind blows
He's frightened and he'd like to stay alive
Somewhere up inside the darkness there's a sniper
Who wants another kill to call his own
Another young man's name
His Armalite takes aim
And one more soldier falls dead on the stone

Soldiers of the islands in their graves
Lying underground or under waves
Soldiers that the battle couldn't save
Soldiers of the islands in their graves

There was some applause, but as much abuse, as more and more people realised they had just heard an elegy to the dead of the British Armed Forces. She was already waving the band on and strumming her guitar by then. 'Well that's just one for you to be thinking about,' she said into the mike as she hit hard into 'Devil's Daughter'.

You can eat your words and swallow your pride
Bathe in holy water
But you can't wash away what you cannot hide
Your love of the Devil's Daughter

•

Dale Freeman woke finally at six, though *woke* isn't somehow the right word, since that suggested he'd been sleeping, whereas all he'd done was to dither intermittently in and out of oblivion. He lay still and listened to his wife's breathing, and he counted money. He counted the incomings and the outgoings, he counted them forwards and then back again. Once he started in the middle and worked both ways at once, but whichever way he did it nothing added up. Two hours later his wife woke too and went downstairs without a word. When she came back she sat down with her back to him at the end of the bed.

'There's a letter for you from the Building Society, Dale.'

He held out his hand.

'So, give a man his mail.'

'I read it.'

'I thought you said it was addressed to me.'

'I read it, Dale.' She had stood up and was facing him, hands on hips. He could make out the shape of her heavy breasts through the shift. 'You're mortgaging the house.'

'Had no choice.'

'Your father gave it to us, as I remember. It was a mere technicality that it was in your name, as I remember. You were always going to change that, and put it in our joint names, as I remember. So what right have you to go and ask for a mortgage on it, without even mentioning the bloody fact to me?'

'I'll get it all back.'

'You'd better get it all back, Dale, because if you don't I'll be leaving.'

Dale walked down the Earls Court Road towards the underground station. He tried to think how much it had changed for Tricia, since she agreed to marry the golden boy with the art collection bequeathed him by his daddy. He had taken her to meet his father in that grand apartment off the Boulevard Saint Germain. She had stared round in disbelief at the collection of modern paintings and sculptures in there. His father, always with an eye for the ladies, had thrown his arm around her shoulder. 'And all this will be my son's, my dear Tricia, and yours too, if you marry him. He has asked you, I trust?'

Now what had he got? Debts, and a lot more of them on the way. He stopped at the newsagent's and bought *The Times*. As he walked away he riffled through to the music pages, then halted, walked back, and bought four other papers. By the time he arrived at the office, he had read all the reviews of Toni Inglish's concert in Dublin. As he walked in, Marilyn pointed to the package on his table.

'Special delivery. By courier.'

He opened it up and looked at Tim's prototypes of an earring, a necklace, a ring and a brooch. The phoenix rising in blue turquoise out of ruby flames. They were all startlingly well made. Five minutes later he was on the telephone to Jack.

'Fantastic, isn't it?'

'What?' Jack asked, not trying to disguise his irritation.

'Come on, guys, you've got to pay attention here. The reviews of Toni's concert. Controversial material, shouting back at the audience, undeniably magnetising performance. We couldn't ask for more, could we? I need you and your mate John round here soonest. I have the prototypes on my desk and they are stunning, boy, believe me.'

'I don't know that Jonathan will be free this week.'

'This week! I'm talking about this morning, for fuck's sake. Come on, Jack, give a dog a bone.'

Jack put the phone down and stared at the floppy disk on his table. He and Jonathan were trying to come up with a concept for CC, Century Communications, to create brand loyalty for their disks. They were rapidly reaching the conclusion that it was impossible. All you could do was to dress them up brightly, make them cheaper, or give away free weekends in Paris to lucky random punters. He called Jonathan.

'Did you ask him why he hasn't paid my bill then?'

'I didn't get a chance. Come on, let's give him one last shot, shall we? Then you can ask him yourself.'

When they arrived and Dale pointed triumphantly to the

jewellery on the table, they both stared at it in silence. They had discussed what he was likely to come up with and were not optimistic. But the prototypes were obviously strikingly well made.

'Can you really match this in production?' Jonathan asked, as he bent down to look more closely.

'That's my problem. I know a man in Switzerland. Old friend of my father's. I'll be seeing him next week. But don't you worry about production. Your worry is how to present this to its best advantage. I've been brooding about which photographer to use . . .'

'I'm not sure it should be photography at all,' Jonathan said, holding up the brooch and turning it round in the light. 'High-quality illustrations might capture more of the mood. They can be more . . . elusive and intriguing sometimes.'

'And you could do that, could you?'

Jonathan stared at Dale in silence for a moment.

'You haven't paid my bill. Is there any good reason for that? You've had it over six weeks.'

'Oh, Christ. Marilyn, as soon as these guys leave, get that bookkeeper on the phone, would you? But I don't want what I've got to say to him going beyond these four walls. He'll have to go, you know. I can't put up with it any more.'

Outside on the pavement, Jonathan and Jack looked at each other.

'Well?'

'Well, at least I know he'll pay me for the work so far.'

'How do you mean?' Jack asked. Jonathan held up the package in his left hand.

'Because if he doesn't, Mr Dale Freeman's not getting his prototypes back.'

Inside the office Marilyn gave Dale one of her looks.

'Shall I get the bookkeeper for you now, Dale?'

'You can always find yourself another job you know, Marilyn, if you really do find all this too much of a strain.'

•

Jack stopped before the reproduction of the portrait of

114

Ambroise Vollard on the wall. He'd once been obsessed by Cubism, by the way time recomposed our faces, took them apart. On his honeymoon in Paris he had stood for hours in front of those canvases by Picasso and Braque, convinced that here time was asserting its vagrant rights. If you walked around an object, or turned it over in your hands, you could see all its facets, so why condemn everyone else to a single, momentary perspective in a picture? Why freeze the face of the clock in only one of its lunar aspects? The Cubists understood that time was not so much a progression as a collage, with the old and the new cohabiting inside the same frame. He knew why Picasso had cannibalised those African masks too. It wasn't for the severity of their simplification of the human face, nor for the savage kick in the teeth they delivered to all the refinements of Victoriana; it was the magic that still accrued about them. They did not acknowledge the dog-days of science, they still propitiated dark powers, they knew sex and violence were the routes to the gods. All beds were altars, all altars beds. The artist was the insomniac priest who ministered over both. Martine came back with two glasses of wine and saw him looking closely at the picture.

'You like that?' she said.

'Yes, very much.'

'I keep it there because it reminds me of my husband. Not the features. Just the fragments. How they seem always to be falling apart and coming together.'

'A blueprint of the world,' he said. 'Well, let's drink to your husband then. Long may he fall apart and come together.'

'Whoever he comes together with next time, it won't be me,' she said. Her English was obviously better than he'd thought. 'All that finished years ago. Here's to Charles anyway. And your wife, maybe? Wish them both a *bon voyage*.'

'Sam Goldwyn used to stand on the boat and shout *bon voyage* to the people on the quayside,' Jack said. 'And who's to say he wasn't right?'

They sipped their wine and Jack turned back again to the picture.

'You like all Picasso, or just that one?' Martine asked.

'I like a lot of it. I'm frightened by his extremes.'

'What are his extremes?'

'Sentimentality on one side; savage violence on the other.'

'Why should they frighten you?'

'Because they're my extremes too.'

'Ah. At least you notice, Jack. A lot of men don't notice. They assume that's what women are here for − to do the noticing for them.'

Jack had only been in her flat for five minutes and the conversation had already turned into a critique of intimacy. He felt a mild alarm. Whenever women praised men for the perspicacity of their self-knowledge, he grew sceptical. It seemed to him that the great power of women over men was that they had at least *some* notion of what they were after. Most men didn't have a clue. They only knew what they wanted after women had already given it to them. They were tangles of confusion, knots of desire and loathing. Labyrinths. Howls and bellows in the dark. Artifice and bestiality. Anyway, whatever else was going to happen with Martine, they were most certainly not going to bed together. There was no desire for it, and no need. He'd decided that much before he came and resolved upon it. They could be friends, though.

She went off to prepare the food and he looked about the room. There was a large photograph of Corbusier's Unité d'Habitation in Marseilles, and an intriguing little drawing at the side of it. A pen drawing of a building he should have recognised, but didn't quite. She came back with red peppers stuffed with rice and they sat down to eat. She started to talk.

It had struck Jack before how erotic intelligence could be. Brightness could irradiate the plainest of features, making them desirable, whereas stupidity could smudge the most perfect good looks. Martine wasn't plain in fact, as he realised the longer he looked at her, but a certain Swiss reserve that went right through her body had always hidden from him the mobility and humour latent in her face.

'The little drawing,' she said. 'It's Corbu's sketch of the Pantheon.'

'Corbu?'

'Sorry. Le Corbusier. We forget he's not everyone's religion.'

'I thought he was just an architect.'

'If Charles were here, you would have to leave now, immediately. Speaking of Corbu in such tones! Really, Jack, you lack respect, you know. Every day of our honeymoon in Zürich we went to the Corbusier House at the side of the lake and we sat in it. It was Charles's temple. The temple of perfect proportion. Not very practical if you have children, I grant you, but we didn't then. So Charles fell in love with me and Le Corbusier, but don't ask me in which order. And he's stayed faithful to one of his loves, anyway. He's in Zürich now for some conference. These guys still want to turn the world into *la cité radieuse*, you know. They've not given up. He woke every morning of our honeymoon at five, to watch them wash the streets. He couldn't believe that they didn't just brush them. He was a new boy in the big city, then.'

'They wash them every day?' Jack said, thinking of Oldham.

'In Zürich, every day. And never use anything cheaper than Evian. And for the rivers, Perrier water, that's what makes them bubble. We are a very clean people. We even launder our money.'

He had started laughing. She refilled his glass and went to the kitchen with the plates. She came back with *chilli con carne* and rice.

'This isn't a Swiss meal,' he said.

'All meals are Swiss, like all currencies. There doesn't have to be a pig in the middle of either, but I'm afraid there often is.'

He'd begun to find the small crescents of blue bruises underneath her eyes oddly endearing. He wondered how many sleepless hours were contained inside them. Her head on the pillow, no one's hands about her, no one's lips. She had a way of raising her arms in sudden, bird-like jerks.

It seemed unexpectedly enticing. Freckles round her high cheekbones, dark hair curling all round her face and down to her shoulders. She'd had it frizzed again since the last time he'd seen her. He remembered the whiteness of Swiss mountains in the photograph that hung on the wall of his school. He could see part of the frosted brocade of her bra as it showed through her red silk blouse.

Later on they sat on the sofa and she put on a Thelonious Monk record. How did she know that? Or was it only an accident?

'Oh, we believed in the city of towers,' she was saying dreamily. 'Geometry was the true language of man. We had emerged from the ages of mythology and decoration. We could clarify life – that's why people became so excited about Corbusier – it really was a kind of religion. After I read *Vers une architecture* – Charles has a signed copy, you know – I did feel as though I'd undergone some kind of conversion. I saw the true shapes of things around me, and the falseness of distorting those shapes with phoney façades. Geometry is the language of man. Corbusier said that, and it's a great compliment he's meaning. But don't ask me why it seemed so possible then, and so impossible now, because I don't know.' She left his hand in her lap, and only stopped him when he reached her breast.

'No,' she said, and he recoiled. Never could take rejection, could you, Jack?

'Not now,' she said kindly. 'Louise is asleep, but she often wakes up, and it would confuse her. On Saturday she is staying with her father. I could come to your flat and you could show me your pictures this time. And give me some Oldham cuisine.' She ran her fingers along his shaved scalp. 'I do admire the Swiss precision of your haircut.'

He started laughing again.

'I won't be one of your women, Jack.'

'Have you been watching through the little lens in your door, Martine?'

'I come from the country of Calvin and Geneva. All Swiss can tell you what their neighbours are up to. We can't help ourselves. We were brought up in *la cité curieuse*. If you want to try me out, Jack, you'll have to be faithful while you're trying.'

'All right,' he said.

'Promise?'

'I promise.'

When he went back into his flat that night, Nadia looked at him askance. He could have sworn her short skirt had ridden even higher up her thighs. Her black stocking-tops were showing. She was playing the slut again. Jealous.

'I know, I know,' he said. 'I have everything I need here. Why get involved with another woman with a daughter who's about to be divorced? I've already got one of those, haven't I?'

•

That Saturday Phil had asked Jack if he could take Dotty over to Merton Abbey Mills for her drama workshop. He thought he had better clean up the flat a little before he set out. He shifted things about, collected dirty cups and glasses that had accrued on various surfaces over the last few weeks, and washed them all up. He tidied the table and closed down his computer. He rearranged the pyramid, the marble egg and the figurine of Ishtar. You could show me your pictures this time, she had said. He stared about him at the pictures he had on the walls – he hardly looked at them from one year to the next. There was the nineteenth-century print of Oldham, with the cotton mills in full production. There was the old French engraving of the ground plan of the Church of the Holy Sepulchre in Jerusalem. He had bought that one day in a strange old shop with Josh. It's good that you should take back a memento of the least spiritual place on earth, Josh had said. There were stills from some of Pelikan's films: Simone Weil in the hospital, Nietzsche draped in his white lunatic's gear, Emily Dickinson in her room at Amherst. How often homes turned into hospitals and prisons in his work, and sometimes the hospitals and prisons turned, by the end, into homes. There was a reproduction of one of the Lascaux cave paintings. An auroch daubed in ochre on the wall of an underground cave in the age of reindeers. Human beings had to shape what they saw about them to make themselves real. It wasn't magic to capture the animals, it was magic to capture themselves, to connect them up again to the great shaping powers, to share in the work of the gods. That had been his argument in his essay and Percy Hardinge had been intrigued by it. There were his portraits of Dotty, done on his Leica.

There was also a little picture of Dylan in the 1960s. Jack picked up his guitar and put it into an open tuning. He ran quickly through 'Arthur MacBride' to make sure he remembered all the words. That was probably his best song; it had been his party piece years back. Martine might be surprised there was another side to him. Another side of Jack Goodrich. Maybe she knew already: she seemed to know everything else. It felt good that she was coming round that evening. He ran his hand across his scalp. He couldn't face cooking, though. He'd order a take-away – and she could choose which species of the world's cuisine she wished to sample. That woman from Leeds had said he might have to start paying soon: well, he could stretch to a take-away at least.

Only at the last minute did he notice Nadia. She had become so much a part of the room, he had forgotten she was there. He might be bringing Dotty back here in the afternoon, so he'd best make sure the little Russian belle was out of the way. He carried her through to the bedroom and put her under the sheets. Only her hair sprouted out and spilled over the duvet. The hair really was very convincing. He ran his hand through it. Blonde hair. It felt as real as Phil's.

'Don't get the wrong idea about this, Nad. I'm not putting you in my bed because I have any untoward ideas. You're not that sort of girl, whatever Josh says, and I'm not that sort of bloke. You're his sweetheart, not mine, and I'm chaperoning you until his return. But with my daughter possibly coming to the flat . . . Well, you've been around.

You know the problems a fellow can create for himself these days.'

He rode over to Earlsfield and collected Dotty. Phil gave him the keys to the car. He looked at her carefully.

'Nice hair-do, Phil. You always told me you couldn't be bothered.' She looked away and said nothing.

They drove over and Dotty chattered away.

'Do you think we go running when we dream, Daddy?'

'How do you mean?'

'It's just that Lupin's legs move, when he sleeps.'

'Lupin?'

'Jeremy's dog.'

'Lupin.'

'He's a golden retriever.'

'Jeremy and Lupin.'

He made sure she was safely in the theatre, and then went to check out the car-boot sale. It hadn't been there the last time he'd brought her. It was certainly there now. Spewed over the huge asphalt car-park were the uninventoried contents of a thousand lives. Old golf clubs leaned out from their tattered bags. A black-and-white television set squatted on a chair, raddled from the memories of the millions of flickering moments it had emitted, all those shadowy figures crossing and recrossing its small screen, fallen silent inside there now: silent gunfire, silent laughter, silent embraces. Dead memories ghosting it in a white plastic box. Cricket bats from fifty years back, the willow almost blackened with the linseed they had drunk. Ice-skates with rusted blades; three-piece suites stained with coffee and beer and the ceaseless scraping of bodies against them. Ten-year-old VDUs stared out blindly at the passing crowds, detached now from their electronic brains. Six antiquated wheelchairs, aimed crookedly one into another, as though evacuated after some catastrophe. A table with twenty white chef's jackets and fifteen white chef's hats, all used, much used in fact, but laundered. A pair of orthopaedic boots, at least three decades old, the platform on the sole of one a good four inches above that of the other, waiting for the right subject to arrive, limping with the precise degree of asymmetry exhibited by the original owner. Mirrors with etched shapes round the edges, lilac or fleur-de-lys in tiny swags, like the one he'd seen his face rise up through every day for eighteen years in Oldham, that pool of silver in which he'd watched each year break surface. A large old wooden spirit-level, the same size as the one his father kept in the garage, its bubbles still swinging gently this way and that, vivid yellow eyes peering out of their small green seas. He could hear the pained lament of family photograph albums, populated by shy smiles peering out of vanished sitting rooms; sense the mild pornography of second-hand silk bodices, still carrying traces of the perfumed flesh they'd shrouded.

An air of pungent melancholy had accrued about the punters, as they poked and skirmished in among the piles, lifting a garment here, handling a screwdriver there. Middle-aged Asian men in ill-fitting suits jostled with large women in white jackets, with cigarettes stuck to their lips, who would turn round periodically to shout at a ransacking child. Jack picked up a Second World War tin helmet from a table. Black, so presumably a fire warden's. He turned it over and saw the webbing that had gently disintegrated, like the head that had once been inside it. He dropped it back on to the table with a clatter.

'You won't dent it,' the old man sitting on the bumper of his car said to him loudly. 'Field-Marshal bloody Goering couldn't dent it fifty years ago. You won't manage.'

Jack felt suddenly exhausted at the pressure of all the lives scattered around him, all the unredeemed chronologies these tawdry trophies represented. He turned and walked back quickly towards the main market. He made his way through the cars. He'd never seen so many rusting estate cars, Nissans and Mazdas and badly wounded Fords. They all looked determined to see in the millennium: enough to make a car salesman weep.

He sat down at a table opposite the theatre and ordered a coffee. He was looking at Madame M, the palmist, crystal-ball gazer and tarot-card reader. Her face was wrinkled into a leathery tan; she had the ancient gypsy features of Mother Teresa. *Find out what tomorrow brings* was embroidered on a banner riding over her stall. A sudden gust of wind blew all the cards from the table. Two landed at Jack's feet. As she scurried about, regathering the pack, Jack carried his two cards over and put them next to her book, *The Tarot and Its Secrets*. She smiled wanly at him.

'I'd have thought you might have seen that coming,' he said.

At twelve he went in, as arranged, and watched as his daughter danced and sang 'There are no strings on me' from *Pinocchio*, the show they were to put on at Christmas. He watched the intentness of Dotty's face as she concentrated on her next move and the words of the song, and found his eyes momentarily moist. You're a bundle of trouble, Jack, he thought, a real sucker to yourself. What was it that you gave this up for?

They didn't go back to the flat that afternoon. Instead, Jack took her for a hamburger and then they went round the shops and he bought Dotty some books. When he dropped her at Earlsfield, and saw Phil all dressed up and ready for the evening, he wished his name was Jeremy not Jack, even if it did mean having a dog called Lupin. But then, who knew what awaited him at home that night with Martine?

●

Two years before, when Martine's husband Charles had been very much in evidence, Jack and he had exchanged spare keys to their flats, on the basis that neither of them trusted the quirky, alcoholic porter, and if they ever needed to allow access to workmen while abroad, or if either ever lost his keys, each could go to the other's door. It was those spare keys which Martine used, once she had seen Jack leave that morning, to let herself in. She was going to put a certain item of nightwear at the bottom of one of his drawers in the bedroom, and then surprise him when she came back into his living room wearing it that evening. She knew that she could surprise men, who usually thought her Swiss and solemn and slow and proper, by the other way she could be when she chose. She had bought it in Knightsbridge the day before. It had been expensive. Twenty years ago she wouldn't have thought it even mattered. Now she wasn't so sure.

She let herself in quietly and walked through to the bedroom. She was about to open the drawer when she looked at the bed. Blonde. Motionless. Her shape clearly visible under the duvet. She hadn't even seen her come in. She folded the black silk shift again, looked down at it sadly (who would she put it on for now?) and left.

When Jack got back he picked up the card.

> On second thoughts, maybe not. Perhaps we live too close. Neither of us has anywhere to escape to. Anyway, my hair's the wrong colour.
>
> Martine

Next to it on the floor was a little polythene bag and in the bag were the four silver denarii.

Jack went running down by the river. He was angry. What difference did it make what colour hair his wife had? Martine poking her nose around the door and peering through her bloody peep-hole at everyone who came down the steps. Jeremy. Lupin. Martine. Jeremy. Lupin. Martine. He turned it into a chant as he sped along. Jeremy. Lupin. Martine.

When he got back he showered and shaved his head again. He wondered if Jonathan might be free that night. They had once met for a meal each week. He couldn't actually work out whether or not Terry had moved in, or if he only stayed over sometimes. He needed to spend the evening with someone. He called, but the answering machine was on, and he rang off without leaving a message.

In fact Jonathan and Terry were standing down by the pond at the edge of Kew Green. Terry had suggested they go for a walk, since Jonathan had been working so hard on layouts for the brochure and his coloured illustrations of the jewellery. They stood staring down at the water.

'You know, I mean those ducks . . .' Terry began.

'I know, I've noticed it.'

'Are they actually provided by Richmond Council? Were they imprinted on Bamber Gascoigne? Trained by some of the local BBC producers? They all huddle together over in the corner there, and then the minute they see someone coming it's splitter-splatter through the water, up and down, formation-swimming, Busby Berkeley routines. I feel as though I'm auditioning them.'

'We'd better go back and switch the oven off.'

'What's in it?'

'Duck, funnily enough.'

'Maybe that's why they're getting so excited. We're baking one of their brothers.'

When they arrived back, the answering machine was flashing, but no message played. Without thinking, Jonathan dialled 1471.

'It was Jack,' he said.

'Are you going to phone him back?'

'I don't think so. Not tonight. Fancied a quiet night in.'

'Maybe he's lonesome.'

'If you'd known Jack as long as I have, you wouldn't be surprised that he was on his own on a Saturday night. The only surprise is that he still thinks he can take being on his own on a Saturday night.'

'What was his wife like?'

'Only met her once. A lot stronger than him. All Jack's strength is in his legs. He just keeps running off.'

'Maybe he's even more lonesome now that his good friend and colleague has shacked up with a big black buck. Have you told him I moved in?'

'You don't have to be psychic to work that one out, surely? He doesn't mind you being black. I doubt he minds you being my lover, to be honest. He could do without you being a writer though, particularly when you get this play finished, and it's put on in Covent Garden. As it's going to be.'

•

Jack went to the big pub over the road and ordered a pint. The barman at the bottom end of the bar walked up towards him.

'Something for you, Jack.' He reached down behind the bar and picked up a thick envelope. 'That little northern piece you were chatting up last week dropped in and asked if I could give this to the nice man with the bald head.'

Jack took the envelope and his pint and went and sat at the table by the window. Inside was a note.

> I'm sorry. I wouldn't have done it if I didn't have to.
> You've no idea what's happening to me. Sorry about what
> I said. I actually liked you. You may not believe me, but
> it's true. If you believe in God, forgive me.

Inside were all the pictures that had been on the film inside his Leica – she had had them developed. Pictures of Dotty in King George's Park. Pictures of Dotty by the river. Pictures of Dotty reading curled up on a chair, her little head bent over the book with such intent concentration. The last six prints were crimson blurs, where the film had been exposed when it was taken out.

Back in the flat he looked at the television listings in the newspaper. They were broadcasting the Toni Inglish concert from Sydney in half an hour. He hadn't realised she'd travelled so far in so short a time. He made himself a couple of sandwiches and poured out a glass of wine, then sat in front of the box. There was the usual palaver and promo hype to begin with, and then she came on, all in black again, strumming her guitar as she walked on to the stage. By the time she reached the mike she was already singing into it. The song was a weird progression through minor chords, some surrealist legend about drug running. Her voice was breathy and urgent:

> You were standing on the corner looking out for the police
> Wearing Chinese slippers, waiting for the man from Nice
> Underneath the lamplight on the midnight run

Half an hour to go before the hit
Found myself half-wondering if I could be the one
The shades I wore were dark enough to fit

The rest of the band began to join in, until everyone on stage was playing with hypnotic concentration. Jack videoed the concert, and when it was finished he simply played it over again. That was the woman he loved, right there, not an ounce of sentiment or spare flesh about her. Why was he pretending to flirt with some Swiss *hausfrau*? Then he went to the door and opened it. He stood there for a minute silently, watching, but for once there was no scuffle behind the door opposite. Charles has come back, he thought with sudden, unexpected clarity, so she has some hands and lips in her bed tonight after all. I read that Toni sleeps alone these days, and I'd best learn to do the same thing. Sooner too, rather than later.

He went to bed early. He had forgotten that Nadia was already there. He turned her round to face him.

'You know, Nadia, you might find this cruel, but that big hair makes you look like an overblown Russian tart.'

He went into the kitchen and came back with the scissors. He cut and swathed until it was all gone, down to a little knotted stubble, a wheatfield cropped by fire. He carried the mass of hair into the kitchen and threw it in the bin. Then he climbed back into bed and switched off the light. He ran a hand over her head.

'That's better, girl. Forget the soft routines. Softness is only for the kiddies from now on.'

●

Down in Earlsfield, Jeremy and Phil lay holding hands in the bed.

'That time you let me in,' he said. 'For the first time, you let me in. Thank you.'

'It's just watching you with Dotty and everything, I realise now I never did know whether Jack had made me the way I was, or I'd made him the way he was. That was what frightened me. He would just dig and dig and dig, but he never could get deep enough down to bury himself.'

Jeremy had let go of her hand.

'Do you think we'll spend much time in bed talking about him?'

She realised what she'd done. 'I'm sorry. I'm really sorry, love. Do you want to talk about your wife?'

'No, I don't think so. She didn't have to worry about how far down she'd have to dig to bury herself, remember. We dug the hole for her. And then we put her in.'

•

*Ashley Simon waited for the violence to arrive. He could smell it. He could smell his own blood, even before his skin opened to let it out into the air. He could already hear the shouts inside his visitors, even though they were still some miles away. Thirty heads of Ishtar looked at him from different shelves and tables. Her eyes were always so wild with delight, with the fury of her own delight: she celebrated whatever fate brought her in the way of gifts. Even her grieving when her lover and son went down in the earth was a type of celebration, a celebration of necessity. Even she, with all her powers, could not choose what was given. What would be would be.*

•

Jack was up early and running. This time he cursed nothing and no one. He wanted to be empty, entirely empty, of everything. How could anybody do that, though? Nothing had ever helped *him* do it. Not prayer, in the days when he still prayed, not politics certainly, and not sex – no sex had ever assuaged that clamour inside him, it only amplified it. Not drugs, with their scheduled oblivions, and not drink. There was only one thing had ever done it. Jack stopped running and stared at the river. His breath steamed on the air. It was October and the bark of the plane trees was turning leprous. Work. Real work, though. The one thing that took the mess inside and then turned it into something coherent outside. But could he still do it?

He ran up through Bishop's Park and, instead of making for the bridge, he jogged into the Palace Gardens and dropped down on to his haunches under the black walnut tree, the one they said was the first black walnut tree in Britain, what was left of it anyway, after the lightning had struck. He ran his hand along the crocodile bark, frozen rivulets from some dark underground current. Then over the bridge and back down into the flat. He showered and dressed. He walked over to the table and picked up the piece of paper lying there.

Buy disks from CC and then see Paree!

He turned the paper over, so that it was blank side up. He wished Josh would phone. He wished he still had some drugs behind the bed in the spare bedroom, anything would do, any diversion from this quotidian momentum. Up, down, technicolour, speedy or slow, powders or weeds, pills or smoke, anything. But he couldn't face the phone calls to old acquaintances that would be necessary to find himself a dealer. And he certainly wasn't planning on hanging around Piccadilly. He wished he was elsewhere, that was all, and somebody else. Out of his head.

He bought newspapers and turned them over idly. Catastrophes. Hatred. Africa. Ireland. Israel. He could hardly bear to touch the books pages, he simply didn't want to know whose face was smiling out at him. He didn't buy books any more. He stuck to Pelikan's *Film* and Percy Hardinge's *Archaeology*. People bought too many books. It struck him there'd been a point to it a few centuries back when they kept mostly to the Bible. If you only had the one book, you might possibly learn something from it. At lunchtime he made himself spaghetti, but he couldn't face most of the bolognese sauce, so instead of leaving it in the fridge to encrust like a small bucket of blood, as he usually did, he threw the lot into the bin. Then he hunted through the listings pages. There was usually one on somewhere; because almost all Pelikan films were short and low budget, having been made for subsidised television in Italy or France or

Sweden, they were an ideal cheap complement to make up a programme. Sure enough *Berggasse 19* was on at that little cinema down the Mile End Road. He had seen it before, of course, three times if his memory was accurate. But he would go and see it again.

He rode his bike through the London streets and up the Mile End Road, past the shifting coloured fantasy of a street market, its quiltwork of national costumes. He parked down a side street and went inside. The unspoken complicity of people in a scruffy auditorium on Sunday afternoon, with what they know to be a classic about to appear on the screen before them. Jack had not seen this film since before he had written *About Time*, and he was startled, when it began, at how much his own portrayal of Ashley Simon's life in Cloth Fair owed to it, for Pelikan had made René Thauss move about under the watchful gaze of all the gods and goddesses whose images Freud had so famously gathered about him. The sphinxes and pharaohs, the shamans and cultic dignitaries stared out with something approaching merriment at his attempted diagnoses. Was this the prognosis of the past that Freud seemed to be hearing when he would turn suddenly to one of the figurines? Whenever a patient left, Pelikan had Freud glance up momentarily at his tutelary deities, and you could almost hear their collective howl through the millennia. The sphinx's expression suggested that this was no Oedipus she was confronting: her great claw was ready to knock him down Clio's cliffside. Oriental heads drifted serenely into meditative sleep, even as he spoke to his patients. A Chinese sage bent low, riddled with incredulity. Only the Attic vessel-heads appeared to be genuinely troubled, their eyes growing wide and wild, as though they had begun to glimpse the approaching catastrophe.

Pelikan was a fragmentarian. In so far as he had a philosophy at all, then this was it. There was the gnomic interview reprinted in *Film* from a small French journal of the 1960s: Jack had once learnt chunks of it by heart:

The machinery of modern life is so vast and compelling,

so inescapable, that the whole cannot be conveyed any more. A director who thinks he can embody the whole in two hours ends up only with rhetoric, a firework display on the site of actual deaths. Reality enters the mind in small pieces now, small sharp pieces, like the millions of pieces of glass on the morning after Kristallnacht.

His camera landed on aspects and facets: the baroque pediment of a Viennese church, the medals on a legless beggar's chest, the way a policeman snapped his fingers at a young worker. It was like the scene at the beginning of *The Third Man*, a scene Pelikan himself had written about in *Cahiers du cinéma*, where the sleeve is rolled back to reveal six or seven wristwatches all the way up the arm. The reality of postwar Vienna was revealed in that shot, without a word needing to be spoken. Whenever René Thauss went to the window and looked out, Pelikan shifted the shot (without a zoom: he never zoomed, saying that the zoom did not correspond to human perception but distorted it) out on to the streets and picked out a detail. The uniforms seemed to change each time the camera examined them, until by the end of the film they were deep enough to enter the skin. They seemed stitched now into the souls of those who wore them. You can't see history anyway, Pelikan had once said, you can only write it. Write it with a camera or a brush or a pen.

Constantly the camera moved from the figures on the street to the buildings around them, that swirl of contrariness over a symmetric ground plan that is the European baroque. Hardly any words were spoken, but this was not unusual with Pelikan: he had his characters use words as though tasting food that could prove poisonous. Then back to Freud, his face darkening, his gestures slowing as though the air itself were growing heavy around him, the pain in his jaw increasing, caressing an admonitory hybrid and saying slowly, 'Mankind. A small disease in time, loving nothing but its own victims.'

Interrogation by the SS. One heard none of the dialogue

here, saw only the backs of the officers, rigid with self-importance, and Freud's face staring up at them with infinite contempt. The cream of this Germanic culture: you could see it in his eyes, he didn't need to say it. On the soundtrack, Janáček's quirky lyricism snapped at their shoulders, as though the notes would bite them, like furies sweeping down through the air. The departure. The journey. Pelikan intercut this sequence with a montage of newspaper headlines from around the world about Freud and his work, the bonfires of books the Nazis were already organising, as though it were a Cubist painting. The hands of Freud on the train, trying to continue writing. How often Pelikan used hands as an image of identity, almost as often as he used faces. The hands often tell the truth while the face is lying. Emily Dickinson's hands laid like a religious gesture on her lap, Simone Weil's quick fingers clawing at themselves over the sheets of the hospital bed in Ashford, where she starved to death in solidarity with Europe's victims. Then the camera had lifted itself up, with what felt like a huge effort, to stare out of the window over the lawn towards Folkestone on the impossible horizon. Or the film about Nietzsche, set in the asylum after his collapse in the street in Turin: the hands pushing at the white lunatic cape from the inside, as though trying to grasp a world that was now forever lost. The gesture where Freud lifted his pen to write and then laid it down again on the blank page said all that Pelikan needed to say. Outside the carriage window it was night, and Freud saw nothing but the melancholy blear of his own reflection.

Then London like a dirty glass the lens couldn't look through. The last few minutes of the film growing more and more opaque – he must have used filters, Jack thought – and Freud's face blurring into the grime about him, all smoke and badly weathered stone, and newspapers announcing the coming war. Finally he faded back into the fog, and as he vanished an air-raid siren sounded, an anachronism that seemed to Jack as perfectly timed as Bresson's tree bowmen at the end of *Lancelot du Lac*, killing once and for all whatever is left of the fellowship of Camelot.

Modernity's machines, however small, which change everything irrevocably from that moment. Jack couldn't face seeing the next film, which he knew nothing about. Forty minutes of Pelikan had been enough.

He rode down by the river for over an hour, then headed back and stopped on the King's Road at the Angler Fish. He parked and went inside, ordering a beer with hamburger and chips. That could be dinner. As he settled down at one of the tables he looked around him at the décor. A huge salmon wearing a soft trilby, smoking a cigar and wielding a split-cane fishing rod reared from behind the bar. When his burger arrived, it was upon a white plate across which blue fish flew grinning. As he chewed and sipped, Jack realised that he had no more ways of distracting himself from the brutal fact of his condition: he was broke and was getting more broke by the day. He had reached the £1,500 limit on his Access card, and he was overdrawn by £1,200 at the bank. His rent was due next week, and he couldn't pay it. He couldn't pay Phil the mortgage money either. The trickle now coming in from his work with Jonathan didn't go anywhere at all. He would have to give up the flat, and ask Phil for an amnesty on the Earlsfield payments for a few months. He never had been much good at copywriting, now he came to think of it. The good copywriters he'd met always believed in what they were doing. Beneath the obligatory cynicism, they believed: they were proud of their work. He wasn't, though, it simply bored him and it showed. And Jonathan wasn't hungry any more. Jack kept expecting him to announce his retirement, so that he could concentrate entirely on portrayals of the male nude. Even if they managed to make a little money from this Toni Inglish project, it still wouldn't add up. Nothing added up. He was well and truly screwed. He took out his pen and wrote on the paper napkin:

> Some are delighted, some are annoyed
> Some know how badly they're screwing it
> And a few turn to face what they cannot avoid:
> The lucky ones aren't too late doing it.

There is a point at which the Fulham Road realises with a shudder that it is leaving behind its blistered cafés and fish and chip shops and approaching the mansion blocks of Putney. It starts to snake then as if uncertain that this progress could seriously have been the one intended. Jack stopped his bike at the lights and stared at the nondescript façades. A Holistic Centre, a bicycle repair shop, and a whole glass-front advertising that here was the focal point, at least as far as this insignificant planet was concerned, of a cult of supreme intelligence from outer space. Jack was back at the flat five minutes later. The answering-machine light was on. It was Jonathan, asking if he could give him a ring.

'Terry and I thought you might like to come over for dinner tonight.'

'That's thoughtful, Jonathan. Has Terry moved in by the way? Not that it's any of my business, of course. I just wondered.'

'He's staying here for the moment, yes. It was my idea – he didn't want to. He pays his way with everything else, but it helps not to have to pay rent while he finishes his play. Had a bit of trouble with accommodation. You're a writer, Jack, you remember the problems.'

'I don't have to *remember* them, Jonathan. If I want to bring them to mind again, I just stand in front of the mirror.'

'In fact I've agreed to work with Terry on his play. I'm going to design the stage sets. Be a new one for me. We'll see, anyway.'

'As long as you don't sign him up to start writing your copy.' Jack laughed uneasily.

'You've got no worries there, I promise you. He said he's prepared to sell everything else, but not the bit of him that writes.'

As soon as the words had left his mouth, Jonathan wished very much that they hadn't.

'Come over, Jack, we could have a pleasant evening.' But he'd already lost him, he knew that.

'No, thanks anyway. Just got a big job in from Germany. Doubt if I'll be seeing you at all for a while, in fact: I need to get my head down. Give it a week or so. Give my best to Terry.'

He put the phone down.

'I think I've just won the Duke of Edinburgh Award for Insensitivity,' Jonathan said.

'How's that?' Terry asked.

'Never mind. Get on with your writing.'

Jonathan carried on airbrushing his illustration. It was for the cover. He had lifted the colours from the Standard of Ur; Jack had once dragged him to see it in the British Museum. There was something about the blues and reds in the phoenix tattoo on Toni's neck which had sent him skimming back through the books on his shelf. He found it in the Mesopotamian catalogue he'd bought back there that day at the BM. He used the same primitive mosaic style to pattern the design, and made the letters look as though they had been cut in cuneiform wedges. Toni Inglish at the bottom, phoenix at the top, one in blue, one in crimson. That was all it said. With the turquoise and reds, you would have seen it from fifty feet away. The phoenix rose from the flames, and her head hinted at the shaved head of Toni.

'It's good,' Terry said, standing behind him.

'I know. Best thing I've done for as long as I can remember. Only problem is, will I ever get paid anything for it?'

He picked up the box that the prototypes had been packed in and read the label once again: Tim Tasker. Goldsmith and Jewellery Designer. 0143 777 948.

'I'm going to do something very unprofessional,' he said, winking at Terry as he dialled the number. 'Hello, could I speak to Tim Tasker please? Ah. My name's Jonathan Hamble, you won't know me, but I'm doing some illustrations of the work you've prepared for Dale Freeman . . . Yes, that's right . . . Exactly . . . Forgive me being forward about this, but I have no one else to ask. Have you been paid by Mr Freeman? No, nothing at all . . . I see . . . Ever worked for him before? No. Are you confident about getting paid? I see . . . Hopeful rather than confident, yes. Thanks

Tim, I shan't keep you from your work any more then . . .
Sure . . . Feel exactly the same way about it all myself.'

'Well?' Terry asked.

'Seems to be the boy from nowhere, our Dale Freeman.
He's not getting anything more out of me, I'll tell you, and
he's not getting these prototypes back either, until I have my
hands on some money.'

That night Jack went to bed early, it seemed like the cheapest
place to go. Nadia gave him her entire attention, her mascara'd eyes intent upon him, as she rose up from her pillow.
He'd come to suspect that her creator had been a devotee of
Egon Schiele. It had taken him a while to fathom her sexual
iconography, but Schiele's *Reclining Woman with Green Stockings* of 1914 came as close as he could find. A lot closer than
de Kooning. Eyes as wide as those of a startled deer, legs
opening as though nothing to do with her head at all, breasts
up and out, and that massive forest tuft down below her
belly. Except Schiele's girl was a brunette, and they didn't
come any blonder than Nadia, even after her scalping. She
was Brigitte with no holds barred, Marilyn plus martial arts.
She was a good listener though, there was no doubting that.
He reached a hand out and took the buckle from the sus-
pender on Nadia's right thigh between his fingers. He needed
something to hold on to.

'Did I ever tell you that you remind me a bit of Dr
Oh? She was my therapist. Very briefly. There's no physical
resemblance, don't get me wrong. She was short, thin, dark-
haired, and with a face like a door that's just shut on your
fingers. She didn't speak at all most of the time; occasionally
she'd open out her palms and bend her head, as if to say, Let
it be done unto me according to the transference. I gather
it's a gesture they pick up at the Tavistock. Creeping Jesus
routine, if you ask me. But I did feel obliged to talk when I
was with her, and I feel exactly the same with you.

'The trouble is, Nadia, I believed in Providence. It's taken
me years to face up to that. That, I think, is probably the
tragedy of the situation. I married Phil, you see, just when

*About Time* had been published. I was finishing the deal with life, can you understand that? I was paying off Eros and Agape for providing for me. And then they didn't — provide for me any more, I mean. I'd signed the deal with Phil, she was Providence's signature, so when Providence let me down, she had to suffer. She'd fooled me, with all her middle-class competence, into thinking she could sort it all out. Success. Money. And she couldn't. Funny, isn't it? I'd lost my faith in Christianity, and then I lost my faith in Marxism, but I still believed in Providence, my own personal Providence. I could be redeemed, even if the world couldn't. And then when that didn't happen, I stopped believing in anything at all. Writing or anything. Sex for one night, then when nothing had changed in the morning, that was enough. Sex with someone else for one night, to see if that could transform me. All one-nighters are in search of magic, trying to fathom entrails. I think people mix up marriage and Providence a lot more than is generally realised.

'You're a good listener, Nadia, has anyone ever told you that? I can't fault you, really. Well, maybe just the one thing. Please don't get upset about this, it's only a little something you might mention the next time you have a check-up: your thighs squeak. Sometimes I hear you when you roll over in your sleep, probably with a bad dream, and it's a definite squeak. I'm sorry, but I'm not the man to oil it for you any more. If only we'd met years before . . . But you're tired, you don't want to hear all my regrets. You should rest. We both need a good long sleep.'

●

Back from his run the next morning, Jack showered and dressed. He picked up the photograph of Phil and stared at it. At the end of Pelikan's film about Emily Dickinson, the camera kept returning to that famous daguerreotype of her in 1848. Emily's eyes had such reality that when the camera returned to Suzanne Legrand afterwards, even her slow movements around the desk seemed theatrical and excessive. In the last frames the camera simply halted on that image of

137

the poet, as the voice-over read, 'I had a terror since September I could tell to none, and so I sing, as the boy does by the burying-ground, because I am afraid.'

He couldn't bring himself to call Phil.

'Could it be that you are afraid of your wife?' Dr Oh had asked him, her face an expressionless white, the therapist's mask.

'I thought all men were afraid of their wives.'

'Even those who beat them?'

'Particularly those who beat them.'

The telephone rang. It was his father.

'I got your lines for your mother's headstone, lad.' He had posted them the week before. There was a silence, then his father read back to him his own words.

'She entered her darkness

'Departed our light

'After her brief day

'Perpetual night.'

More silence.

'What do you think?'

'Sounds a bit morbid to me.'

'She is dead, Dad.'

'She's not *that* dead. Anyway I've done one meself.' He coughed and then read his own lines out.

'Dorothy Goodrich.

'A wife to her husband, a mum to her boy

'She's gone to the realm of perpetual joy.'

'That's better, Dad. Yours is better. Use that one.'

'All that education.'

'Waste of time and money, I know.'

●

Dale Freeman lay in bed and watched his wife dress. It always intrigued him how she turned away from him to lift first one and then the other breast into her bra. He supposed they must have teased her about it at school. He had seen those photographs of her when she was thirteen. Her new-found womanhood must have made her conspicuous. It wasn't as though she was tall. She buttoned up her Jermyn Street striped blouse and zipped herself into her chalk-striped skirt. They hadn't touched in weeks. He had started watching her face closely and had come reluctantly to acknowledge the growing evasion in her expression. It wasn't that she didn't love him, he knew that, it was just that the person she had started loving was being so radically redefined, and she found it hard to recognise him any more. That person had been assured a grand inheritance; that person was going to own one of the finest art collections in Paris and a large apartment down the Boulevard Saint Germain. That person wasn't meant to have to deal each morning with factors' letters and unpaid warehousing fees, and the ceaseless litigation expenses leaking over from those lawyers in France. He marvelled at himself, at not holding anything against her, and he also made a decision, there and then. Sometimes you had to.

His wife left without a word. It was just as well they'd decided not to have any children yet. Dale bathed and dressed and made coffee and toast. He stared at what looked like a bowl of dried grass on the shelf. Some herbal infusion, no doubt: she was on one of her diet jags. He picked up the paper and turned to the back page. It struck him as a sign of his intellectual decline over the last year that the first, and sometimes only, thing he read in the paper was the television listing and the report on the previous night's viewing. Perry Biscay was barking on as usual.

> *Tracey Garrett remarked, à propos her life with comedian husband Peter, that they rose in the morning laughing and went to bed at night laughing. There is something unaccountably grim about this, like the prospect of a life sentence at Butlin's, that concentration camp of merriment. One is reminded of G.K. Chesterton's smiling philanthropist, assassinated finally by his own valet, who simply couldn't take any more universal* bonhomie. *It might also go part of the way to explaining the epic unamusingness of Garrett's television series, another episode of which was screened last night: the fellow's evidently all chortled-out before he even sets foot in the studio.*
>
> *Off-stage, comics should surely sink into a life of melancholy*

*self-destruction, with the single notable exception of Morecambe and Wise. Hancock drowning in vodka or Lenny Bruce choking his veins with heroin seem somehow healthier options for the home life of the comedian than this round-the-clock stargazey pie of Peter and Tracey. To greet each day laughing and lay down your head in the same state suggests psychosis rather than humour. One only has to imagine Ben Jonson or Max Beerbohm guffawing so incessantly to realise how swiftly the doctors would have been called in. Voltaire (or for that matter P.G. Wodehouse) may have started and ended each day with a smile, though a pretty bleak one in Voltaire's case, but audible laughter? Presumably if one starts the day laughing, and ends it so, one must carry on in pretty much the same state through all the hours between. How then ever get through* King Lear *or* Wagner's Ring, *not to mention the knottier scenes in Strindberg? And what on earth would happen (as Eric Morecambe, bless him, would have asked) should one find oneself unexpectedly attending a Des O'Connor show? Laughter might well be the appropriate response to his songs, but to the jokes?*

Dale opened his case and took out the chequebook for Freelands Marketing. He had received the money from the building society two days before. There were certainly plenty of funds now. His father had always told him, 'A man who's not prepared to risk all he's got will always be someone else's employee.' So, it's risk time, he thought. Let's get on with it then. Let's show Ferdie Lockyard that there are still some balls in the Freeman family, even if he's dispensed with his own. Let's see how deep the worldwide devotion to Toni Inglish really is. He telephoned Jonathan Hamble. Jonathan was wary.

'You want to come over now?'

'Yes.'

'Why?'

'To see what you've done, of course. And collect my prototypes.'

'I think there's something you'd better know.'

'And to give you a cheque for all your work so far.'

Jonathan wasn't expecting that.

140

'You're going to pay me this morning? There's been quite a lot of work, you know. Illustrations. Page designs.'

'Give me a clue.'

'Nearly ten thousand. Three of that's for Jack.'

'That's a relief. I was expecting it to be more. Tell you what. Why don't you get your mate Jack over and we can all have a chat about where we go from here?'

Jack was about to pick up the telephone and call Phil when it rang.

'Maybe we've all got Mr Freeman wrong. He's on his way over here now to give me a cheque for the better part of ten grand. How much of the copy have you done?'

'About half. I've got notes for the rest.'

'I've said your part's three, so far. That would mean you've got another three coming, on completion. He sounds amiable on the subject of money this morning. Why don't you come over, Jack? He says he wants to have a chat about where we all go from here.'

Jack started laughing.

'Have I said something funny?'

'It's your timing, Jonathan, that's all. It's what distinguishes all the great comics.'

Dale Freeman drove the TVR down Talgarth Road. Traffic in London had improved over the last ten years, but it still wasn't fast enough. He thought of Paris, where the cars surged forward in a single wave as the lights changed. Brussels wasn't too bad. Madrid was exciting: chicken-runs at every crossroads. It was possible to speed in New York, but only with specially reinforced tyres for the pot-holes. Worst of all was Canada. The cars you could hire in Canada said it all. Great sulking beasts, with drowned suspension, automatic transmission and a two-minute gap between turning the wheel and noticing any effect. It was like steering a water bed. He'd rather drive in downtown Lagos than Canada. Rather be stuck in a traffic jam in the centre of Bangkok than cope with that whole sensible continent, keeping below fifty in their super-safe estates. Best of all was Italy; he loved driving there, where they'd made driving, like everything else, a form of reckless self-expression. Dale had a car that was just too sappy for its country of origin, he knew that. He managed one single surge of acceleration before he hit the roundabout.

It was a nice little house. When he went in, he noticed Jack there already with his head freshly shining, and a tall, well-built black man, early twenties. That one was introduced as Terry.

'I don't owe you money as well, do I?' he asked with a smile. Terry didn't smile back. A chippy black, he thought, that's all I need.

'I don't think so.'

'Good. What *do* I owe, exactly, Jonathan?'

Jonathan handed him the piece of paper containing the costs so far. He had hurriedly cobbled it together after Dale's telephone call that morning. Dale had a feeling that a finger had been stuck in the air to see which way the wind was blowing, but this wasn't the time to argue about it.

'Nearly ten thousand, then. And that's including Jack's copy?'

'Three thousand of it goes to Jack. That's for copy he's written so far. He's still not finished.'

'How much have you done, Jack?'

'About half.'

'So, you've another three thousand coming. You guys *are* an agency after all, at least in the billing department.' He laughed again. Jonathan had gone into his study area and pulled out his layout boards and illustrations. On one he had set a whole page of copy that Jack had fed him. Dale whistled as he looked at the cover.

'Worth every penny. No doubt of it. That really is good. And those illustrations . . . who did those for you?'

'I did them for myself. Or for you, I suppose. A special aptitude you won't find in many designers.' Dale was already reading Jack's copy.

'If I didn't know you better, I'd think you'd fallen for this girl, Jack. This isn't copy, it's a love letter. It's a poem. Well,

I'm delighted. I am really. Despite the hole you fellows are about to scorch in my pocket, I couldn't have hoped for better. Now I have something to hit Toni Productions with.' Dale was writing out the cheque. 'What's become apparent though is that I can't get through this project by myself. I need an assistant. Well, more of an associate. For a lot of the things that need doing.'

Jack realised that everyone was looking at him. He was about to be definitively negative when the facts of his situation came back to him. He could only continue to live in his flat in Putney as of today because of the work coming his way from Freelands Marketing.

'What would you have in mind, Dale?'

'I already owe you for consultancy on the direct-mail side, don't think I've forgotten that. But we don't have to go through Jonathan there, do we? It doesn't apply. We need to come to our own arrangements. Could you come over this afternoon, around two?' Jack said nothing. 'Right then, that's settled.'

He was gone, with the prototypes and layouts, and they looked at each other.

'Well,' Jonathan said finally. 'Looks like you may have found a job after all. I'll put this in the bank right away. You might as well have your cheque now. Seem to be flush with funds at the moment, for some reason.' Jack appreciated that. Jonathan knew how desperate he was for the cash, but he was being delicate in front of Terry.

Terry had lifted up the Ayrton bronze from the table and was caressing its smooth weight in his big hands. Jack noticed for the first time how well manicured his long black fingers were. Without considering his words, he said to Jonathan, who was writing out the cheque for him, 'You should have an alarm fitted in this place, you know.'

Terry looked across at him then, unsmiling.

•

Martine couldn't understand. She had watched carefully, but blondie had never emerged. She had seen them come and go before, Jack's women, his various bimbos and waffle-heads, including a few of the blowsy pick-ups from the pub over the road, but this one had not come out. When she saw Jack leave that morning she waited five minutes to make sure he'd not forgotten something, then she took the spare key and let herself into his flat.

She was nervous and walked around his front room for a moment. There were used glasses on the table, which she picked up without thinking. She looked briefly at the marble egg and the little stone pyramid, and at the figurine of Ishtar next to the photograph of his wife and daughter. Then she carried the glasses to the kitchen and put them in the sink before stepping briskly through to the bedroom.

It was only the hair which had been entirely lifelike. Cropped now, and with patches of plastic showing through, Nadia's head was no longer so convincing. Martine walked up to the bedside slowly and then pulled back the sheets. There was something oddly mutilated about that skull, with the yellow stooks rising out of it, the roots the scissors had left behind. Martine ran her finger gently across the stubble. Where had it all gone? She walked back into the kitchen and opened the plastic rubbish bin. Great swathes of Nadia's hair lay there in tangles, bloodied and clotted with the bolognese sauce from the day before. Martine stepped back and let the lid drop. She went into the bedroom once more and studied the figure lying there supine, in such vacant invitation. The black lingerie, the stocking tops, the coloured nipples, and the little pouting lips of the mons. So you're the fuckable artificial woman are you? she said softly. Stupid. Stupid bastard, Jack. She walked quickly into the kitchen and hunted through the drawers until she found a sharp enough knife. Then she returned to the bedroom.

'I hope he was worth it, my dear,' she said as she brought the knife down in one swift arc into Nadia's neck. Nadia let out a gasp as the air rushed through the puncture in her throat. The manic invitation in her eyes suddenly started to crumple into the features of a small child about to cry, and her breasts were going down too, like mountains sinking into the sea, as though the years were spinning back again. And Martine speeded their return by pounding on her chest as though she were a patient whose heart had stopped that instant in the theatre, and Martine was the surgeon who'd just been wielding the lancet. Soon there was nothing. The stockings shrivelled around dead plastic as those legs wheezed back to two dimensions, and the face with its mascara moons, flattened out into a charcoal drawing that had been left out in the rain. In one final lunge, Martine stuck the knife through Nadia's belly right into the mattress below, then calmly left the scene of the murder.

•

Jack had taken a taxi over to Jonathan's, since he'd thought he'd better look reasonably presentable, given the amount of money they were asking Dale for. He now found the nearest branch of his bank in Kew and deposited his cheque. Solvent. He thought he'd better not try to take any money out for a few days, but all the same he was solvent. He almost danced out on to the street. He bought an envelope and stamp at the post office and posted the next cheque to Phil. Solvent and acquitted. He'd better have a brood about how much to pay Access, but for today, he could act like a free man. He took the train up to London.

He had plenty of time before his meeting so he walked up through Soho towards the Charing Cross Road. Nadia's sisters were frozen in various tableaux in the windows. They weren't all as lucky as she was, with a flat to themselves down in Putney. He walked along Denmark Street, looking at the guitars displayed in the windows, but didn't go inside. He had found out by bitter experience that all the assistants in those places were usually highly proficient, and extremely unsuccessful, guitarists. Their speciality was to hand you an acoustic, tuning it in mid-air as they swung it down from the wall, and then watch you sceptically as you played your party piece with great concentration, only to pick out a riff infinitely better than anything you could ever play, as they swung the guitar back through the air on to its hook. Just to let you know who had the expertise around here. Just to let you know they didn't *have* to do this job; it was only a temporary filler before the evening gig.

Jack walked through Trafalgar Square. Twenty feet from one of Landseer's monumental lions, an armoured vehicle daubed in camouflage colours was dappled all over with poppies. 'Help heal the wounds,' the British Legion banner said. Flowers of oblivion sprouting from the killing machines: it seemed unlikely. Jack walked on. As he turned into Villiers Street there was a young man in a sleeping bag, crouched in one of the doorways. He was shouting, 'No, leave me alone. Shut up and go away.' Jack turned to look. He was talking to a particularly obese pigeon, which turned and walked off unsteadily, as if bored now with the relationship.

Just down the road from Dale's office was an underground wine bar that appeared invitingly dark as Jack peered in. He went inside and bought a glass of wine. He looked around him. Half the tables were old barrels and half the chairs had broken backs. The brickwork was dirty and unfaced. He sat underneath one of the high, dark windows. He stared at the uprights and crossbars, so webbed with spidery filth that lacework patterns appeared whenever the October sun shone outside. As his eyes grew used to the gloom, he noticed that the window, which had at first seemed monochrome, was in fact a subtlety of blacks and blues and vellums, and when the light leaked through, its effect was that of sombre stained glass. Beyond where he sat was another section of low arches, and he started to wonder if they might have met the river's edge once, before the embanking began. York House had been here, he remembered that much at least. He had two drinks and then said goodbye to the young barwoman. An actress, apparently.

Marilyn opened the door and gleamed at him. Dale was there at his desk, a big smile on his face.

'I gather that instead of working for us, you're going to work with us now,' Marilyn said.

'Hadn't thought of it like that,' Jack replied as he sat down. Dale handed him a cheque. It was for £250. 'For your consultancy work re the direct mail,' Dale said. 'How tightly scheduled are you over the next few months, Jack?'

'Well, I have work on, obviously.' Dale's bright blue eyes scanned back and forth across Jack's face.

'Obviously. Look, I'll be frank, because the fact is, if you don't want to do this work, I can soon find someone else who does. But I have a feeling I can get on with you. We could work together, I sense it. I need an assistant — an associate — to help me co-ordinate this project. That means no standing on ceremony, no demarcation disputes. Copy-writing, trips to mailing houses, printers, presentations at Toni Productions, even liaising with Toni herself, the whole caboodle. Want to do it? Call it twenty quid an hour, plus expenses, with a very substantial bonus coming shortly when we get this thing off the ground. Your copywriting's separate, it goes without saying. That's whatever fee you're used to charging. Another two grand for the brochure copy, and then presumably the same rate for the other stuff.'

'Three grand.'

'What?'

'We agreed three grand for the rest of the brochure copy.'

'We did?'

'We did.'

'You're a hard man, Jack, but I admire that.'

Jack was no longer sure why he had disliked Dale so much to begin with. It could have been simple prejudice about the word *marketing*. Anyway, it would have been an act of grave irresponsibility to turn down this offer now. After all, he had liabilities, he was a father with bills to pay, and certainly no other way of meeting his debts.

'Let's try it for a month anyway.'

'Good,' Dale said, and reached across the table to shake his hand. 'You're part of the firm. Now, the first thing we have to do is to go and present these prototypes and your mate John's artwork to Toni Productions.'

'What's the nature of the agreement you have with them?'

Dale took the letter he had once waved at Jack out of the drawer and handed it to him.

Dear Dale Freeman,

It is not our policy to license people at Toni Productions, only products.

For this reason, we would be happy to see the range you are proposing, and make a decision as to whether it is suitable as a TP product.

When you have some material ready for presentation, please contact us here, and we can make an appointment.

Yours sincerely,

David Seltzman,
Promotions Licensing Division

Jack looked up at Dale, bewildered.

'You mean you've done all this and you don't even have a licensing agreement?'

'No, not yet, but we'll get one. You need *cojones* in this business, right, Marilyn?'

'If you say so, Dale.'

'We have an appointment tomorrow morning at nine sharp at TP down in Kingston. Get the address from Marilyn. I'll bring all this stuff. You go away and think your way through the rest of your copy and a letter to accompany the mailing from TP, a serious selling letter. There is, Jack, one advantage to TP's draconian policy about product licensing.'

'What's that?'

'We don't have to explain who we are, because we don't need to exist. We're only the manufacturers, you see, not the sellers. This product comes straight from the bosom of Toni Inglish's nearest and dearest. It's a family heirloom. Got a suit, by the way?'

'One. Not exactly new.'

'Wear it. Seltzman's a Yank. They can be funny about these things. See you there. Oh, before I forget, don't miss *Top of the Pops* tonight. Seven-thirty. Toni's doing a new number on it.'

Dale Freeman drove his car to Fulham, where he had an

appointment to have his hair cut with Simon. He thought he'd better look the part for TP the following day. He climbed the stairs of the mansion block, once council-owned, now private, and readied himself. He had been through so many hairdressers. They had these odd ways of lifting the curls up from his collar, then staring over his head into the mirror and saying, How do you actually *feel* about your hair, Dale? Dale didn't feel anything at all about his hair, except that it needed cutting from time to time. He was glad that it was beautiful and curly and blond, and that women he had gone to bed with ran it through their fingers and said, 'You have beautiful hair, Dale. Make any woman jealous.' It was certainly a better deal than the full-moon shine of old Jack, who was beginning to look more and more like a method actor auditioning for a Soviet film about the Stalin years, but beyond that he had no feelings about it. Certainly none that he felt like discussing.

Simon's flat was conspicuously tidy. It was necessary to kneel on cushions on the floor of his bathroom and bend your head into his bath, while the hair was lathered and Simon, his own hair and beard trimmed to perfection, regaled Dale with all the women queueing up to have him, or all the women he'd once had, and how now that he was married at last with five children, all of that was behind him, thank God, what with all the diseases out there which, given the incessant nature of his activities once upon a time, he was now statistically bound to contract should he ever again slip between forbidden sheets, even once. First it had been NSU, then herpes, now it was AIDS. Dale listened to this, and made the odd murmur, as his head was towelled and he walked back through to the living room, where the cutting took place. On the walls were prints of Parisian female dancers in what were meant to be erotic poses. In fact they were asexual, antiseptic. On various shelves and tables were photographs of Simon's children and his place in the country, his wife, his tennis court. Except that Dale had come to the opinion some time back that Simon was lying, that he wasn't married, had no children, and certainly no place in the country. There was something about those tales that didn't ring true. Why was he working here for £10 a cut, cash in hand, if he really did have a pile like that one in the photographs? The wife and children were probably a sister, nephews and nieces, which would explain why Simon was there in those wedding photographs, in his top hat and tails, grinning away. Whenever Simon spoke of his marriage, the birth of his children, or his country life, the words were chosen with great care, as if he were remembering a script. Reported speech. He came into his own, and his features became mobile again in the mirror, when he started to describe his nights out in London. Which were always with the boys, Dale noticed. Dale had himself grown wary of saying anything at all to him, because he was reasonably certain that whatever he said would resurface as first-hand experience with the next customer. This fellow was a fantasist; he enjoyed the manipulation of his customers' credulity. He was a movable feast, and varied the dish according to what he thought was the taste of each listener. He could cut hair, though. And it was intriguing, the way he shaped his stories at the same time that he shaped people's heads. Dale's face smiled gently at him in the mirror, and Simon's smiled back as he talked. Here was a fellow who decided what you wanted, then invented it to keep you warm. You were paying him though – he wasn't paying you.

'I had a real stunner in here yesterday, Dale, you wouldn't have been able to take your eyes off her, honestly.' *Snip snip* went the scissors. 'Works for the BBC, one of the new producers there. Asked me if I might be free any evening. I said, if only you'd caught me ten years ago, my love, when there was still a spare seat in my old E-Type . . .' *Snip snip snip*.

Jack went back on the tube. First he sat in the underground station, reading his paper. An announcement stated that there were extensive delays to the District Line service. The man with the shaved head next to him (where were all these shaved heads coming from?) stood up and started yelling at the people around him. He stopped in front of Jack after a few minutes. 'Look at you, you cunt. You sit there like a fucking automaton. Why don't you *do* something?' Jack briefly considered standing up and kicking him in the balls. He resisted this, only just, though certainly not through any charitable impulse. The two things that had propelled him out of the Catholic Church were his incompetence in regard to chastity, and his complete inability to go round forgiving people: he was simply no good at it. But the last time he'd involved himself in an underground brawl with someone who was evidently demented, he had lost. Painfully. Finally he was on the train, staring at the figures hunched behind papers and books, or with closed eyes, trying to forget the day. The man standing next to him had a mobile. It bleeped. 'Hello, yes, I'm on my way now. That's right, Sue. Oh absolutely. We're just coming to a tunnel actually. Phone you back on the other side.' Which he did, and explained again that he was ten minutes away from where he had been, and ten minutes shy of where he was going to. 'That's right, Sue, that's my point too. Hit the nail on the head. See you then.' Jack got out at Putney Bridge and stood for a while leaning on the parapet, staring down at the water, and at the little boats bobbing up and down on their moorings. As he approached the flat, he decided to go for a drink first. He went to the usual place over the road, bought a pint and then carried it over to the table by the window where he normally sat. He was thinking about Toni Inglish, and so he didn't recognise that familiar figure at first, and she hadn't noticed him at all, but then as he slipped quickly from his seat and started towards her, she caught sight of him and darted out of the door. He ran outside to see her legging it down along the river. She was on his running circuit – that was a mistake. He caught up with her by the boathouse and grabbed her hair.

'Let me go, please, you don't understand.' Writhing and pulling away from him. Looked as though she was going to cry.

'I understand that I had a Leica and I don't have it any more. Where is it, you scumbag?'

'I sold it.'

'How much for?'

'A hundred pounds.'

'It was worth two thousand.' She looked at him in disbelief. He gripped the back of her hair a little tighter.

'I have a little boy. In Leeds. He's not well. He's got problems. In his head. I can't even pronounce the words for what he's got wrong with him. I don't know what's going to happen to him now. I can't go back to his father, not this time, not after what he did. I've got to get some money.' Jack had let go of her by now. They were both getting their breath back. 'Don't turn me in, please. I'll do anything you like. Anyway you like it. I'll come back each night.' Jack saw the true fear in her eyes, though who could tell whether she was telling the truth or not?

'Forget it,' he said, and started walking away. She ran after him and pulled his arm.

'What do you want?' she said.

'Nothing. I hope your little boy gets well, but just don't ever work this pub again, all right? I know too many people who go there, and they probably all have cameras. Some might not be as forgiving as me.'

He couldn't face going back to finish his pint. He went to the flat and put a meal in the oven. At seven-thirty he switched on the television and the video. He watched the jigging mannikins under strobe lights, as hands hammered synthesiser keyboards in rhythms seemingly unrelated to the music. A man and a woman shared a breathily irreverent introduction, then it was over to the solemn waltzing of the bass player, as behind him the lead guitarist tried to give the impression of being above it all by looking far away. Suddenly there was film of stretches of London wasteland. An air balloon took off in a freak arousal of artificial wind. Then it cut to three attack dogs snapping. The song changed, though it made little difference. Now a man opened a briefcase and a fish swam slowly out of it, then an eagle filled the sky and covered the sun. The music seemed to be nowhere, a mere adjunct to this succession of images, the audible inflation to their vacuity. Each song could have been composed by a computer, and most of them sounded as though they were played by one. A frog leapt in slow-motion on to the deck of the *Mary Celeste* and a black man in big, tinted glasses started ranting into the mike. Girls, dressed inexplicably in football kit, pirouetted and jumped in the air behind him. Now suddenly all the women were in shiny leather suits. They jigged and rotated with as much syncopated eroticism as a combine harvester. How could Toni Inglish possibly fit into all this? She didn't, of course. When her spot came, they showed a clip from one of her concerts on the international tour. She was playing an electric mandolin and was accompanied by her new Serbian accordionist, the Irish fiddle player and a man with bongos. Some strange gypsy rhythm, swooping and gliding. All of the musicians' eyes were glazed. They played together with sinister hilarity, as they turned to each other bowing. There were two whole choruses before Toni started singing.

> I waited for you near the Angel
> Where the crowds swarm home at five
> Waited for you in a wine bar in Fleet Street
> Wondered were you still alive
> Waited for you by my telephone
> And I waited for you by my door
> But oh my cheri
> You can take it from me
> I won't wait for you any more

In the middle of the song, they all seemed to be taking off in surreal improvisations, particularly the Serbian accordion player, who was on his own planet, working to his own time. This was obviously as near as Toni Inglish came to being happy, but she still wasn't smiling. Then she was back at the mike:

> With your hand on your heart
> Can you tell me you're living alone

153

Or have girls from the band in that exotic land
Gone and taken my place by the phone?

I waited for you in the winter
And I waited for you in the spring
I waited for you in a chapel in Crewe
But my prayers didn't answer a thing
I waited for you down in Brighton one night
At the Firemen's Fancy Dress Ball
But I'm tired of the wait
And you always come late
So I won't bother coming at all.

It wasn't until nine o'clock that he went in to say hello to
Nadia. At first he simply thought that all the spirit had gone
out of her, then he saw the bulge below the duvet and pulled
it back to where the knife had stuck her through the gut.
He looked at her face, but it was beyond caring. He had to
think for a minute. He went round the flat, checking that
nothing was missing. The door was unforced. Whoever had
done it had let themselves in with a key. There were only
two people with keys: Mrs Johnson from the letting agency,
and Martine. It seemed unlikely somehow to be Mrs
Johnson. He had a feeling he'd been wrong in thinking that
Charles had come back.

He gave Nadia a decent burial in a black bag and opened
a bottle of white wine, then he picked up a second glass,
and the bottle, and went over to knock on Martine's door.

Half an hour later they were lying side by side in the bed.
They had said nothing, so as not to wake Louise. He was
surprised at her frenzy, and at the fluent yielding movements
underneath him. She had learnt to dress herself in heavy
gestures, like winter clothing, but underneath everything was
different. They lay on her bed, the bed where, presumably,
she had lain side by side with Charles for so many years. He
liked Charles. Still they said nothing. What did you expect
her to say, Dr Oh had asked once? *My God, that was the most
extraordinary experience of my life*? Or perhaps, *I never knew a
woman could come so many times*? Bloody Dr Oh.

'Now you don't have to kill anyone, Jack,' Martine said at last, very quietly. Her hand was floating gently up and down his belly, and he was starting to move again. 'I did your assassination for you.'

# 3

# Tertia Scriptura

*Akkadian*

JACK WAS BACK IN HIS OWN FLAT AT SIX THE FOLLOWING morning, hurriedly making notes. He had bought another book, *Toni: A Life on the Edge* by Dick Dooley. Dick explained in the introduction that, although his technical designation had been that of a mere roadie, he had come much closer to Toni than his official occupation could possibly suggest. In fact, according to his own account, for a period of a year she had been entirely dependent upon him: for her drugs, her emotional stability (didn't look as though he'd done too well there) and, one had the clear impression, for his unparalleled athleticism in the sack. Jack started reading the first chapter: *If Toni Inglish were an animal, she'd already be extinct.* He stopped reading there, and carried on with an outline of his mailing letter.

The post came at the same time that his cab arrived. There was a card from Josh in New York; it was a picture of a funerary statue from the Egyptian section of the Met. On the back he had written:

> Coming to think all archaeology is no more than poking about in other people's holocausts. Ashes and gold. And gold and ashes.

> Love, Joshua – not the one from Nazareth.

As Jack stepped out of his door, Martine's opened and she walked across to him. She kissed him on the lips, leaning into his chest, her flesh still fragrant with sleep. 'Whenever,' she said and stepped back into her flat.

Jack sat in the back of the minicab as the traffic jerked and juddered towards Kingston. Toni Inglish, who was she exactly, and what had she turned herself into? It had always been part of the fascination surrounding Dylan that the man had made himself up. Gave himself a new name, turned mere fortuitous biography into the essential data of mythology. Jack had never had any problems understanding how myth and fact were always getting married and divorced. It was this, more than anything else, which had made him a Marxist: that at least was a way of trying to discover the facts beneath society's mythology. He had taken to the Trotskyist variety because it maintained its purity through its spectacular, global failure ever to achieve any power at all. History's ceaseless oppositionists. He remembered standing in Mrs Kennedy's fruit shop in Oldham on the day after J.F.K. had been inaugurated as President.

'What does it feel like, Pat?' some old lady had asked, as two pounds of potatoes were dropped into her leather shopping bag.

'Wonderful,' she had said. 'That the Catholic son of Irishmen should become the most powerful figure in the world. It's wonderful.'

He remembered the night of the killing too. He had been to the swimming baths and when he arrived home, with his damp towel rolled up in his hand, his father, who normally treated anything on the news with contemptuous indifference, said quietly, 'President Kennedy's been shot.' The television was still on. They both sat in front of it in silence – his mother was at bingo that night. Ten minutes later came the announcement, 'President Kennedy is dead.' It was the end of the world. The funeral, the broken bugle call, Kennedy's little boy stepping forward and saluting the cortège. It seemed that no one could ever again watch an open limousine, with the state's alumni waving and smiling, without a catch in the throat. Then all the revelations began, all the words that mired his memory in subterfuge, mendacity, corruption. It was his father's dollars that had elected him. Dirty wars in Latin America and south-east Asia. Jackie went off later and married a fat old Greek with a rosary of philosophical names. Money then. Money.

Dale was already waiting in the reception area of TP's riverside offices when Jack arrived. Two minutes later David Selzman strolled in and introduced himself. They both stared at the tall, heavy American with his ponytail half-way down his back and his white shirt fastened at the collar with a black Wyatt Earp necktie. He wore blue jeans and brown suede boots. Jack felt uncomfortable in his ten-year-old suit, newly pressed for the occasion. Selzman's face was cratered from the devastations of acne a decade before.

'Come in, guys. Come into my office. Let's see what you've got.'

Dale opened the packages that held the prototypes and layouts. Selzman whistled.

'Hey, this stuff is pretty. But you know, Dale, you've gone a long way here, without a TP licence.'

'Look, David, my attitude is simple. If you want this in your catalogue, we can do business. If not, not. Yesterday I was talking to one of the directors of Asprey's. He thought this stuff was wonderful, and he's never even heard of Toni Inglish. What I'm saying, David, is that if you look carefully at what we're proposing here, you'll discover that there's nothing that I actually have to get permission *for*. There's no trademark on a phoenix, is there? TP don't own that.' David was reading the copy.

'But this is all about Toni Inglish.'

'It is at the moment, but Jack here, my Projects Manager, can soon get it all changed so that it's all hints and guesses in the shadows. I'm sure you know what I mean. We've created a beautiful product and I'd be more than delighted to share it with TP, but don't imagine for a second I'm going to throw all this away if your people don't want to play. I've spent too much money, too much time. It'll still come out, believe me, but without you instead of with you.'

David Selzman's pocked face slowly relaxed into a smile.

'Well, thanks for coming to the point so quickly, Dale.'

'It's my way, David.'

'Can we keep this here, for a day or so?'

'Afraid not. Too many security worries with the artists who prepared it. Anyway, we have another appointment this afternoon. An Egyptian chap with a rather large shop. Knightsbridge area. If there's anyone needs to look at this, you'd best bring them through while Jack and I are here. That's the way we work.'

Two hours later they stood on the pavement outside TP's offices, clutching their packages. Five different executives had been brought in, one by one, to examine what Dale had taken to calling the Phoenix Collection.

'Are we going to meet the Egyptian now?'

'What do you think, Jack?'

'Did you really show that stuff to Asprey's?'

'What do you think, Jack?'

Jack started laughing.

'They're biting, boy, did you see their faces in there? Time we were biting as well. I'll take you for lunch. I seem to remember there's a place just further down the river here. Should pass muster, even for a Projects Manager, and they can be very fussy, I seem to remember.'

They sat at a table overlooking the river.

'What do you want, Jack?'

'This is fine.'

'No, I mean what do you *want*?'

'Ah.' Jack put down his knife and fork and looked out at the boats swaying and bobbing on their moorings. 'How about my life over again? Get it right this time.'

'Can't manage that. How about money?'

'Money would help.'

'Money always helps. Work hard enough on this and, assuming it all works out the way I expect, come in with me. I need someone I can trust on the inside. Something about you – we can get on.'

Jack was flattered. He smiled and sipped his drink.

'A lot of work, though. Over the next couple of months.

A lot of work. You're on the edge aren't you, financially I mean?'

'Yes,' Jack said, too weary with the subject to prevaricate any more.

'Your mate John's not on the edge though, is he?'

'No.'

'And you depend on him for most of your money, right?'

'Right.'

'Not a good idea. One hungry, one just finished eating. Doesn't work out in the long run.'

'You hungry then are you, Dale?'

'Ravenous. Compared with me, the wolf and the bear are vegetarians who've had enough. You in or out?'

'I'm in.'

'All the way, then.'

'Wherever that is.'

'Never know till you get there. That's the beauty of it.'

Two days later Toni Productions telephoned Dale Freeman to tell him that they wished to do a deal. Later that day, Dale phoned Jack.

'We're away. Knew we would be. Dust yourself down and take your vitamin pills. We've got a lot to do. You're going to have to start coming in each day, Jack. We need to be in the office together. Regular hours. Regular *long* hours. Then in a few months we can sit down and count the money together.'

•

They were staring at Jonathan's visuals.

'Incredibly tasteful aren't they?'

'Yes,' Jack said. 'Yes, they are.'

'Ever been to a rock concert, Jack?'

'One or two.'

'Tasteful, were they?'

'Not usually, no.'

'Not the word that automatically springs to mind, is it?'

'No.'

'What I mean is, your mate John has done a fine job for

163

the Royal Academy Annual Report or the British Museum Catalogue. But I do wonder if we're hitting the average fan of Toni Inglish in the right place.'

'Toni's bright enough, I'd have thought. Tasteful too.'

'She may well be. We're not trying to sell the stuff to her though, are we? Doubt she has much interest in the matter at all. Too blitzed most days even to notice, from what I hear. Who was your main man, musically?'

'Dylan.'

'Me too. For a while. Ever meet any Dylan fans, the real hard core, the ones who go to every concert?'

'Yes.'

'And?'

'Cretins.'

'Exactly. Use Dylan to fill up all the holes in themselves. Let him do their thinking for them. It's just the same with Toni Inglish. They don't like her because they're bright: they like her because *she's* bright. Bright as a fire in your bedroom. She lights them up, like throwing the switch on a Christmas tree. They don't even have their own bulbs. She takes their chances for them, takes their risks for them, dreams their dreams for them, breaks their husbands' jaws for them. She sings their song, Jack, because they don't have one of their own. Not a single one of them – otherwise they'd do what she does.'

'So?'

'This brochure design is not the one to reach them.'

'It got you the contract with TP.'

'Indeed it did. Which is why I'm not bitter about the money. TP, by the way, don't know their arses from a hole in the ground. Read their promo gear and see for yourself. Their imagination fades away a few inches after the T-shirts. Which is why they're buying into us. If they could do it themselves, they would. We're going to have to start again.'

'With Jonathan?'

'No, not with Jonathan. He's given it his best shot, but I reckon it's time your friend was retiring. What's he planning on doing when he quits?'

'Nude portraits, I think,' Jack said quietly, and thought of Terry.

'Well, there you are then. Says it all, doesn't it?'

'You're just going to drop all Jonathan's work?'

'All the way, Jack, remember?'

They started again. This time they used photographs of the jewellery, with artificial highlights. Jack had to start from the beginning with the copy too, but Dale supervised each column. He also hunted through the books on Toni to find the quotations that now stood at the head of each page. 'These days I sleep with my phoenix.' 'I like things hard: hard like metal.' 'Pay me in gold and silver. Save the words for your wife.' Dale was right – it was better. It was brutally persuasive.

All the forms about the divorce came through that week and Jack signed them. He couldn't see the point in making any fuss. Phil had been a better mother than he'd been a father. What would be would be. And parents shouldn't prey upon their children, hawking their love around.

Jack walked across to Martine's flat and let himself in with his key. He watched as Martine talked in French to Louise. He noticed again how everything speeded up, her gestures, the flow of the words, the animation in her face. It must be the English language that slows her down, he thought, she's entangled in it as though it were a great invisible net all around her. That was why she didn't use English when she murmured in his ear sometimes: she made love either in silence or in French. And what language did he make love in? No language at all. He didn't even make love in silence: it wasn't *in* anything. Was it love he was making anyway? He didn't know – he never had known. Louise looked up at him finally. She didn't smile. She preferred her own daddy, even though she didn't see much of him. Her large wire-rimmed spectacles made her look even wider-eyed. Glasses on small children seemed to magnify their vulnerability. She walked off to her bedroom without speaking.

'Don't worry,' Martine said, stroking his cheek, 'she'll get to like you. She already likes you. She's confused, that's all. Why don't you have your daughter round to stay?'

Jack used Martine's phone.

'Can we have Dotty round to stay this weekend?'

'We, Jack? Never mind. I was actually going to ask if I could leave her with you on Saturday and Sunday. We've been invited down' and I want to introduce Mum and Dad to Jeremy. Dotty wants to say hello.' Her voice was suddenly on the line.

'Hello, Daddy. Can I stay the weekend?'

'Of course you can, sweetheart.'

'Can Lupin come as well?'

'Lupin.'

'He's my friend, Daddy. Can he come?'

'He can come. Bring the parrot if you like. And Uncle Tom Cobley and all.'

•

Martine had insisted. 'We can take the girls somewhere, Jack, it will be nice for them. They can get to know one another.' He was uneasy about it. He imagined Dotty telling her mother all the facts when she was back home. Finally, he gave in. 'We could go on a boat.' 'No boats,' he had said, 'we have Lupin too. My wife's fiancé's dog.' 'Then we'll go to Richmond Park, and afterwards I'll make us all a meal. You can buy the food.'

When Phil arrived that Saturday morning, Martine opened her door and put out her milk bottles just as she was handing Dotty over. Phil turned and said hello, and she saw some flicker in Martine's face, some sheen of a conspiratorial smile as she looked at Jack. Phil turned back as the door closed behind her. She dropped her head on to her shoulder.

'Have you been having an Alpine roll, Jack?' He ignored her.

'You wouldn't happen to know where that script I wrote for *About Time* was, would you? It wasn't one of the things I left behind at Earlsfield?'

'You probably left it under one of your floozy's beds, Jack. Forgot it in all the excitement.'

'Have a nice time down in Cornwall. Give my regards to your folks. You'll pick Dot up tomorrow evening, yes?'

'Tomorrow evening. Here's the dog food. Jeremy's outside in the car. I'll introduce you soon.'

'Something for me to look forward to, then.' She ran off up the stairs.

Lupin was a golden retriever, who was wagging his tail so hard at Jack that his whole body was undulating back and forth.

'So you're Lupin, are you?' Jack said, with the two tins in his hands. The dog wagged and wagged. 'Oh, get inside, you great blond prat.'

The girls started talking to one another, a little shyly at first, then more easily as the laughter began, as they all walked through Richmond Park. By the end of the afternoon, they were romping together with Lupin. When the dog ran off, they both seemed equally distraught, and Jack went sprinting after him. He'd needed a two-mile run anyway. The dog was hovering about under an oak tree, sniffing and circling.

'LUPIN!' Jack yelled and the dog seemed for the first time to register his voice. A biker was walking along with his arm around his girlfriend, their crash helmets dangling from their hands.

'*Lupin?*' repeated the man, incredulous.

'Not my dog, and not my name for the dog, so don't give me a hard time about it, all right?'

Afterwards they went back to Martine's flat. She made food for the girls and put out Lupin's meat. Jack had bought a present for Dotty, as he always did. And before leaving the bookshop he had walked back and found the six-year-old section, and bought one for Louise too. When he gave it to her, she stared up at him through her big lenses, but said nothing.

'Say thank you,' Martine had said, but she still said nothing.

'Leave her,' Jack said. 'She can speak when she's ready.'

'Louise has asked if you would like to stay in her room tonight, Dotty,' Martine said. She'd not said anything to him about it. 'You could all stay in there. There are two beds. And Lupin could sleep on the floor.'

'Oh yes,' Dotty said, not even looking up from the book she'd been reading to Louise. 'That would be nice, wouldn't it, Daddy?'

Something happened that night. After he'd taken Lupin for his walk down by the river, and the girls had been put to bed, and Jack and Martine had had their Chinese meal with white wine, something happened. As his hand pressed into her breast and she pushed and murmured so hard beneath him, he could feel Louise's lips at the same nipple his fingers were grappling, could feel Charles's fingers there too, for so many thousands of nights before him. *Jacques, Jacques, Jacques*, she moaned in his ear quietly as he dug deeper inside and below, and then just at the moment that his surface scattered, he said, 'Martine.' That was all, but it was more than he had ever said before. With anyone. She pushed her tongue into his mouth and he accepted it. Feed my sheep.

●

In Cornwall that evening, Phil couldn't stop looking at her father's face, over there at the other side of the table in the candlelight. It was in his eyes, and she knew. That was why he had asked her down. What an idiot she had been, not to bring Dotty. He'd probably wanted to see her more than anyone else. He ignored it of course, as he ignored any force presumptuous enough to threaten him. But she could see it there, for it filled the whole room now: that was death rehearsing its one good line. He wasn't going to be here long. He *would* evacuate the universe after all. Could Jeremy fill the space he was about to relinquish? Nobody could, she knew that much at least. No one in the whole world would ever fill the spinning vortex that her father was about to leave behind him when he finally crashed to earth.

When Phil drove back up with Jeremy the next day, they had her mother in the back seat.

'I don't think Dad should be by himself, you know.'

'Oh, he's all right, Phil. I know he's aged a bit since you last saw him, but he's a tough old bird, your father. And he absolutely insists. He knew how much I wanted to see Dotty again. I'm so pleased about you two getting married, Jeremy, I can't tell you. Jack gave Phil such a hard time, you know . . .'

'Come on, Mum.'

'Well, he did, my love, let's be honest. He wasn't *there* for you. That boy was never properly trained in the basic arts of life.'

'He wasn't there for himself, Mum. Didn't know who he was.'

'Oh, poor old him. Pity he didn't have a war to go to, like your father. That would have taught him not to sit around brooding about who he was. What difference does it make, who a person is anyway? One still has to get on and do things. All I said was, I'm pleased, that's all.'

Phil had never sought her mother's approval. It was not something that interested her. Her mother followed where her father led. They collected Dotty. On the way back in the car, the little girl told them about staying the night in Martine's flat, with Martine's daughter. Phil was stroking Lupin's head and she realised that she was both jealous and pleased at the same time. They were all diversifying, symmetrically. She started to laugh. Jack.

Later that night, Major Hubert Dawlish sat at his window staring out into the dark. He'd not been able to face that trip up to London and had thought that if he could be alone and quiet for a while the pains would simply go away. But they hadn't gone away – they were increasing by the minute. He had walked around the telephone trying to bring himself to dial 999, but something stopped him. He realised he couldn't face going back into hospital. His hand touched the receiver and then lifted off again. He'd been in with this business twice before. Tubes stuck into his wrists. Enough.

Everything was settled. He didn't like it any more, this palaver with his body, it humiliated him. It was time then. If not now, then later. He did wish that Phil had brought Dotty down. They'd have to drive straight back again now. Made the best fist of it I could, he thought, and if some of it turned into a bugger's muddle, well there we are. Phil and Jack, what a bloody muddle *that* was. All the same, you've been C-in-C of a lot more bugger's muddles than I have, with respect.

He filled the glass to the brim with whisky and drank half of it down before he started coughing. He could see out across the lawn to the wood beyond. The moon was almost full and he made out the trees in silhouette. Two larches and a spruce. God, it is beautiful down here, he thought. Thanks for all of this then, for the tenancy of this little patch of earth. Where was that damned owl? She would normally have hooted by now.

He knew those sensations inside only too well. Bits of the body breaking ranks, whining that they've had enough. Well, maybe they had. He couldn't bring himself to try to bring them to order any more. They weren't pumping him full of anything this time. Time to get it over with. Time to be done with waiting. Never could abide being kept waiting. Particularly not for that murderous little sod inside with the balaclava over his head swinging his pig-iron. Have done with it. He took another swig of the whisky. Phil had bought him those glasses for his sixtieth. Irish crystal.

The war was the best of it, he had no doubt of that. Make what you can of life when you don't know from one day to the next what's coming. The Middle East. Then that great charge through Europe at the end. France. Germany. Those months were probably worth all the rest of his life put together. He sometimes thought it was a pity the shrapnel from the mine hadn't done for him there and then, same as it did for his driver. But those clever young chaps had picked it all out of him.

Afterwards there was Africa as a director of Naumgate, organising the shipping up and down the east coast. A lot of fellows from the war there. Still knew how to behave. And when not to. Then Jennifer, England and Phil. Never seen anything so beautiful in his life as his little daughter. 'She's not a boy, Hubert,' his wife had said to him over and over, as he took her out and taught her what he knew. 'Be as good as any boy, when I'm finished with her.' Jennifer couldn't have any more after that one. What life gives.

Phil was bold – he'd liked that. Climbing every tree, swimming in all the forbidden waters. If he had a heart, and the dwarf inside in the black balaclava seemed to think so, more and more by the minute as he went for it, he'd given it to Phil. Later on, it seemed as if she hated him. Why? 'You never looked at me long enough to notice who I was, Dad,' she had shouted at him once. Could that be true?

He lifted up the whisky to his mouth and sank the lot. Let's get this business over with, shall we? If you're as good as your word, Lord, then tomorrow I could be meeting chaps I've not seen since Normandy. Pity about Jack. Always liked the fellow, but there we are. Maybe Phil had over-whelmed him, he could understand that. She's more of a man than he is, Jennifer had said, you made sure of that, Hubert.

He felt it coming, felt his blood spill over from his veins and start to burn and then his breath start to swoosh like a bellows as though his lungs were being sucked out into a vacuum and he gripped the sill as that malignant savage little man smashed and smashed again with his sledgehammer at his heart and Hubert Dawlish's head finally crashed down on to the windowsill.

And that was how the cleaner found him the next morning.

•

'I'm sorry, Phil, truly sorry. I liked your old man. Liked him a lot more than I ever said. Admired him, too.'

'He liked you, Jack. He thought you were wasted.'

'He said that?'

'He said you were one of the casualties of Britain in peacetime. Said you could have led men, instead of . . .'

'Instead of what?'

'Dreaming up names for toilet rolls. He said you were all tactics and no strategy. Didn't know the difference between a setback and a failure. He thought he'd be able to sort you out, given time, but you never hung around long enough for him to make a start on it. We're going to stay down there for a week or so, and make sure Mum's coping. You know. Taking Dotty, obviously.'

'Phone me when you get back then.'

Jack set off to the office on the tube. Dale had asked him to start coming in each day in his suit, just in case. When he arrived, Marilyn appeared uncharacteristically morose. She merely nodded at him. In fact, she had spent the weekend with the son from her second, though by no means final, marriage. She had driven him around Oxfordshire in her Morris Traveller. She could no longer think back accurately enough to the thirty years before, when she had been at university herself, to remember whether all male undergraduates were moronic, or if this was merely another distinguishing characteristic of Martin. She felt as though her brain had been lengthily drained out of her left ear. She had plied him with food and drink, but his incessant, self-regarding drone remained unimpeded; she had almost been goaded into asking if he didn't have some drugs he wanted to take, but knowing him they would all have been amphetamines, and the drone would simply have speeded up, without even the prospect of sleep to quench it. Family life, she thought, no wonder I kept escaping.

Marilyn was aware that her age, and a certain thickening of her figure, had shifted her from affairs with men whose wives did not understood them, to affairs with men whose wives understood them only too well. But she had no intention of retiring. It was her one true pleasure, and she felt entitled to it, even at the cost of some social friction from time to time. On two occasions she had actually needed to move house. So much for the permissive society, she had thought to herself. She finally spoke.

'Dale won't be in. Other business to attend to. Gone to Paris. Could you go down to the printers? They're pulling proofs today, for the brochure.'

'How well do you know Dale, Marilyn, just out of interest?'

'Known him ever since he was a little boy,' she said.

'I didn't realise.'

'Knew his father,' she said. 'A *very* attractive man. Bald as a coot, funnily enough. Just like you.'

Jack went over to the printing company, using the new cab account which Dale had opened. 'Don't turn up on that bike, Jack,' he'd said. 'If it were the latest Kawasaki 1200, and you were dressed up in elegant leathers, I could take it. But not that clapped-out 250 of yours, and that knackered jacket. It doesn't work, mate, believe me. I know the impression people make – that's my job. You look like an unemployed Hell's Angel on his way to the dole queue on that bike.'

Jack watched as the buildings went by. Micawber Street. Was that where Dickens had taken it from? Then blocks of council flats with washing draped over the balconies. It reminded him of Oldham. Tom Dell met him and took him straight through to the six-colour machine where the proofs were being pulled. The Phoenix Collection. The jewellery gleaming out at you, and the background tint of a woman with a guitar, who was unmistakably Toni Inglish.

'Very striking,' Tom said. 'You fellows stand to make a mint, I'd have thought.' As they made small adjustments to the colour over the next hour, and pulled one sheet after another, it struck Jack for the first time that Tom might actually be right. When they had finished and the machines were running, Jack called another cab on account and had it take him to Putney.

When Jack arrived back, he laid the proofs on his table and looked at them again. You fellows must stand to make a mint. Was that really possible? And what was his part in all this? His answering machine was flashing. He played the message back.

'Hello, it's Jonathan. Remember me? Just calling to see how my brochure's coming along. I do have a certain paternal interest in it, you know. Give me a ring, would you?'

Jack changed quickly and set off running down the river. Martine had noticed him come in and then go out again. When he got back, he telephoned Jonathan after he'd poured himself a drink.

'So how's it all going?'

'I'd been meaning to tell you actually. Dale dropped your designs. He decided he wanted something . . . different.' There was silence at the other end of the line for a moment.

'That's interesting. Thanks for letting me know. So how far have you got?'

'They've been printing the covers today.'

'And the inside pages?'

'On Friday.'

'Quite a long way down the line then.'

'I suppose that's right.'

'Well, I'd like to see it all obviously. Out of morbid curiosity, if nothing else. At least I got paid. Maybe you could come over sometime.' Jack said nothing. 'Or I could always come over to you.' Jack still said nothing. 'We'll try to meet soon anyway.'

'Definitely.'

Jack went out alone that night and ate in a little restaurant half-way up Putney Hill. He wanted to put Martine out of his mind for a while. He couldn't think clearly about it, about what he seemed to be getting involved in, and so he decided not to think about it at all.

Over the next weeks they put the whole package together: brochure, letter, order form, envelopes. Discs holding the database of the Toni Inglish fan club were transferred, with a great hullabaloo of security, from Kingston to DMS in Deptford. David Selzman and his colleagues were full of praise for the quality of their work. In fact, everyone was. People kept muttering about how much money they were bound to make. So many people said it, Jack had started thinking that it must be true and wishing Dale would be more specific about future arrangements. Dale kept telling him not to worry. Jack didn't see Jonathan; he avoided Martine.

Tens of thousands of images of Toni Inglish flew out of the presses; her throw-away remarks were printed over and over again at the top of the glossy pages. The women in the noisy hangars of DMS fed machines with stacks of envelopes and brochures. Franking machines thwacked their postage-paid impressions. Hundreds of grey Post Office bags were crammed full of their mail shots. The Phoenix Collection finally went out into the world, so as to entice the devotees of Toni Inglish to part with even more of their cash and so prove once again their loyalty to genius.

'That's it, then,' Dale said on the day that the last of it was posted. 'Now we just have to sit back and wait for the orders. At 0·2 per cent we break even. At 0·5 we're into the money. At 1 per cent we're into real money. So cross whatever bits of yourself it is you cross for luck, Jack.'

'Don't cross your legs till you die,' Jack said distractedly. Marilyn looked up and smiled at him. She was wearing a blue and red scarf round her neck, secured with a black leather woggle. Still scouting after all these years.

'I'm off to La Chaux-de-Fonds to sort out the manufacturing,' Dale said. 'Marilyn, guard the phones. And Jack, take a break for a few days. You've earned it. You all right for money?'

'At the moment.'

'Let me know if there's a problem.'

Early that evening, Jack was running down the tow-path. Snow came tumbling down in swerving gusts out of the nacreous sky. The crystals landed on his hot face and dissolved. He wished each mile were a year, and that he could run his way back into his marriage, back to the days when Hubert Dawlish wanted to teach him to fly, and sail. Maybe he would even have taken to riding, who could say? And he would be down in Cornwall now, arranging the family affairs, helping himself from time to time to a whisky out of one of those crystal glasses. Going down to the river to check that the old man's boat was all right. Maybe taking Dotty with him as he drove Hubert's Rover, explaining to her about life and death, watching her little features so intently taking in the great themes her father was expounding. He started to run faster. Maybe Jeremy was doing precisely that with her now. Fucking Jeremy.

Phil had always been oddly unimpressed by Jack's temporal symmetries.

'Typical of you, Jack, that you can only go backwards. If you could just go forwards, then there might be some purpose to it. We could work out who was going to win the Grand National next week and make some money. But you can't stay home, can you? Can never stay wherever it is you're meant to be. Even in time. What's the point in being able to tell people what's already happened in the world? We can all see the bloody mess around us – we're looking for somebody to teach us how to clean it up, not go back into it. You see even less of the future than I do.' It was true that he never did know what would happen from one day to the next. Keep on running, Jack, whatever you do, don't stop running.

When he came back, sodden and breathless, he saw something lying by the mat which he had missed that morning. It was a card from Josh. A photograph of an excavation. Foundations of some sort. The caption was in Hebrew and he couldn't read it. He could only just make out out Josh's wild writing.

> At Cherith Brook, they have a picture on the wall as you go in. Guess who? Baruch Goldstein. Remember him, do you? The nice fellow who massacred 29 Arabs in the mosque in Hebron. He's a hero to these boys.
> Give my love to Nadia, and keep her warm for me.
> Back soon.

Jack went out and bought a paper. He stopped outside the shop and stared at the photograph covering half of the front page. It was the Captain's Tower, blasted and mangled, its thousands of windows ragged with shattered glass, its whole frame buckled and bent and stooping. IRA BOMB EXPLODES IN DOCKLANDS.

•

Jack turned the pages of Dick Dooley's book. Dick, it seemed, had often come across Toni crouched in meditation and muttering her mantra. He'd not been able to understand this at first; it had sounded like someone reading from the bottom of a road map. Only gradually did she reveal to him the secrets of her litany. She often sat cross-legged on the floor, murmuring.

'Brighton and Southsea, Bognor and Ryde, Bournemouth, Yarmouth, Shanklin and Deal. Cromer, Clacton, Morecambe and Blackpool. Hastings, Eastbourne, Colwyn Bay.'

All the piers her father had performed on. Some of them already tumbling into the sea.

An hour later Jack was on the underground to Victoria, with a small overnight bag at his feet. Halfway there, the train squealed to a halt in a tunnel. Eyes long accustomed to stay fixed on their books and papers flittered around in a brief panic of premonition: was this a bomb scare, or perhaps even another bomb? Jack could make out a cluster of black sooted cables, like the ossified intestines of some chthonic giant down inside the earth's coal seams. He took the train from Victoria to Brighton. The snow had stopped, but rain had taken its place. By the time he had walked from the station to the front he was soaked. He found a little hotel and booked in for one night at thirty pounds. The man at reception looked at him sceptically. 'I'd better come up and put your radiator on, it could get a bit chilly in the night. You'll be here by yourself, pretty much.'

He walked on the pier and stared down at the great grey thrashing flank of the sea. He remembered how he had escaped once to Blackpool with Denise. They had slept in his sleeping-bag in the dunes near the South Pier. Denise's sluggish thighs had received him. They had laid their cries on the salt night air. Then he had known all that life afforded. Afterwards her father, the local shopkeeper, had shouted through the door of his house never to come near his daughter again, or he'd do for him, God help him he would. Neither his father nor his mother could ever bring themselves to speak to him about it. That much had been a blessing anyway. Denise's father hadn't let her out on to the street after that. She was under house arrest for a year. What was he doing here? What was he doing anywhere, if it came to that?

He lay in the cold of the hotel room that night, constantly pulling the sheets around himself, trying to keep warm, and listening to the wind and the tide. The next day the weather had calmed down and he walked up and down the pier for hours. He thought about Denise again, and Phil. Northern men — how they surrounded themselves with a mythic aura of stability. In fact, they were scared to death half the time. Of sex, of childbirth, of responsibility, of women generally. Jack started to walk back to the station. He took the first train back to London. He felt like a tube with all the cream squeezed out of it.

As he was letting himself into his flat, Martine appeared. The blue crescents under her eyes looked very sore.

'I have something for you, Jack. I'll bring it over.'

When he opened the door to her a minute later, she handed him a card.

'A man came to see you. An old man. He left this note. Can I come in for a moment?'

He looked at the card as Martine walked through. It was from Harry Trench. Martine stood by the window and talked with her back to him.

'Are you sorry that the plastic lady has gone?'

'Nadia,' he said quietly, without looking up. Martine turned round to look at him.

'Ah, so she had a name. You said my name too one night. Then you went away.' Jack was still staring at the card. Martine had picked up the rosary beads which had once belonged to Jack's mother and which he had dumped on the windowsill when he'd come back from her funeral.

'Were you raised a Catholic, Jack? I've been out with a few Catholic boys. You always got two for the price of one: the one who wanted to go to bed with you and the one who felt guilty about it afterwards. Are all Catholic men celibates breaking their vows? Maybe you should try remembering the *felix* and forgetting the *culpa* for a while. What is it, Jack? Is it fear?' He looked up finally and met her eyes.

'Yes, I think so. Fear.'

'Of what?'

'Failure. All over again. Affection and its demands. More children. Expectations. Responsibilities. Money. Having to start up on what you thought you'd closed down for ever. And fail again. Having to pay for it, and not just with money. I'm sorry, I should never have . . .'

'No please. If it's just the exit sign you want, then you have it. I won't bother you. Louise was upset that you might have been angry with her because she didn't say thank you for the book. She asked me to say it anyway – she likes it. She said she'd like to see Dotty again sometime too. And Lupin.' She had walked over to him. She ran her finger down his cheek. Why did her body always smell so sleepy? Did drowsiness have its own perfume? She scratched his neck gently with her nail, the way she'd done that night. 'It's not long we're here, you know. Warm beds. It's a lot longer down there in the grave, it'll be cold enough there even for you Catholic boys from the north – it'll be just like home. I think we should try to make the best of things for a while, that's all. Nothing's ever perfect. Nothing and nobody. You can come over if you like, but you'd better make it soon if you're coming.' She left and Jack read the card once more:

*Please forgive my long silence. It was unavoidable. A medical matter. Could we meet finally? I am staying on a boat that belongs to a friend of mine, along Battersea Reach. Here is the telephone number. Any time. Harry Trench.*

Jack phoned and rode over on his bike that evening.

It was a narrow boat called *Albertine*, the only narrow boat in among the barges. It was already dark by the time he arrived, and her deck lights were on. The tide was coming in and she was rising and falling gently on the lapping waves. Jack walked aboard and knocked on the door. Harry Trench opened it. Jack had seen a photograph of him twenty years before, but he had been in good health then. The figure before him now was bent and ravaged, though the brown eyes were still alert enough. The flesh on his scalp was mottled with purple and brown patches.

'Jack Goodrich?'

'Harry Trench.'

'We meet at last.'

They sat in the cabin drinking coffee. Jack tried to give the impression that copywriting was merely one minor aspect of what he had been doing over the past ten years, amidst a score of more intellectually reputable projects, all a little too complicated to go into now. Harry Trench didn't seem to care much either way. Jack wasn't entirely sure he was even listening. He often looked through one of the port-holes at the river outside. Lights blurred on to the water. Finally, Jack came to the point.

'You wanted to discuss *About Time*.'

'That's what brings us together, I think. You know about my relationship with Pelikan?'

'His cameraman for the last ten films.'

'Ah, you're well informed.'

'He became something of an obsession of mine.'

'Yes, I can understand that. I thought for a while I was just his cameraman. I worked for others too, of course. Truffaut, Godard, Bresson obviously. Even Welles once. It wasn't until Miro died that I realised how fully I had entered his world.'

'How did you first meet?'

'He invited me to his hotel in London. He had seen some of my work and it had impressed him. There was a television in the corner of the room, and for the first ten minutes he flicked channels with the sound off. He made me tell him who was an actor, who was not. It was easy — it's still easy. "I want the reality of the people who aren't acting," he said. "Would you like to help me put that down on celluloid?" That's all he said, and I understood completely. By then he'd already made a name as the director who wouldn't touch actors. When some people he used, like René Thauss, went on to become professionals, he was furious. It meant they had insulted everything he held sacred. It was strange to watch him when they first came on a set. People used to say to me, How does he teach them to act? And I used to explain that the battle at the beginning was to teach them to stop acting. Either well or badly. People have learnt so much of the manner, the rhetoric of acting, that they do it when they order a sandwich or climb on a train. Miro used to say that even the insides of their dreams were the walls of a cinema. He was obsessed with stripping away the falsehood, finding the one true gesture and filming that. That was his credo, that short film about stained-glass windows. Nobody appeared there at all, and yet by the end you understood the drama going on in each frame, the spiritual movement of it. He wanted to make his films as much like stained glass as possible: frames through which the light passes to illuminate a gesture. He had studied with Rouault as a young man, but then you already know that, presumably?' Jack nodded.

'Miro hated cinema and all it stood for. The more they ran and shouted and shot and sexed, the less reality was conveyed. The more effects the less effect. He used to point to these moments of maximum reality, like Welles as Quinlan in *Touch of Evil* dipping his hands in the filthy sewage of the border town, as though to wash away the filth with more filth, and then falling into it himself, a great bloated bladder of corruption; or Dick Powell in *Farewell My Lovely* after he's been knocked out and drugged, fighting his way through that spider's web of smoke as he falls deeper and deeper into the dark. There were no effects there at all — well, Dmytryk had to buy a couple of door frames and a two-dollar filter — but all the *effect* you could ever dream of.

'I suppose you could say Miro converted me to his way

of thinking, his philosophy. I learned how to be very still as his cameraman, stiller than I'd ever been before, working for anyone else. Things became simplified in the light of what he believed, the way he directed: the meaning of man is his life, his love, his hate, his atonement, his death. The great modern myth is making these things relative. But that simply puts them in the context of other people's lives, loves, hates, atonements, deaths. It doesn't make them any the less absolute for each one of us.

'Did you ever see his film on Joseph de Maistre? Then you're one of the few who has. The Left in Paris hated it, of course, but they didn't understand it, they didn't *want* to understand it. Miro had seen both fascism and communism, and he wasn't keen on either. He believed the dark orders, as he called them, came about when the great pessimistic truths were forgotten: that people, if they are lucky, grow old, their bodies rot away from the inside and they die. That's if they're lucky. That they need to live in an order of signs, to quieten their own tumult and incoherence. But the order should be for their benefit, they shouldn't be for the benefit of the order, otherwise you end up making a fetish of death. Uniforms and lethal goddesses. The priests of destruction.

'He saw your *About Time* as an allegory of the dark orders. Did he manage to tell you that?' Jack shook his head. 'The man who could steal the past. Hitler did that, of course, as did Stalin. They took away the past from people and, after that, corralling them to march into the future was easy. Women banished to the status of a goddess. And the figures who get employed to make such worship possible are thugs and gangsters. Finally the man is done to death by his own tomb robbers, the ones he sent down into history's graveyard in the first place. The scene at the end where the shadows come up the stairs and Ashley Simon simply sits with his back to them staring at the heads of Ishtar, saying, What will be will be. That's absolutely right.'

To Jack's astonishment, Harry reached under the table and took out a large battered envelope, from which he took a copy of *About Time* and an old typescript he recognised. Jack leaned across to read the title of the typescript. It was the screenplay he had written for his own book and sent to Pelikan ten years before. There *was* still a copy of it.

'Miro liked the way Ashley was a criminal, but a criminal who found out the truth, who, having travelled back and forth through history, then turned away entirely from it. Just accepted his death as one more punctuation point in time.'

Jack could not help himself asking the question.

'Did he read my screenplay before he died?'

'He did, yes. He hated it, I'm afraid. He said you'd missed the point of your own book. He said your novel was film, pure film, but the screenplay was cinema from beginning to end.'

'That was his ultimate term of abuse,' Jack said, as he bent his face down on to his knuckles.

'Yes, it was. He couldn't see how you could so misunder-stand what you had created. You put women in the screenplay. At one point someone actually makes love. And things keep happening. But nothing *happens* in the book at all – that's what Miro loved about it. Your fellow travels in and out of time and lives amongst the shadows, in one sense he *is* a shadow. Surrounded by his loot, surrounded by Ishtar. But Ishtar's not a woman; she's the goddess men invent so they don't have to look at real women at all. When they turn women into woman. And it was right too that in the novel, when the murder scene comes at the end, you simply described the shadows climbing the staircase. Because these people are shadows too. Shadows out of the shadows of Ashley's darkness. They are from the present and that is the most shadowy thing in the book, the most insubstantial part of all. So Miro ignored the screenplay, I'm afraid, and worked directly from the novel.'

'He did some work on it?' Jack said, looking up again.

'He filmed it.'

'He *filmed* it? When?'

'It was at the time we were working on *Arthur*. It was an extraordinary time, for me anyway. All these characters spending hours getting into their armour and on to their horses, then Miro would have me do a tracking shot of their knees. Just their knees, clanking up and down as they rode along. Faces smile and frown too much, he said, even with visors on. Knees can't lie. The metal is articulate enough. Did you notice, in his films, how often he shoots the hands or the legs, even the hair sometimes? Anything but a face. I'm sure there's less of the human face in his work than any other director. It was a joint production, as so often with Miro, and we'd agreed to do some filming in Ireland, some in France and some in London. It was all stipulated in the funding agreement. Well, by the time we were done in Ireland and France, we'd finished. We had two weeks in London and Miro had read your book and made notes on it. So we filmed, in black and white, no soundtrack, using Christy O'Connell as Ashley. You remember him?'

'He was Merlin in *Arthur*.'

'Yes and he was perfect. Thin, grave and looking as though he came from any period but this one.'

'No soundtrack?'

'No, we couldn't run to it. We had the 8 mil. film, but we were always short of cash. It didn't bother Miro anyway. He said your book was a series of tableaux with a monologue spoken over them, so it seemed to him appropriate to film the images, then put the sound on after. He said it should all be filmed from inside Ashley Simon's head, because that's the way you'd written it. He could escape his time but not his own consciousness, which he was imprisoned inside. He thought it was a surrealist work. Pelikan felt you had taken a collector, an antiquarian even, and had simplified his relation to the past as one of theft. Money, after all, is so often the cosmetic that covers up the criminal's face. So even Ashley's journeys back in time amount to a form of theft.'

'But theft of what?' Jack said.

'Theft of the attention that he owes the present, that's the way Miro put it. He is alone. He pays attention to none but the dead. Miro used a striking phrase about it to me. He said, "The silence that surrounds him should be filled with the voices of need."' Jack said nothing for a moment. Then he spoke again.

'What happened to the film?'

Harry bent down again under the table and, not without effort, lifted up three spool-cans.

'It's here. He died before we ever made it to the edit or the sound stage. But he marked the passages in your novel where he could see the words accompanying the images we created.' Harry handed the copy of *About Time* over to Jack.

'This was Pelikan's copy?'

'It still has your inscription to him in it, and all his notes.' Jack flipped through the pages. Many of them were marked. Comments were scrawled across margins, usually in French, sometimes in another language he couldn't make out. He presumed it must be Czech. He looked at Harry again.

'So now, finally, after all this time, I'd like to edit that film and put the soundtrack on to it. And see it at least once in a cinema. A very small one, probably. But for my old friend Miro's sake, and for my own, to be truthful, since it will be the only film I'll come even close to directing, I would like to do this before I die. I need your permission and collaboration, it goes without saying. I can't pay you any money. I have just enough left to put all this together. I would be happy to sign over the rights for the film in their entirety to you. But I wouldn't expect that to make much difference to your finances, judging from the box-office revenue on all Miro's other films. Subsidy was our lifeblood.' Jack was holding the book in his hands. He had never expected it to come back to him, particularly not with Pelikan's annotations. The past was turning back again, or maybe the present was finally coming to life.

'Can I think about it?'

'Don't think too long, my friend.' Harry pointed a finger down below his own midriff. 'Inoperable cancer. Six months at the outside. That's why all the hair from my head has . . .' He stopped and looked at Jack's scalp in mild alarm.

'Don't worry,' Jack said. 'That's nothing. Just a style.'

'A style? Do you think I could call mine that?' He smiled

and Jack could see why Pelikan had kept him as cameraman for film after film. 'Good. You'll let me know over the next few days then?'

'Let's do it,' Jack said and Harry smiled again.

'You're sure?'

'I'm sure. For his sake, as well as ours.'

Harry reached down for the last time under the table and took out a foolscap notebook.

'Miro sketched the scenarios in here. If you look in your novel, you'll see the codes that correspond to the scenes in the notebook. One to thirty-two. He put all the numbers in the margins. He made suggestions, about cutting the text, splicing some of it, even at times enlarging it. A lot of it's in French. Do you know French?'

'A little, but I'm close to someone who knows a lot.'

'Could you please work through this as soon as you can? I still know Christy. I think he loved Miro as much as I did, even though Miro wouldn't talk to him after he became a professional actor. He's agreed to come over from Dublin and lay down his part of the soundtrack for nothing, as soon as we've agreed on the script. I have some recordings to fish out, but I can do that, I know the music he'd have wanted for it. I was a very *observant* cameraman. I studied everything he ever did.'

Jack rode back towards Putney. He stopped at Fulham Broadway and went into the Slug and Lettuce for a beer. He wanted to think for a while – somewhere a little distance from home. He sat by the window and stared through the window across the road to the Swan, or what had once been the Swan. Its golden name had now been deleted back to blue on the fascia. A green banner stretching unevenly from the scaffolding proclaimed: BOOTSY BROGAN'S OPENING SOON. He looked down at the big notebook and *About Time* and he realised how elated he felt. He would tell Martine. They could have a glass of wine together and look through the notebook. She could help him with some of the French. Cold down there in the grave, as Harry knew only too well. Or would soon. And every time you run away, you only run a little faster towards it. The silence that surrounded Ashley should have been filled with the voices of need. He finished his drink and rode back. Inside his flat he took off his leather jacket and picked up the notebook and the novel, then walked over to her door. He knocked and she opened it, but only after a few moments.

'Something to show you,' he said and smiled. Her face was dark.

'It's Louise, she's not well. She's lying on the sofa in there. I'm sorry, Jack. Maybe at the weekend?'

'I'm sorry too. About everything. At the weekend then. Give her my love, would you?' He leaned over and kissed Martine, and then Louise's little ashen moon-face appeared behind her in the hall, as she walked along slowly in her fluffy pink nightgown.

'Thank you for the book, Jack.'

'You get better now, and there'll be another one for you soon.'

●

Dale was on the train back to Zürich. He had seen Paul Delmonde in the factory above the hills near La Chaux-de-Fonds, and gone over the manufacturing details with him. They would have to lose some of Tim's fancy filigree work, and use enamel where he'd used stones, but they could come close enough to the prototypes to make the project credible. Twenty-five grand to tool up, though. 'We'll have to wait till the orders start coming in and there's some indication of the response rate,' Dale had said. 'I'm reasonably certain this one's a winner. Just be ready to go as soon as I pick up the phone.'

Afterwards they had sat by the window drinking coffee and gazing across the snowy valley below. This was the one bit of creation where the Almighty had worn rubber gloves while he was at it. Nature as sanitised contrivance.

'Still no settlement from your inheritance, Dale?'

'No, they stitched me up.'

'How?'

'My father left half the collection to me, half to Françoise. Then he dies. Suddenly a mysterious codicil appears attached to the will. It stipulates that so long as his wife is living alone in Paris, then the collection shall remain with her for the duration of her life.'

'Is that legal?'

'Only just. And only if the codicil was witnessed by a properly qualified figure.'

'Was it?'

'Before my father died, my stepmother was already knocking around with a new boyfriend. It was no secret. All Paris knew about it.'

'Who was he?'

'A young lawyer.'

'It wouldn't be the same one who witnessed the codicil?'

'Yes. Also the one she lives with most of the time, though I can't prove it. So the amendment to the will is probably invalid on two grounds, since she doesn't even live alone in the first place.'

'But why did your father do it?'

'The writing's very shaky. It was probably near the end. Maybe that was the condition of her affections one last time. You know my old man.' Delmonde smiled.

'Yes, he was very fond of the ladies.'

'I've heard it put a little stronger than that.'

'Beautiful ladies. Your mother was very beautiful, of course. You have her hair. Before the codicil, he had specified precisely what you were to get?'

'An inventoried list. Two actually. One for me. One for my beloved stepmother. I knew it by heart. The early Picasso, two Matisses, the Braque. And the collection of erotica. I'd been looking forward to it all.'

'Maybe she will die.'

'She'll never die, believe me, not as long as there's any money left to spend on this earth.'

Now Dale looked out of the window as the train neared Zürich. He had booked himself in for the night at the Hotel zum Storchen and he intended to enjoy himself. With Toni

Inglish he was either going to make a lot of money or go bankrupt. Didn't seem to be much point sparing any expense at this point.

There was a little club up a cobbled street, which he remembered from the days before he was married. It was still there. The champagne was even more expensive, and the floor show even more explicit, than the last time he had been. It was the tall black one who caught his eye, writhing dementedly in what seemed to be a white leather bikini with chains holding it together. Afterwards, she joined him at his table for a drink.

'Do you always wear that?' he said, jingling the chain that dangled from her left breast.

'No. Sometimes I take it off.'

'Four hundred francs,' the woman at the desk explained.

'That's for the night, is it?'

'That's for an hour, sir.'

When he arrived back in Kensington, there was a note from Tricia saying she had gone to stay with a friend. That didn't surprise him. She had left a bowl of what looked like desiccated scutch grass, presumably from her holistic feast before she departed. He picked it up and threw it into the bin.

He had noticed in the paper that there was a programme about Swarm on the television. He'd decided to watch it, purely with an eye to the marketing of modern icons, since that now appeared to be his business. He microwaved some pasta and poured himself a glass of Chianti. It was strange the way he always sensed the house in terms of her presence or her absence, each room wired to the distance from her body or her disapproval. The building was a sheath about her that went limp as soon as she left. If they were getting divorced, he'd have to move. He curled barefoot on the sofa with his wine glass in his hand and picked up the remote control.

Swarm were extolling the exemplary extremity of their existence. Drink, pills, heroin, detoxification units, three suicide attempts in two years. One gay, three straights, all united at least in relentlessly exasperating whoever their current partners were, multiple or single. Tal, Freddie, Jasper and Geoff were separately interviewed, as were all their parents and a gallimaufry of relatives and friends.

'Never thought he could play the guitar much myself. Still don't, to be honest.'

'Play the drums? Freddie needed the assistance of both parents before he could time an egg.'

'At school Jasper couldn't hit a note if you put it two inches in front of his nose and gave him a hammer and a miner's lamp.' It didn't seem as though the band had inspired much loyalty in their home town.

Each of the boys responded to these reported encomia with a slack nodding smile and some comment of transcendent non-specificity: 'Yeah, well I suppose they're right really. I mean they're as right as anybody ever is – which isn't *very* right of course.' Dale wondered if he was getting old, though he'd felt young enough the night before.

Jasper's mother was firm in his defence.

'The only thing that's ever been important to Jasper is his art. He'd sit there in the kitchen for hours at a time just learning chords. Wouldn't even eat -- just smoke. And he had to learn them from diagrams because he's dyslexic. People talk about drugs and things but he's just dedicated to his art. I think he's like a priest sometimes.'

The director cut to live footage of Swarm at the Marquee. Jasper was swaying drunkenly before the mike stand with a can in one hand. He had already removed his shirt so he could perspire with greater freedom. Periodically he grabbed the mike in his non-drinking hand and screamed into it:

> There are dead men outside looking in on me
> Dressed in uniforms of shadows, talking history
> But I can't join the army, father, I'm not free
> And I always shoot myself in the arm

The only one who held Dale's attention was their manager, Giles Gifford. He must have weighed twenty stone.

'You find them difficult sometimes?' the BBC interviewer

said demurely. He looked at her for a moment in silent incredulity.

'Difficult's hardly the word is it?' Giles said finally. 'Imagine four able-bodied men, then give them an emotional age of about five and a half, shoot them full of junk, speed, champagne; give them cars, hotel rooms, aeroplanes whenever they need something substantial to break to bits. I regard myself as a sort of Christ-like figure – I've taken on the insanity of the modern world. And all this for only fifteen per cent.'

At the Caine Mutiny, downstairs in the grotto where Dave David took his women and his drugs, he and his old friend Giles Gifford had just done their second line of coke apiece, and were sufficiently charlied up now to hoot with hilarity at the television screen every time Giles appeared on it. When any of the boys came on, they booed loudly and held their noses.

●

Phil had arrived back from Cornwall. Many things were now beginning to trouble her. Jeremy came downstairs after reading a story to Dot. He saw the expression on her face. He walked over and took her by the hand.

'Look, you have to accept that if we move over to France next year, as we've been talking about doing, it would be a nightmare if Jack starts insisting on his visiting rights and what have you. It's not as though anyone's going to keep him from her. All I'm suggesting is that we cut a deal that removes his financial responsibility and gives us a little freedom.'

'Not by cutting him out, Jeremy, you can't do that.'

'Try to remember something, Phil: I'm about to save that feckless husband of yours a lot of money. What with the CSA and everything else at the moment, I'm probably the nearest thing he's got to Santa Claus.'

●

Jack moved backwards and forwards through his own pages. He remembered Percy Hardinge's lectures on writing in antiquity. Nothing is ever merely written, they had been told, it is always written-over. As Jack read his own book, it was as though he was reading a book by someone else, someone long gone and buried. And yet it was him too, he knew that for sure, as he sorted and cut and edited. Pelikan was a good critic, and had seen in the text everything he needed for his film, and had simply discarded all that was inessential. He had seen exactly what to pull out from the rubble and what to ditch. In some way he'd grasped the real story better than Jack himself, even though it was still Jack's story, and they were still his words. The man who had written them, though, had been much transcribed by the subsequent years. Almost to illegibility in some passages.

He had not read it straight through like this since its publication and he began to see the point of Pelikan's comment: it was all filmed inside Ashley's head. The words were merely the monologue he provided as a voice-over to the images. Ashley Simon was entirely alone, for precisely the same reason that he could move so fluently through time: he was anchored to nothing in the present, he could float. The only things he made any real attempt to communicate with were the effigies of Ishtar, and they were not of the present, even if they were in it. Jack remembered all those plastic statues of the Virgin Mary which his mother had placed about the house in Oldham, how she would mumble her prayers and invocations before them at odd hours of the night or day. Talked to them sometimes more than she did to either him or his father.

That weekend Jack rode down on his bike and collected Dotty to go for a walk and a meal. No burgers, Jack, Phil had said, not while this BSE thing carries on. Give her chicken nuggets. In the park he stared at her on the swing. Suddenly he tried to work out how old she was, precisely how old, how many months had passed since the day of her conception. All those years he'd spent learning how to date things thousands of years away from him, but he couldn't work out now how many days and weeks his daughter had been alive. Surely that was more important? Later they sat side by side in McDonald's and she ate her chicken nuggets, dipping them with liturgical precision into the tomato sauce, while he had a hamburger.

'Why can't I have a hamburger, Daddy?'

'Because it might affect your brain.'

'Why won't it affect your brain then?'

'Nobody would notice, even if it did, sweetheart.'

He took her to the Wandsworth Museum. They looked at the flint arrowheads and the Roman swords; at the Battersea Shield and the Roman quern. They studied the photographs of the way Earlsfield used to be.

'It's funny how things change so much, isn't it?' Dotty asked him, squeezing his hand as she peered and peered.

'Yes, Dot,' he said, 'it's funny.'

Later they walked around the Arndale Centre. Jack always studied the consistency of its tackiness. It didn't even have the courage of its New Brutalist parentage. The premature Christmas decorations appeared secondhand and weary, the reds and greens anaemic and ersatz under the artificial lights. A fairy in her frills on top of an acid-rained-on pine tree smiled a smile wearier than that of even the weariest King's Cross tart. A Frank Sinatra song was spooling itself away, but without a Frank Sinatra voice to warm it. Everything appeared cheap and cheapened. The only part of the building he found at all compelling was the inside of the car park, where the scarred sparseness of the concrete retained at least a bleak integrity. Graffiti decorations. He bought her two books in the bookshop and then went and picked one from the six-year-old section. Dotty looked at it with interest.

'Is that for Louise?'

'Yes,' Jack said uneasily. 'She wasn't well this week.'

'Are you going to be Louise's second daddy, like Jeremy's going to be mine?'

•

Dale Freeman stood in the middle of a pile of mail bags in

the basement of TP's offices in Kingston. David Selzman stood by the door.

'This is the first few days' response?' Dale said.

'That's right. Post Office delivered it all at once. Looks pretty promising, eh Dale?'

'They can't all be filled with dogshit and used condoms, can they?'

'I wouldn't have thought so. Hope your manufacturer can keep pace with your promotion, otherwise you'll have put me in an embarrassing position.'

'Whether or not I keep my house depends on fulfilling these orders.'

'I feel better already. That sort of thing concentrates a man's mind. So, rummage and count away. Enjoy.'

An hour later, still only a tenth of the way through the orders, Dale telephoned Marilyn.

'Get me two temps pronto for the rest of the week. I'm setting up a little office down in the basement here. I need these orders properly logged. I want them both here tomorrow morning at nine sharp. I need to show them what to do, then I've got to be on a flight in the afternoon to Switzerland. This thing's going to be big, Marilyn. Get Jack, wherever he is, and tell him his holiday's over. You can have the airline tickets and six hundred Swiss francs sent over to me here by bike tomorrow morning. A lunchtime flight.'

Marilyn was about to ask a question, but Dale hung up. She sighed as she put the phone down: she'd rather enjoyed the quiet spell, but it looked as though it was over at last. She booked Dale's flight and ordered his francs and then called Jack.

Jack and Martine were sitting together on the sofa in her flat, where she was deciphering some of Pelikan's more crabbed writing in the margins of *About Time*.

'Emphasise how Ashley turns away from the present,' she said. 'When he sees the drunks in the graveyard . . . when people interrupt him in the crypt . . . even when the shadows are climbing the steps to kill him . . . he must turn each time back to his stolen books, and his statues of Ishtar . . . this is the whole gesture of the film . . . gesture of his journeying through time . . . even the gesture of his death . . . he has chosen . . . the dead.' She stopped and looked up at him. 'Did you know where Ashley Simon ended and you started?'

'No,' he said.

'Do you know now?'

'I might be learning. Possibly.'

'Your telephone is ringing. Leave it.'

'It may be Harry.' Jack went out of Martine's door and into his own. He hoped it would be Harry. He knew that by the end of the week his script would be finished.

'Hello, Jack, it's Marilyn here.' Marilyn put so much sex into her voice, Jack wondered that there was anything left over for her affairs. 'We seem to be all systems go. Dale is most anxious for you to return to us. I've missed you myself, to be honest.'

'That's nice, Marilyn. Look, tell Dale I'm delighted it's all working. I've something else on this week, but I can start again next Monday.'

'I don't think that will please him much.'

'It's important, Marilyn, honestly can't tell you how important. Something I've been waiting ten years to do. And the man I'm doing it with is dying – it's a genuine deadline.'

'Well, I'll tell him, Jack, obviously. All I'm saying is, he might be on to you himself quite soon.'

Jack walked back into Martine's flat, and slumped down on the sofa next to her.

'So, what's the problem?'

'Mr Dale Freeman requires my services again. The devotees of Toni Inglish are obviously banging on the door.'

'Let them bang.'

'I have to finish this script for Harry.'

'I'm aware of that, I think. I'm the French-without-tears part of the operation. So, finish the script, then.'

'What if he makes it a condition of going back with him that I go now, tomorrow, no delay? It's the only money I've got at the moment. I can't pay for anything without that.'

'You can always move in here, and then you won't have to pay any rent for a while.'

'It's too early, Martine.'

'Everything in life is either too early or too late, Jack, it's never on time.' Her hand was moving up and down his thigh. 'Don't make a decision by not making any decision, because then you'll find you made a decision after all. I've watched you over the years. I used to watch you running outside sometimes. Like watching a dead man running. It's only these last few months your face stopped being a mask.'

'What about Louise?'

'She likes you.'

'I bet she loves her daddy though. If it was a choice between me and Charles . . .'

'She said, Will Jack start sleeping in the big bed with you like Daddy used to? And I said yes, I said I hoped so. And she accepted it. You underestimate them, Jack.'

'Who?'

'Little girls. Maybe even big ones. The flat is mine now, no mortgage. I'm still the English secretary to the architectural firm. It's quite good money.'

'I couldn't live off you, Martine. I'm a working-class boy from Oldham.'

'You can live with me for a while though, and get some writing done. I won't be keeping a list of everything you owe me. If I thought you were, what do you call it, a sponge, then I wouldn't offer. But I know you better than that. Don't start with all that northern proletarian bullshit again, Jack. It's the only thing about you I do find truly boring.'

Jack was back in his flat, hammering away at the word-processor when the telephone rang that evening. It was Dale.

'All the way, Jack, remember.'

'Look, Dale, I know what I said and I meant it. It's just this week, that's all.'

'Not just this week, Jack. All the way's all the way. I trusted you, now deliver for me. There's over two thousand orders down in Kingston and that's the first few days of response. Most of them are multiple orders, for more than one item. I haven't even managed to add it all up yet. We've hit the button, son, and I've been most impressed by your part in it all. We can work together, I told you that at the beginning. I always trust my instincts about these things. But nothing's more important than this right now. Meet me tomorrow at nine down at TP.'

'Or?'

'Or don't bother meeting me at all. Your choice. You can be my partner and make a lot of money, or carry on doing whatever it is you're planning on doing this week. It's up to you.' He put the phone down. Jack changed and went for a run, out in the dark along the tow-path, and tried to forget for a moment what was going to happen when his run was over.

•

Earlier that day Phil had registered the faces turning towards her during the reading of her father's will, when the solicitor indicated that she had been left a quarter of a million pounds. She didn't expect anything at all, she assumed everything would go to her mother for as long as she was alive.

'Daddy wanted you to be secure, that's all,' her mother said afterwards, 'he was always very shrewd with his investments, and I thought it was a good idea that you weren't in any way dependent on dear Jack Goodrich. We weren't expecting Jeremy to come along then. So we agreed. I've got everything I need anyway, I've always been well taken care of.'

Phil was alone with Dotty that evening when they arrived back in London. She stared at the little girl as she sat at the table reading, and realised that she could pay off the mortgage and still have enough money to put away as security. She could carry on working at International House, but wouldn't have to worry any more about bills. It would be the first time since she could remember that she would not have to worry about money each week. And she realised something else too, something she did not want even to think about. She telephoned Jack, but his answering machine was on.

He's probably humping Lady Geneva, she thought. She left a message.

'Jack, it's Phil. I need to talk to you about the house. Don't worry – what I've got to say might actually cheer you up for once.'

•

Later that evening Martine let herself into Jack's flat. He was sitting at the table, staring at his little monuments in silence. Pyramid. Egg. Ishtar. He couldn't even face listening to the messages on the answering machine. He knew they'd all be from Dale. He didn't look up as she came in. She ran a finger along his neck.

'Have you made a decision, Jack?'

'No.'

'What are you frightened of this time?'

'Same as I was last time.'

'Me or the writing?'

'Maybe both.'

'I'll tell you one thing, Jack Goodrich. I don't know this for certain, you understand, but I think if you turn away from me now, and turn away from Harry Trench now, just for the sake of next week's rent, you'll be finished. You're going to have to let somebody down. Who would you prefer it to be, Dale Freeman or Harry Trench? Not to mention yourself. Or me. You might make a lot of money with your Mr Dale Freeman, but you'll never write another fucking word, believe me.' Jack reached up behind him and took her hand.

'I like it when you talk dirty,' he said. 'That was my wife's one erotic ploy. I've never forgotten.'

'Your first wife, Jack, remember. Come to bed.'

'What about Louise?'

'She's already asleep next door.'

'I don't like the idea of her being by herself in there.'

'I meant, come to bed next door. You might as well start getting used to it.'

And so it was that when Dale Freeman kept looking

at his watch the following morning, between handing out response sheets and explaining mailing codes, it gradually occurred to him that Jack Goodrich really wasn't coming. It hadn't struck him as possible before. Money was flying in from all over the globe, and Jack had decided not to bother turning up to meet it. He telephoned Marilyn.

'You have a note there of what we owe Jack?'

'Up to now, yes.'

'So make out a cheque and bike it over to me to sign. I want him settled and out of the way.'

'He's definitely finished then?'

'He's finished.'

'Shame. I liked him.'

'I liked him too, but he's a loser. He's another one whose bride is failure, and I really haven't got the time.'

●

Jack was out running at six o'clock the following morning. When he got back, he started work on the script straight away. He wasn't merely editing what he had already written. Some new things were coming out too – it was the first time he could remember writing anything for so many years, apart from flummery for other people's bric-à-brac. Helping to fill the world with junk. In between, he contacted the letting agency. There were still three months to run on his six-month renewable lease, but to his surprise they said that if he wished to move out at the end of the month, that would be fine with them. Obviously he'd been there too long for their taste, and they reckoned the rent might well be a little higher for any future occupant.

Then he phoned Phil, having finally listened to the message she had left. She asked if he would sign the house over to her, since she planned to pay off the mortgage. That would be the end of his liabilities there.

'The Major left you something then, Phil?'

'The Major left me something, Jack. I'm checking it all out with Deakins now, so that you can't be hit by the CSA for anything else later. Then you can pay a few hundred a month towards Dotty's upkeep. It takes the pressure off both sides, doesn't it?'

'Looks like Jeremy's marrying into money then.'

'What are your plans, Jack?'

'I'm writing.'

'Kitchen roll? Tinned vegetables? Washing-up liquid?'

'*About Time.*'

'I thought you'd finished that one.'

'It's the film script. The second and definitive film script. It's a long story. I'm moving in with Martine.' There was a silence. 'Can Dotty come over again and stay this weekend? Louise would like her to come and stay. She can bring Lupin, if she likes. Give you a weekend all to yourselves.'

●

*Dear Jeremy,*

*It all moved too quickly, I think. And all these ideas about going to France – the more I've thought about it, the harder I find it to imagine taking Dotty away from her friends and school like that. I've also started to realise something I've never really faced up to before: I like it here and I like my job. I can't imagine not doing it. What on earth would I do all week? Maybe I even like being alone with my daughter for a lot of the time. Perhaps we do end up with what we need, and only tell ourselves we lack something else so we can carry on complaining. You helped me to learn all this and I'll never forget you for it. Honestly I won't.*

*We were both very confused, I think. Maybe we still are. You helped me to stop blaming myself for everything which had happened with Jack. I sometimes think the world's divided into those who blame themselves for everything that happens, and others who never blame themselves for anything. I'd like to think I helped you walk away finally from your wife's grave. I think in some odd way you held yourself responsible, as though by marrying her you should have been able to keep her alive. The same way I always thought, if I'd been more of a lover, Jack would probably have stayed home at nights. I was confused about my own sexuality. I often thought I was frigid. You've taught me that it wasn't my fault – and what happened to you wasn't yours either. Anyway, that's enough time in the graveyard for you. You're still young, you know, and attractive – and successful. Half the women in London would jump at the chance.*

*Can we be friends, Jeremy? Let's be friends. Let's not leave it all in bitterness like this. I like you too much and so does Dotty.*

*Love,*
*Phil*

●

Jack turned up at Battersea Reach on Saturday morning, as he had promised he would. He had the script in his bag. He'd done it – he'd got it right. Now he had no job, and he was about to have no flat, and he had no wife, but he'd got this one thing right. A cheque had arrived from Freelands Marketing for £3,000, in full and final settlement of his labours, and since Phil didn't want any more money for the mortgage, he could live for a while. 'Write,' Martine had said. 'Stay here and write.' But write what? His themes began and ended with the material in that bag. Things were changing quickly all around him.

Harry looked frail, he'd had a bad night. Sometimes the cancer from his bowel sent electric pains rooting down his leg like lightning and he would dance on the spot until it stopped.

'Never mind that,' he said, when Jack asked him how he was. 'You remember Miro's motto: the difference between the psychotic and the artist is that one yields to the forces of destruction aimed at him, while the other rides them. It's a pity you never got to meet Miro: he'd have liked you. He did like writers who delivered on time. I knew that you would.'

'I'm not sure that I did.'

'No, but I *knew*. Can't explain. You're a serious person. You should trust yourself more, do you know that?'

Jack stood on deck and watched the river while Harry sat down in the cabin and went through his script. Trust yourself, Jack, he said over and over. Martine trusts you and Harry trusts you, so trust yourself. Occasional boats shifted down with the tide; occasional figures waved. Finally Harry called him down. The mottled skin was stretched into a smile.

'You've done it,' he said. 'Did you see what it was Miro was trying to point you to?'

'Tell me anyway,' Jack said.

'From time to time you tried to explain Ashley, and there was no need. His gestures and his language gave us all the information we needed. The whole point of him was a refusal to explain or be explained. Miro said to me it reminded him of Iago's silence when he's questioned, or Hieronimo in *The Spanish Tragedy*, remember, when he bites his tongue out so they will understand there's no point asking him anything at all any more. Remember what Marlene says about Quinlan at the end of a *Touch of Evil*: "He was some kind of a man. What does it matter what people say about you?" Miro thought the search for motivation had turned what should have been a lawyer's trick into a modern religion. He was more interested as a film-maker in what people did than why they thought they did it.

'Anyway, you've pulled it off. Now you've done something to be proud of, so you don't have to lie to people any more about what you've been doing for the last few years.'

'You knew I was lying then?'

'You don't spend the years I did with Miro searching for the truth in people's features without learning how to notice when it's absent. Christy's arriving on Monday to start the voice-overs.'

'On Monday?'

'Yes.'

'You really did trust me to deliver on time, didn't you?'

'Yes.'

'What would you have done if I hadn't?'

'Oh, got on with dying, I suppose. But a little sooner than I plan on doing now.'

'Can I come and watch?'

'As long as you promise not to tell me what to do.'

'I promise.'

When Jack arrived back he opened the door of his own flat and Martine's door opened at the same time.

'There's a friend of yours here to see you,' she said. Jonathan appeared behind her.

'Thanks for the coffee, Martine,' he said and walked across to Jack, smiling.

'I think I remember the face.'

'Sorry, Jonathan, but with one thing and another . . .'

'Oh, don't apologise. I just wanted to see what had happened with my brochure.' They walked inside and Jack pulled one of the mail shots out of his drawer and handed it to Jonathan. He slid the brochure out of the envelope and looked at it carefully.

'Yes, well this certainly is a bit different isn't it? He's cut the cover weight by a half for a start.'

'He was keen on getting production costs down.'

'It works,' Jonathan said, evenly. 'What was it about mine, out of interest?'

'Too tasteful.' Jonathan started laughing. Jack had forgotten how much he liked him, how much he missed him. Maybe he'd been ashamed at going along with Dale so easily and letting him be cut out like that. 'Oh well, if you have to be rejected that's not a bad way to go, is it? And how are you getting on with our Mr Freeman?'

'I'm finished.' Jonathan looked surprised. 'I had to make a choice. And for once in my life, I actually made one.'

'I can't give you any more business, I'm afraid. I've retired. From that stuff anyway.'

'I don't want that sort of business. Sick of it. Been sick of it for a long time. Think if it came to it I'd prefer manual labour.'

'I thought you'd come to admire Toni?'

'I did. And the more I admired her, the less I admired myself for doing this stuff.'

'Is it going to work?'

'Apparently, it's already working. The money's rolling in. To those who have . . .'

'How will you make a living, Jack?'

'Search me. I'm giving up the flat this month and moving in with Martine.'

'Ah.'

'How's Terry?'

'Gone.'

'I'm sorry.'

'Don't be. He was honest enough about everything. He wrote the play with his old lover in mind for the lead part, and now that it's being produced at the Donmar, he's moved back in with the fellow.'

'It's being produced?'

'In the spring. You will come, won't you? I've done the stage designs. Quite proud of them, to be honest.'

'I'll come.'

'Bring Martine. She seems very nice.'

'We should have you over for dinner.'

'Some time, yes. Must get off now.'

They stood together in the doorway.

'Looks like anchors aweigh for both of us then,' Jonathan said.

'Looks like it. You've got a bit more behind you in the way of resources than me though. That house of yours is like the Tate. Did you ever get that alarm fitted?'

'Funnily enough, I'm seeing a bloke in the pub about it tonight. I'm told he does the job cheaper than anyone else in London.'

That afternoon Phil dropped Dotty off and immediately left, saying her car was parked on the yellow line outside.

'Why didn't you bring Lupin?' Louise asked.

'Lupin's gone.'

'Gone where, Dotty?'

'He's gone. Lupin's gone and Jeremy's gone, and Mummy says they won't be coming back.'

Martine turned to see Jack staring at Dotty, and tried to

work out what the expression on his face meant, as his hand went up to his mouth and he turned and walked slowly into the kitchen.

That night in bed when he was asleep, she lay on her back and said quietly, 'Ne repars pas là-bas, Jacques, n'y retourne pas. Après tout ce qui s'est passé entre nous, ce n'est pas possible.'

•

Scarborough in December. The blades inside those north-easterly winds made sure that no one was around who didn't need to be. So Toni Inglish had the harbour wall largely to herself, apart from one or two fishermen with their lines twitching in the wind. She stood up there and let the weather whip her face. Salt acerbities. The distillation of all her years of recollection.

She walked over to the old theatre where her father had performed, but it was closed now until the spring. Most things were. It would reopen with a new bill of musical comedy. So she read on the tattered billboard: Bogo and his Monster Cat. Something for the Yorkshire holidaymakers to look forward to. They weren't millworkers any more though, were they? There were hardly any mills left. They'd all moved to somewhere in south-east Asia.

She remembered the shops. There was one where her mother had bought an enormous leather purse. This she had kept through all the subsequent years. Toni remembered its gilded catch and the layers of polished leather, dirtying and darkening as it aged. She couldn't think any more why she had come to hate it so much. Perhaps it simply never had enough money inside it. Not for her anyway. Most of the items in the window were made of plastic now. She took a tram down to Peasholm Park, white with cold at this time of year. Even the ducks, it seemed, had gone into retirement. Then back again to the open-air swimming pool at the end of the south bay, near where the organ used to open like an orchid when the sun came out. How she had hated that organ, and the manufactured smile of the man who played it, in his shiny suit and purple bow-tie, as though music were no more than a sycophantic bleating from the pipes; what the central heating would say if it could sing and count shillings.

She could have checked into the most expensive hotel on top of the hill, but she had found somewhere close to the place where she had stayed with her mother that last time, after her father had gone.

'It'll be a bit chilly, love,' the lady with the big glasses downstairs had told her. 'Not many lodging houses even stay open this time of year. Not round here. Only keep the sign in the window for form's sake, to be honest. Never expected anybody to actually *come*. You're not what's-her-name by the way, are you?'

'No,' Toni said. 'No, I'm not.'

'Didn't think you could be, coming here, but you do look like her. She some kind of hero of yours, is she?'

'No.'

Toni sat by the window. She could see down to the sea-front from there. She picked the strings gently and hummed until she found the tune. The tune had been ghost-scrolling inside her head for a long time now anyway. And she had notes for this one in the bottom of her guitar case. She'd written lines down for the lyrics for over a year, all the different places she wanted to bring together: her litany of mayhem and slaughter. When she finally found that tune it was as though something had triggered at last inside her. She stitched the lines together for the whole of that evening and played it over and over to herself until she felt she had completed something. Something had been made whole. Then she made her preparations, filled the needle (what a little baby's gurgle it made as it sucked) and shot up.

The next day Mrs Gryson found her in that chair by the window, the needle lying on the carpet beside her. Three grams of lethally pure heroin had hammered through her veins, hitting her brain and heart at once, and she'd gone out, even before the lights down on the harbour. On the table, in her careful tiny handwriting, was her last song, though no one now would ever know the tune she had created for it.

### 'After the War'

It's after the war, there's flags on the promenade
And they march to the beat of the band
Black capes a-flutter like a battered umbrella
I once saw blown across Scarborough sands
Well it rolled and it flapped like a broken-winged bird
Like these veterans back from the line
Who brought all their memories back here to Scarborough
But had to leave part of their bodies behind

Ypres and the Somme and Arras and Passchendaele
Flanders and Picardy, Lille and Verdun
The graves and the silences all the way out from
Siberian snow to the Scarborough sun

I was just gathering leaves for the autumn
In a valley in Flanders last year
When the deaths of so many husbands and brothers
And sons swept over the countryside there
White wooden crosses like a thousand dead forests
Murmured complaint to the sky
Which looked down as before through those days of the war
With not a word spoken, not even a sigh

Arnhem and Alamein, Katyn, Gallipoli
Hiroshima, London and Dresden in flames
Smoke over rubble in Greece and Manchuria
Scarborough's wrapped in its mist and its rain

I was just gathering Japanese roses
To give thanks for the end of the war
To the men of the line I drink German white wine
And an iced Russian vodka to the brave and the poor
Slow English sunlight rolls over Scarborough
Touches the faces I love
I hope and I pray that this peace today
Blows over the world like a wind from above

Stalingrad, Burma, Warsaw and Serbia
Bombers like death birds across Germany

Chemical rain and the graves of Cambodia
The wind across Scarborough blows hard and free

Sabra Chatila Beirut San Salvador
Tiananmen Square Bucharest Tripoli
Bullets in Belfast and bombs in Jerusalem
The wind across Scarborough blows hard and free
From the wastes of the grey northern sea

•

### TONI INGLISH FOUND DEAD IN SCARBOROUGH HOTEL

*The rock star Toni Inglish was this morning found dead from
a drug overdose in a small hotel in the Yorkshire holiday resort
of Scarborough. Her body was discovered by the landlady, after
the famously difficult singer had failed to respond to repeated
knockings.*

*'I didn't realise it was her,' Mrs Gryson told* The Times.
*'I thought it looked a bit like her, but then so many of them
do these days. It was a shock, I can tell you. Drugs in my
lodging house – that's the first time there's been any of that,
and the last.'*

*Toni Inglish was about to start a world tour next month to
launch her new album* Carnival. *Her agent Seth Waterhouse
said it was a great tragedy to happen at this stage of her career.
The hospital in America where her ex-husband Kurt Illen is
believed to be battling with his own heroin addiction stated that
he was heavily sedated and unavailable for comment.*

Dale stood against the railings outside Earl's Court Station
and read it for the fifth time. Then he took the first taxi he
could find and gave the driver the address of TP's offices in
Kingston. He had been on his way to meet Jim Torrance at
his new mailing house over in Reading, to discuss the
fulfilment of the issue, now that its success was assured.

David Selzman's face was grey. The craters on his skin
were now lunar in their unsunny desolation.

'I want to know where it leaves me, that's all,' Dale
shouted.

'In the shit with the rest of us,' he said. 'Read your
contract, Mr Freeman. All TP arrangements are valid only

as long as her performing career continues. That's what it says down there in the little words at the bottom of the page. I don't know how good your lawyers are, but they'd have to have very special gifts indeed to argue that Toni's performing career is not, well, let's say pretty much fucking finished, wouldn't you say? Even with virtual reality, we haven't managed any posthumous concerts yet.'

'I've spent twenty-five grand on tooling, not to mention the fifty this last mail shot has cost me. Are you seriously telling me . . .'

'As of now, baby, you can forget the lot. Start renegotiating with the estate if you like.'

'Who's the estate?'

'Her mother.'

'I thought she hated her mother.'

'I thought so too. I think she did. Maybe that's why she passed it all on. Her little joke from the grave. Who knows? We phoned the old girl this morning.'

'And?'

'As a mark of respect, considering the death of her only child, no promotional material may be issued for the next year and that's flat. As of now, I'm out of a job, Mr Freeman. So don't start giving me a hard time, all right? Maybe you should go see that Egyptian friend of yours in Knightsbridge. What was his name again?'

●

The newspapers were littered about the room. Jack had read six different accounts of Toni's death, and he'd read them all three times. Had she deliberately taken enough pure heroin to kill herself, or was she only looking for the biggest fix she could find? Didn't matter much now. Nobody really knew her, one of the reporters had said, but he still felt as though he did. That evening he asked Martine if he could borrow her car to drive Dotty back to Earlsfield. He called Phil and said he might as well save her the drive over. She was happy to come, but he insisted. Just before they left, Dotty turned suddenly to Louise.

'Do you want to come and see my house, Louise?'

'Yes,' she said. Martine looked at him.

'All right,' he said. 'Why not?'

As they drove over, Dotty stopped talking to Louise in the back seat and leaned forward.

'Daddy, why do tickles make you laugh?'

'Well,' Jack said, 'it's because . . .' He stopped and thought for a moment. He'd learnt over the years not to offer explanations when he didn't have any. 'I can't explain it, Dot. I'll have to look it up.'

When they arrived at the house, he sent the children ahead of him into the front room. He and Phil stood looking at each other in the kitchen.

'I hear you've split up with Jeremy.'

'No secrets with kids around are there?'

'I wanted to say something, Phil.'

'And I want to say something too, Jack. You've started with Martine. She's even got you writing again – more than I ever managed to do. She must have something I don't – who'd ever have thought it of the Swiss? Stay with it, stay with her. Don't go in for any sentimental crap about the past. You can't go back there anyway. Neither of us can.'

Jack smiled. 'And now you'll never know what it was I was going to say.'

She walked through into the other room and brought the girls out in front of him.

'Do you know what Dotty always wanted more than anything else in the world, Louise?' She shook her head slowly from side to side. 'She wanted a little sister. So maybe now she has one. Would you like to be Dotty's sister?'

Unsmiling, her face taut with the gravity of this decision, Louise thought for a moment and said, 'Yes.'

'Well then, I think you two had better spend next weekend here, and Dotty can show you all her things.'

'I'll have to ask Mummy.'

'Then you go back now with Jack and ask your mummy. So you see, Dotty, we often do get the things we really wanted, but sometimes not in the way that we expected.'

•

Louise was with Phil and Dotty. Jack sat in the kitchen as Martine cooked dinner.

'You wanted a Swiss meal,' she said, 'so you can have a Swiss meal. Pork and *rösti*.'

'Pig and potatoes,' he said.

'You understand my culture too well.' Jack was turning through the pages of Pelikan's copy of *About Time* – there were still a few notes in French he couldn't understand, and he wanted to know everything Pelikan had said, even though he'd finished the script. She walked over to him. 'So now you want me to give you French lessons.'

'Are they expensive?'

'For me, yes,' she said and left the room. When she came back she was wearing the black silk shift she had bought that day in Knightsbridge and never yet put on. He was impressed once more at the ease with which she slipped from Calvinist citizen to Parisian show-girl.

'I'm hungry, Jack,' she said as she bent down. He was stiff in the warm wetness of her mouth and waiting for the next curl of her tongue, when her head suddenly came up again.

'There's someone pressing your buzzer.' He looked down at her in disbelief.

'In a week's time it won't even be my buzzer any more.'

'It's for you.'

'How can you know that?'

'I know.'

Painfully, he pulled himself back into his clothes, as Martine disappeared into the bedroom. He walked out into the stairwell and up the stairs. And there, looking even wilder-haired than he had the last time, stood Josh.

Ten minutes later they sat at the table together, drinking Josh's duty-free, while Martine added more ingredients to her Swiss meal. Josh was meditative. Or maybe exhausted.

'When I was in New York I was invited to a gallery to see an installation. It was the latest work by Leroy Dwight. We all stood around for twenty minutes drinking white wine and eating canapés and then we were invited to make our way through into the installation itself, which turned out to be videos of us all drinking white wine and eating canapés in the atrium twenty minutes before. The videos were all out of sync with each other, so it was a sort of visual roundel, I suppose, and the soundtrack was a monologue by Leroy about seeing the city through his car window. How life became a silent movie you were driving through.'

'What amazes me with all this stuff', Martine said from the cooker, 'is that it was all done seventy years ago. In my country as a matter of fact. While the rest of you people were killing each other, we preferred to stay home and count the money. So all the ones who didn't feel like going to war came to us. Remember the Café Voltaire in Zürich? I sometimes think that all they really invented there was modern advertising. Maybe Switzerland rubbed off on them after all. But now I can't tell the difference between the advertisers and the artists.'

'I went to an exhibition in Whitechapel last week. Rachel Singer. When you went in you were all asked, men and women, to go into the back room and put on a T-shirt she'd designed. It was a white T-shirt with the word TWAT printed raggedly over it in black. Then you went back into the gallery. In the centre of the room was a perspex block and mounted on the block was a banana, already peeled, but with the skin still hanging off it. The banana had already been there a few days, and had started to rot. You could smell that sweet gas they give off. What is it, methane or something? There was an inscription underneath it that said: Without skin, man grows beautiful. It took a while before someone realised that all the *T-shirts* had a tiny hole down near the bottom at the front. It was called the Marsyas Project.'

'I think I can explain the inscription,' Josh said, smiling and leaning forward. 'You see it's often been pointed out to me, by women who've experienced both sides of the equation, that the member of a man who's been circumcised is far more . . .'

'Josh, we are about to eat,' Jack said, smiling. 'And Martine and I have already swapped dance-cards for this evening.'

'Story of my life,' Josh said, still staring at Martine's hips with frank appraisal. 'At least I'll have Nadia to keep me company next door.' Martine turned around towards the table.

'Actually, Josh,' Jack began.

'I killed her,' Martine said abruptly and took a long drink from the glass she'd just refilled. Josh looked at her quizzically.

'You killed my Nad? My little sex toy from the Russian steppes? What had she ever done to you?'

'She was coming between me and Jack, that's all. Let me pour you some more wine.' Jack had a feeling Martine was getting drunk, something he'd never seen her do, and he was curious as to what effect it might have. 'She was a bit of a tart, Josh, to be honest, and I'm surprised a man of your intellectual distinction thinks he needs to slum it with girls like that.'

'The daughter of Calvin finally speaks,' Jack said. Josh still hadn't taken his eyes off Martine's face.

'It has been my experience, Martine,' Josh said grandly, 'that inside every tart there is a librarian waiting to emerge, all they ever need is the right night-school teacher; and that underneath the blue stockings of every intellectual lady there is a tart waiting to grab you between the legs in the lift.'

'I've never understood', Martine said, 'why black stockings arouse you fellows so much, while blue ones make you think of the *Encyclopedia Britannica*.'

'If you hadn't killed Nadia, she'd probably have told us.'

'Her English wasn't so good, actually Josh,' Jack said, half to himself.

'I speak Russian, you schmuck, or have you forgotten everything about me? I could have translated. Or you could have sent her to International House for a month. Phil would probably have looked out for her. How did you kill my girl?'

'Stabbed her with a kitchen knife,' Martine said proudly. 'Straight through the throat.'

'The throat?'

'And the belly.'

'You always liked tough women, Jack, but you should have mentioned we were dining tonight with Lucrezia Borgia. Has she made you agree to sell your soul?'

'You might like to know, in relation to my soul, that I rewrote the script for *About Time*.'

'I thought your man was dead.'

'His cameraman isn't, though. He turned up with the film Pelikan made, and last week he finished editing it, using my new script.'

'Good, Jack,' Josh said and smiled a weary smile as he held out his glass for it to be refilled. Jack poured wine from the bottle and Josh raised his hand for a toast. 'To my old friend Jack, who might be beginning to remember who he is at last, after all these years. You'll never know how much I missed you.'

Later that night they were all sitting in Martine's front room. Now they had moved on to Josh's duty-free cognac. Josh was drunk, Jack certainly wasn't sober, and Martine seemed to have lost what Swiss inhibitions she'd had.

'I reckoned it all out, Jack, about this time business,' Josh said. 'You were going in and out of wormholes, that's all, not even anything to write home about.' Martine's hand lay on the inside of Jack's thigh and she kept fidgeting. Josh's eyes were fixed with an undeviating stare on that hand. He wanted a hand on the inside of his own thigh, Jack knew that. With the warmth of the drink inside him, Jack almost invited his friend over on to the sofa, to sit on the other side of Martine, and have his own thigh caressed. He had the odd feeling that Martine was probably now in a state to oblige. Just how Swiss was she? he wondered.

'Time we went to bed,' Martine said, standing up, and Jack was suddenly glad she'd said it. 'You can come over for lunch tomorrow, Josh, we'll give you the works.'

'You can tell us all about Ravens Inc. and Cherith Brook,' Jack said.

'Then I'll have to get drunk again because I can't face talking about it sober.' He stood up, uneasily. 'Jack's staying in the present with you then is he, Martine? Congratulations. He has been known to stray. I think I'd best take this bottle with me, since I'm required to sleep in my sweetheart's grave.' Jack helped manoeuvre him across the stairwell as Josh started to sing 'She Moves Through the Fair'. His rendition was surprisingly tuneful. As he slumped down into the armchair, Josh looked up mournfully at Jack.

'I know the truth about Nadia, by the way.'

'What?' Jack said, swaying slightly.

'She committed suicide, thinking if she didn't I'd probably come back again and bore her to death all night, like last time. That's why my last girlfriend left me. She said I talk too much in bed.'

'It's not just in bed you talk too much, Josh.'

'A friend, Jack, you always were a real friend.'

In the morning when Jack woke, Martine was already sitting up in the bed.

'I have a sore throat, Jack. Probably from Josh's cigarettes.'

'I read in a scientific magazine that there's one foolproof cure for a woman's sore throat.'

'What's that?'

'It involves the use of the tongue.'

'But maybe that's only the cure for the man.'

'No, if the man has a sore throat, then the one foolproof cure involves the use of his tongue. It's all been documented. I'm surprised you know nothing about it. I thought the citizens of Helvetia were systematic about these things.' His hand was already underneath her shift. Nipples, the points of them waking too. And then the nest of soft hair in the warmth down below. How quickly she responded at his touch, her fingers already twitching at his neck, her legs moving across him. Not Phil.

'Have you an itch at all, then, at the moment, darling? At the back of your throat, I mean?' Her fingers were stepping in tiny Swiss military formations up his thigh now. How precise her nails were. She had rolled over on to her back again and was pulling him on to her, and pressing his head down lower and lower.

'So this is what you call bed and breakfast in Geneva, is it?' His lips moved upwards now in a damp blur from her knee, where he'd sunk down beyond her bidding. A snail's wet track, the silver bubbles of his saliva. She flicked the silk up from her belly with sudden urgency and his hands moved back up to her breasts, where they remained, kneading and stroking and gently remembering their generous asymmetric sag, the little peaks of stiffened red flesh, and the mild tang of sorrow on his lips from the night before.

'It's a continental breakfast,' she said softly, pressing both index fingers into the lobes of his ears, and pushing up in a firm jerk as he fell silent and his tongue found her. 'Later I'll give you Sunday lunch, I promise. English style, Jack, I promise.' She was moving now, like a boat lifting quickly on the waves underneath his closed eyes, and she had almost forgotten to think about Charles for that moment. 'I'll be as missionary as you like. I know some hymns. I'll show you how to talk to God in French. Oh, She's nice, you know: you'll really like Her. You will, *Jacques*.'

●

Jack ran down the tow-path. He stopped at one point and stared at a shrivelled condom lying in the dirt. Pink and moist, like cherry blossom when it's fallen to the ground. Passion had won out over the chill in the dark here last night. Condoms. He felt an electric charge of panic go through him. Martine. The subject had never arisen.

When he stepped briskly down the steps to the stairwell, he stopped in brief confusion, forgetting which door he was meant to go through.

Martine was already preparing lunch. He walked over and kissed her on the back of the neck as she bent over the table. He was sweating.

'You either had a good run or you have another girlfriend down on the tow-path. Go have a shower.'

Afterwards he wandered over to see Josh. He had thought

he might still be asleep, but Josh had found a news broadcast on the television and was watching it intently, while sipping coffee and smoking.

'Have some coffee,' he said to Jack, who nodded. Jack stared at the screen for a moment and watched the emaciated African bodies, and the shallow graves they had started to excavate. Hadn't all this happened before? He walked into the kitchen in time to see Josh pouring cognac into one of the mugs. He looked embarrassed and held up the bottle.

'You want some? It's a French habit I picked up. Only at weekends, you understand.' Jack shook his head.

'You don't look too good, you know, Josh. You should try to take it easy for a while.' Jack looked at the skin around Josh's eyes – it was as grey as his hair.

'There are things to do,' Josh said. 'Things that have to be done.'

They ate lunch in silence at first. Yorkshire pudding and claret. Finally Jack spoke.

'You promised us a story, my friend. Your mysterious figures in New York and Jerusalem.'

'You really want to know?'

'Yes.' Josh filled his own glass with wine.

'Do you remember, Jack, how Percy Hardinge started the first lecture of each year by holding up that ammonite with the head of a snake carved on to it? A medieval priest had carved it there, not out of any sense of deception, but simply to emphasise the point that this was the remains of a snake. He knew it, so he was entitled to make it absolutely clear. How not to do archaeology, Percy said, don't carve your own preconceptions on to the evidence. We do though, don't we? Well now, our wonder-boy of a Prime Minister over in Israel opens up the Herodian Tunnel, which is really no more than a sewer, under the Muslim quarter of the Old City. And people start blowing one another's brains out, and I decide that I've had enough. I suppose I'd had enough a long time before, if the truth were known. But I'd been sleuthing after these fuckers in Yesodot Mikdash, this invisible

American group funding half of this so-called archaeological activity, and I decided I was going to find them – no one else seemed much interested. And I did find them, in New York, in a set of very large offices.

'The gentleman behind the chequebook is called Solomon Asher, and after staking out the joint for a week, I finally got an interview, though not for long. He thought I was a nice Jewish boy over from the Motherland, come to kiss his fat arse for all he was doing for the people of Eretz Israel. Come to worship his holy wallet. He's made his money out of disposable towels, apparently, made millions out of them, and now wants to fund the search through time for the remains of our people in Jerusalem.

' "What you are funding", I told him, "is the dispossession of people whose families have lived there for hundreds of years. What you are funding is terror, intimidation, black-mail. I've seen their faces when their houses are bulldozed and it's the nearest I'll ever come to knowing what it was like during the great round-ups that this century of ours has been so good at."

'He looks at me, from behind his big polished desk, and says, very quietly, the way a man with his own security guards can be quiet, "You are a disgrace to your people and your faith. You do not understand, do you, how quickly the end for the likes of you is coming? Israel is the edge of the world for the Jew. If we do not defend it, we will be pushed over into the abyss again, as we were fifty years ago. You understand nothing, with your liberal ideas about tolerance and progress. You are a parasite upon those who have died, and those still living who fight to keep the Jews alive. If we had left it to you, there would be no Judaism. No people in the world have ever survived without defending themselves. Do you imagine, if the early days of the United States or Great Britain were shown on television, that everyone in the world wouldn't be shouting at the injustice, the slaughter, the genocide? We are the only people who ever tried to live out there amongst them, with no rights or territory of our own. For thousands of years we tried. And

what did they do? They decided to exterminate us completely, every man, woman and child. Systematically.
Laughing as they did it. You come in here whimpering about
justice. Go back to your smart friends who believe in nothing
at all. Go back to your girlfriend, whoever she is. Go and
put seed in her womb, and if it's a boy don't even bother to
get him circumcised. Let him become one of the rest, see if
he can get away with it this time. Now clear off. As long as
there's money here to use, I'll use it to support my people
in the homeland they've returned to." '

Josh fell silent and Martine used the opportunity to serve
him some more food.

'And he made his money from disposable towels?' she said
gently, as she put Josh's plate back in front of him.

'A worldwide franchise,' he said. 'Probably even got them
in Switzerland.'

'My people don't need disposable towels, actually. They
are so clean already.'

'What will you do, Josh?' Jack asked, sipping his wine.

'Go back to Jerusalem. Write my article. Maybe try
putting my body in front of one of those men with guns
guarding the next archaeological site, since my words don't
seem to make much difference. Maybe find myself a girlfriend and put seed in her womb. Well, why not?'

'And if he's a boy, will you circumcise him?' Martine
asked, sitting down again.

'Yes, I will,' Josh said. 'If only to show that son of a bitch
in New York that there's more than one sort of Jew. I still
believe in it, you see, still believe in Israel, but not in Zionism
any more. We've been so good at remembering the past, it's
time we started remembering the future. Some of those old
boys over there think we have to get rid of everyone who's
not a Jew to make it Israel. I know one thing for sure: if we
do get rid of the rest of them, Israel will be dead for ever. I
hate the Jewish National Fund and the trees it planted round
Jerusalem, so it could throw Palestinians off their land. When
they were asked who owned the trees, do you know what
they said? "Trees represent people who aren't here yet." So

there you are again: a land without people for a people without a land. But I still believe in it somehow. In the museum in Tel Aviv, if you look at the paintings, the only Jews who were born and died in the same place, died in the Holocaust. I still believe in it, believe in some Israel that can live without oppression. I have to believe in it.'

Later Jack ordered Josh a taxi on the Freelands account to take him to the airport. (That would be the last one of those he could get away with.) Jack stood outside on the pavement with him. They put their arms around each other's shoulders briefly, then stood back again.

'You know the greatest tragedy of my life, Jack?'

Jack shook his head.

'I reckon Nadia would have converted.'

●

Dale Freeman left the bank with his face even darker than it had been when he had entered. When he arrived home, he took out his piece of paper. There were still two names on it: Ferdie Lockyard and Tricia. He called Johannesburg. The black maid's English wasn't good, but he kept on until she said she would go and retrieve Ferdie from his study. Jack suspected he was in fact probably lying by the swimming pool. It was hot over there at the moment.

'Hello, boy, how's it going?'

'Hit some problems, Ferdie, to be honest. I need forty thousand badly.'

'No, Dale. Go to the bank.'

'The bank says no. Can't you help me? Not even for old time's sake?'

'Let's be honest, it was your dad I had the old times with, not you.'

'You know, Ferdie, if my old man were here to tell you, he'd say you were a disloyal, spineless, self-serving, self-important apartheid-loving . . .' The phone went dead, and Dale crossed Ferdie's name off his list. Then he called Tricia.

'Let's meet for dinner at Marino's.'

'Not tonight, Dale.'

220

'Tonight, my love. You are after all my wife, unless I hallucinated that sequence at the registry office. I have something to tell you that may change your life. Tonight at seven-thirty.'

Marino led him to his seat.

'And your beautiful wife?'

'My beautiful wife is joining me, I think. I'll have a Bacardi and soda with lots of ice so I can jingle it about while I wait.'

He stared through the window at the late shoppers. Christmas soon. With or without her? That was up to her. He saw her on the pavement and remembered what it was that had made him chase her around London until he had her in his bed. Marino took her coat, and stood joking with her as he pointed over to where Dale sat.

'I deliver the beautiful Mrs Freeman to her rightful owner,' Marino said and laughed. 'Your usual?' She nodded.

'So, Dale, what have you to tell me that will change my life so much?'

'Let's have a drink and something to eat first, Tricia. And you can amuse me with what you've been up to over at Claudia's place. Or maybe I'm not old enough to know.'

'Why do men have such lurid imaginations?'

'It comes from studying women as closely as we do. So do tell me, has Claudia been introducing you to her famous young men?'

'I don't need anyone to introduce me to young men, Dale. I can do that well enough myself.'

'Temper, temper.' She wore a necklace he didn't remember. Had he bought her that? She saw him looking at it.

'Fresh-water pearls,' she said. 'I like the asymmetry. The way they look so . . . natural. They used to call them unions, you know, because each one is unique.'

'Recent?'

'Fairly.' She had brushed the hair from her forehead and

he could see the freckles there. On their honeymoon he had counted them. Twenty-four.

'What will you have?'

'What are you having?'

'*Fegato*.'

'You know, Dale, I think I've told you before, but if you eat an animal's offal, you're eating the poisons it couldn't get rid of. Years and years of concentrated poison. All the liquid and solid waste. And with the toxic material they're being fed these days . . .'

'You should open an Italian restaurant, Tricia; your patter would have them queueing at the door. You left some of your magical herbs behind by the way.'

'Get on with it, Dale.'

'Even before dinner? All right. I've screwed it, sweetheart. Toni's dead and all my one-time creditors have gone deaf. Spent the money from the mortgage, I'm afraid. Bank won't touch me, and neither will Ferdie. I'm sorry but we'll lose the house. I want to draw a line under it all. Start again. Maybe with more modest aims. But definitely with you. I've come to realise that much: definitely with you.'

Those grey eyes stayed fixed on him. She rolled the rim of the glass containing her gin and tonic back and forth across her mouth. Her lipstick was pink. He preferred her to wear the dark red. It's a mouth, not a wound, she'd once said to him. He had forgotten how tiny her fingers were. His flesh could still remember them closing around him as he grew.

'I want a divorce, Dale.'

'Don't you have any faith in me at all then?'

'No, Dale, I don't. You're a loser. Now you've even lost the house, half of which wasn't yours to lose in the first place. And I want a divorce. Soon. I'll see my solicitor tomorrow.'

So it was that Dale Freeman ate his *fegato* alone in Marino's that night. All the poisons of the years, he said to himself as he cut into it. All the poisons that can't escape. Certainly makes it tasty, though.

'Where did your beautiful wife go?' Marino asked as he served him the cognac.

'To find another husband, my friend, a solvent one.' The Italian threw back his head and laughed. Odd how often people do that when you tell them the truth, Dale thought.

●

It was a white Transit van that pulled up outside Jonathan Hamble's house in Kew. One tall black man and one small, much older, white man climbed out. They walked up the path to the door, and then the white man took out a number of small tools from inside the leather bag he was carrying. It only took him twenty seconds to prise the door open, because Jonathan was still inside, down in his cellar, staring at one of his drawings and asking himself whether he had gone too far with this one, or maybe not far enough. He hadn't put the extra locks on.

They didn't realise he was there. As they pulled the paintings from the walls and collected the sculptures and the electronic equipment, he heard the scuffling sounds above him. He emerged from the top of his cellar steps to see the tall black man in the white coat taking down the Lucian Freud from above his fireplace. There were patches all around it where other canvases had already been removed. He stepped across and grabbed the man from behind.

'What the fuck do you think you're doing?' he shouted as the face turned fully towards him. The white man, frightened now that they were about to be identified, picked the Ayrton minotaur from the table and ran up behind Jonathan. He brought it down upon the top of his skull with greater force than he had expected. The back of Jonathan's head smashed open and blood spattered on to the Persian carpet as he sank down twitching, then lay there motionless. The black man looked down at Jonathan and then up again at the white man, who was still holding the bloody bronze in his gloved hands.

'You stupid cunt,' he said quietly. 'You've only gone and killed him.'

Jack was watching the news on the television while Louise sat next to him on the sofa with a book when Martine shouted out, 'Someone at your door.' It's not my door any more, he thought. He'd never seen the man before. Middle height, thinning hair, in his late thirties. Wearing a long white raincoat.

'My name's James,' he said. 'You won't know me. I'm Terry's partner. Terry was a close friend of Jonathan Hamble.'

'Ah, you must be the lead man,' Jack said, smiling.

'That's me, yes. You haven't heard then?'

'Heard what?'

'Can we step inside for a moment?' Jack beckoned him in and they both went through to the kitchen and sat down. James told him about the attempted burglary, the attack, and how Jonathan was now on a life-support system with a dubious prognosis. They thought he could be irreparably brain-damaged, but they couldn't say for certain yet.

'And Terry's at Paddington Green Police Station. He's the prime suspect.'

'What do you want me to do?' Jack said finally.

'Come with me to Paddington. Tell them they've got it wrong. One of the neighbours, you see, saw a tall black man leaving the house.'

'And Terry's a tall black man.'

'Who was seen at the house a lot until recently. And the police and these elderly neighbours do sometimes find them very difficult to tell apart, you know, tall young black men. Will you come?' Jack nodded and went through to tell Martine what had happened.

'I don't know when I'll be back. Don't wait up.' She looked anxious and he kissed her gently. 'Get some sleep for God's sake,' he said, 'those bags under your eyes are big enough as it is.'

As James drove them over, the Detective Chief Inspector at Paddington Green was sipping his coffee and staring at Terry, his interrogator's eyes a brilliant blue, but his face registering nothing at all, whatever anyone said or did. Terry could see how he had passed the audition.

'I don't know how he got his injury,' Terry said again. 'I've already told you that.'

'Well, we can probably help you a little bit there,' the DCI said, leaning forward again. Terry noted his out-of-London accent, and the way his blond hair was cropped at the front, Roman-style. 'He received his injury when a bronze sculpture of a minotaur by', he looked again at his notes on the table, 'by Michael Ayrton was brought down with such force upon the back of his skull that the pieces of bone went flying around inside, probably causing irreversible brain damage. We don't expect to see our Mr Hamble eating grapes or reading Get Well cards or chatting to his old mum over the next few weeks, to be honest, Terry. We expect him to be in PVS, or what we call a persistent vegetative state, probably for the rest of his life – which might not be much longer anyway. Only kept alive at all by the plug in the wall and the tubes stuck into him all over the place. Of course if he doesn't manage to stay alive, we switch from looking at burglary with GBH to looking at murder, and I'd be happy to outline the usual length of sentence being handed out for that, at the moment. We are doing our best to discourage it.

'Now the funny thing is, from our point of view, that the bronze minotaur that made that journey half-way through to Mr Hamble's brain had your fingerprints all over it. Yours and Jonathan Hamble's, and no one else's. So, assuming he didn't try to beat himself to death in a little tantrum, that seems to point the finger pretty much at you, wouldn't you say? Looking at it from here, your involvement does seem to fit the evidence very neatly. So, if you wouldn't mind taking another trip down memory lane and telling us where exactly you were at two o'clock this afternoon . . . What was it by the way, sir, a lover's tiff? Or had you taken the opportunity to have Mr Hamble's collection valued while you stayed there with him until recently? Worth a few bob, I'm told, though I'm no expert at this sort of thing. The neighbour, a Mrs Jenkins, has identified you as one of the two men who got out of the white Transit. For the tape, Mr Field is shaking his head from side to side, and closing his eyes.'

After they arrived, Jack and James sat at the end of a corridor and waited. Uniformed figures came and went, striding back and forth amidst the clatter of the law. Jack had said to the Sergeant that he had information relevant to the case. After a little more than an hour, the DCI had Jack brought into his room. He had left Terry with a junior officer, to give him time to think it all over.

'You have information regarding the assault on Mr Hamble?' he asked Jack. James had been told to remain outside. Jack registered his accent.

'Yes, Terry Field didn't do it.'

'You psychic then, are you, Mr Goodrich?'

'More psychic than you are if you think it was him. Where are you from, by the way?'

'Stockport. You?'

'Oldham.'

'The neighbour's boy. Been acquainting yourself with the gay community down here have you, sir? Best not let your mother know.'

'I worked with him, that's all. For a long time.'

'And you got to know Terry as well?'

'He moved in with him for a while.'

'So we gather. And when he was given the boot, popped back to pick up his compensation money. Palimony, I believe it's called these days.'

'He wasn't given the boot. He chose to move out.'

'How do you know that, sir?'

'Because Jonathan told me. It wasn't like that. I really did know him very well.'

'*Very* well, sir?'

'Believe it or not, we weren't interested in one another's dicks at all. I go the other way myself, as I'm sure you do. Why are you so sure it's him?'

'Mr Hamble was attacked with a bronze by . . .' he didn't have his notes in front of him.

'Michael Ayrton,' Jack said.

'You really *are* well-informed.'

'Like I said, I knew him well: he only had the one bronze.'

'The only fingerprints on it were Hamble's and Field's.'

'Hardly surprising,' Jack said, wondering if there were anything behind those blue eyes, except more blue. 'Terry used to pick it up all the time. I remember watching him do it. Presumably your burglars might have worn gloves.'

'The old lady next door, a Miss . . .'

'Jenkins,' Jack said wearily. 'Old Joan.'

'There before me again, Mr Goodrich. Miss Jenkins said she saw Terry Field climb out of a Transit van with a white man and enter the house.'

'Let me tell you something about Joan,' Jack said, snagging the other man's eyes with his own for the first time and feeling as though he were back in the playground up in Oldham, squaring up for a fight. 'Joan has taken to calling me Dave over the last few months, because Dave is the milkman and Dave is bald. I've only just started shaving my head. It's only the better part of ten years she's known me, you understand, and now I'm Dave. So I think you can take it that one tall young black man looks pretty much the same as another to her. Know what I mean?' For the first time, Jack registered a flicker in the man's face, some trick of doubt crossing his features.

'You must understand, Mr Goodrich, statistically in cases like these . . .'

'Cases like what?' Jack said. 'Cases like a white middle-aged designer who decides to live for a couple of months with a queer nigger . . .'

'Those are your words, not mine.'

'I think there's probably a few lads around the nick here who'd be happy to use them, don't you? That's certainly what they'd have said up in Stockport and Oldham when we were there, and you know it. I'm telling you it wasn't like that. I knew them, both of them, and it was Terry who left – he didn't want to get back in and he's not a thief. The love of his life is sitting outside this room on a bench. I'll introduce you if you like. Jonathan made a point of telling me that Terry always paid his way. He wasn't on the make. This isn't Joe Orton and Halliwell. The situation's just not that predictable.' Jack suddenly stopped. 'Was there an alarm? In the house, was there one fitted?'

'No. Why?'

'He said he had a man coming round to fit one. Last time I saw him.'

'When was that?'

'A week ago. Said he was meeting a bloke at the local pub that evening who was supposed to do it cheaper than anyone else.'

'Thank you for your co-operation, Mr Goodrich. Now I must get back. Mr Field and I have a conversation to finish.'

The next day, Jack went to St Mary's Hospital, but he couldn't get any closer than the door at the bottom of the ward. He saw the mound of Jonathan's body, the monitor screens with their endless hopeless bleeps all around him, and an old woman crouching on a seat at his bedside, still wearing her coat. That must be his mother, Jack thought, the one who always proudly introduced Jonathan to her neighbours by saying he was too sensible to get married. Jack left and rode his bike down to the Coach and Horses in Kew. He ordered a pint and, as casually as he could, asked the barman if he knew anyone round about who fitted house-alarms at a reasonable price.

'You from the press, are you?' he said. 'You're too late, squire. The police have already been round asking those very same questions earlier today. We're fed up of talking about it.'

By that evening, Terry had been released. The tall black man had presented himself to the police, having decided that whatever he had to do for taking part in a burglary, it would be considerably less than what he'd have to do for GBH or murder. It also entered his considerations that with him being black and young, and of no fixed abode in the Brixton area, and his partner being older and white and married with kids, the sooner he turned up and gave his own account of things, the better it might turn out for him. Six days later, on the advice of the doctors that Jonathan would never lift a finger nor blink an eye again for the rest of his days, his mother agreed to have the respirator turned off and he was declared officially dead.

•

Dale Freeman walked past the *For Sale* sign into his house. An offer had been made on it. It was too low, far too low, but he was probably going to have to accept it anyway. He had given Marilyn three months' salary that day, and she had agreed to sort out the closing of the office — he honestly couldn't face going in there any more.

'Out of interest,' he had said as he left that day, 'did you ever actually . . . with my old man, I mean?'

'No,' she had said brightly. 'I would have done, mind you, but he never asked.'

'Don't ever change, Marilyn,' he'd said at the door. 'Stay just as you are.'

Inside, he poured himself a glass of wine and went over to the answering machine. It was a message from Pierre, his lawyer from Paris, asking to be called that evening at home, as a matter of some urgency.

'It is your stepmother's boyfriend,' Pierre said. 'Or rather, it *was* your stepmother's boyfriend.'

'Was?'

'It seems their happy days between the sheets are over, my friend. And in a little burst of principle we never noticed before, the young man has let it be known that he has had his doubts about the codicil for some time now. He says he always thought his signing was merely the preliminary to taking it to the notary. A sort of provisional gesture, no more, to help out. He said he never imagined even for a moment that such a hasty and *ad hoc* arrangement could be used to reverse the previous terms of a will. He says he would most certainly not go into court to defend it. After all, his reputation is at stake.'

'They really have fallen out haven't they?'

'They have. So we are hearing now from many different

sources. And your stepmother has suddenly become very nervous indeed.'

'She has contacted you?'

'Her lawyers have. Today. I indicated of course that were there to be even any suggestion of an attempt at any point to pervert the testator's intention . . .'

'And?'

'I am happy to tell you that your stepmother would like to settle according to the original terms of the will. She has come to feel that your father's last thoughts on the matter were perhaps not as well judged as they might have been, in the light of his final illness.'

'She's accepted a reversion to the original will?'

'She doesn't merely accept it — she seems very anxious to have the matter proceed as soon as is possible. Over the next few months, in fact. She's a troubled lady today, and she does not want to be made a fool of in front of the whole of Paris. It seems the young man has an awful lot of stories to tell. From what I've heard of them so far, one can only envy any man who was at the receiving end of your stepmother's versatility, however briefly. Your father was greatly blessed, in the twilight of his years. Anyway, with Christmas coming, she seems to feel that, like your famous turkeys, she's about to get stuffed. And she'd really rather not. So, Dale, *félicitations*.'

Dale put down the telephone and went to his study, where he picked up the folder in which he kept the inventory of all the artworks his father had originally bequeathed to him, along with little photographs of each one. Braque, Matisse, Picasso, Modigliani, Arp, Giacometti. And after he had turned the last page he started, very softly, to laugh.

●

Christmas Eve. Jack pushed himself down the tow-path faster than usual. He crossed Hammersmith Bridge and started up the other side of the river. At the east end of Bishop's Park he dropped down on to his hands on the damp grass and did his twenty press-ups. Then, breathing deeply, he walked over to the embankment wall and stared across the river.

The last year was, he was sure, the longest he'd ever known or ever would know. His mother's death. Jonathan's death. And Toni Inglish's death too – he had come to feel connected to her in some way he couldn't define. But he missed Jonathan the most. He kept making notes to telephone him about something. Then he would find his eyes blurring unaccountably. And now he was divorced. And a professional writer. By the time Harry Trench had died, they had at least finished that film between them. And Harry had given him the book he needed to write.

'I'm leaving you Pelikan's papers,' he had said. 'I hope that's all right.'

Jack had looked at Harry's pale face, with the veins on his head throbbing, and had not been able to think of anything to say.

'I've had them ever since he died. Kept thinking one day I'd sit down and sort them all out, so I could do that book on him that I always meant to, but somehow it never happened. Bit late now, isn't it? Anyway, they're yours. They'll be delivered to you next week. Promise me you'll do something with them, Jack.'

'I promise I'll try,' Jack had said finally.

'If you try, then I reckon you'll succeed.'

'Maybe that answers your question then,' Martine had said to him later.

'What question?'

'The one about what you were going to write. That's your book, Jack, so get on with it.'

He stared over at the mansion block where Martine was having breakfast at the table with Louise and his father, who had come down to spend Christmas with them. He started to run again and was back at the flat three minutes later.

Phil turned up with Dotty half an hour after he had come out of the shower. She hadn't realised Jack's father would be there and was momentarily confused. Then she gave him a kiss.

'If I'd known you were here, Michael, I'd have brought a present for you too.'

'Don't you worry about that, love,' he said. 'You just look after yourself and little Dotty here.' Jack watched as his father's eyes stayed on the face of his only grandchild. How seldom he'd ever taken her to see him – or his mother. Dotty sat on the sofa with Louise, showing her one of the books she had been given. They handed each other their presents.

'Can we give you a Christmas drink, Phil?' Martine asked her.

'No thanks. We're leaving to drive down to Cornwall to stay with Mum. I don't want to doze off at the wheel. Well, Jack, we finally got unmarried after all. You're a free man.' Jack smiled and looked at Dotty and Louise on the sofa.

'More to the point, you're a free woman,' he said.

'I always was, though. That's what you didn't understand.' Jack saw them both out into the car.

'Suits you, Jack,' she said.

'What does?'

'Staying put in the present. Try to keep at it.'

Back in the flat, Jack watched as his father gradually made himself understood to Louise. She had found his accent strange, but soon enough she was showing him her books, and he was talking to her as though she were his grandchild.

'You go get another of them books then, love, and we'll sit together and read it.' Louise left the room. Martine was out shopping. His father turned towards him.

'So, you going to marry her then?'

Jack shrugged.

'If a lass is worth living with, she's worth marrying, that's always been my view, and I'm not about to change it now.'

Later that night, Jack and Martine lay in bed together.

'Your father wants you to make an honest woman of me, you know.'

'Can we think about it for a bit?'

'Not too long, *chéri*.'

'Why not?'

'I'm pregnant, Jack.'

# Coda
# Sumerian

DALE WALKED FOR THE FIFTH TIME THAT EVENING AROUND the walls of his new apartment in Paris. The paintings had been hung and the sculptures mounted. He stopped in front of the little watercolour landscape by Cézanne. The prismatic brush-strokes had recreated a copse of trees – it turned into a honeycomb of light as you stepped back from it. It was a spectrum. Next to it was the small Cubist still life by Picasso, dated 1914. Pipe, wine glass, table. Only three colours and all of them matt and provocatively dull. A sandy geometric mystery. There was the Bonnard that turned a room into a rainbow, and the Ben Nicholson relief, shadowing its own whiteness. And then that portrait of a woman by Matisse, her lips and her thighs rhyming in full and fleshly invitation. It always reminded him of Tricia. Or could it have been, since he had grown up looking at this image, that Tricia had reminded him of the picture when he met her, that she seemed to be the painting come to life? Tricia. He had made sure the divorce was out of the way before the will was enacted – that had been his one condition. His stepmother had found it amusing. At least she wasn't the only one in a compromising position.

He remembered how, as a child, he had assumed everyone had such pictures hanging on the walls of their homes. He had been surprised when he entered the first house that didn't.

He went into the kitchen and poured himself a glass of wine. It was a very good claret. This was France after all. He walked back through the hall, past the monumental head by Modigliani, and stared up at the video entry-monitor. Only the flickering shadows of passers-by. So he stood over at the window again and looked down on to the blurred lights of the Boulevard Saint Germain. Someone watching carefully from the street could have seen the tall thin figure with blond curly hair, standing alone as he raised his glass to the whole of Paris. Dale Freeman was toasting himself at last in his victory.

•

The degree of self-doubt in Miro Pelikan had come as a surprise to Jack. He sat now at the table with a pile of the film-maker's papers in front of him. Pelikan had been greatly troubled until his death by his own decision to stay in Paris after the German occupation, and to work as a film-maker under the Vichy regime. He wasn't alone in doing that. Bresson and Carné did the same. Renoir had left though, as had others. Pelikan had started to wonder if he hadn't decided to forget life in order to be able to make films. In truth, he had suspected that the Germans would certainly win, and he was trying to create an art that might still be possible in a fascist world. His main project of those years was *Lady Godiva*, and Jack had begun to ask whether it wasn't his own inability to face himself naked which had driven him to make that strangely woman-hating film.

Martine walked into the room with a piece of toast in her hand.

'Someone's pressing your buzzer.'

'It's not my buzzer any more, love, I keep telling you that.'

'All the same.'

Jack walked out of the flat and peered up the stairs to the door. Josh.

Five minutes later they were sitting around the kitchen table together. Martine leaned across and touched the scar, still red above his eye.

'My cicatrix,' Josh said proudly. 'The battle during the arrest.' He took the paper out of his bag and threw it on to the table. Jack read it carefully.

Joshua Segal was one of the people arrested yesterday
over new excavations which have just begun in East
Jerusalem. Segal is a freelance journalist who has made
himself notorious recently with his argument that Israel
is not a historic territorial entity stretching back to
antiquity, but an invention of Zionism, aided and
abetted by the work of nineteenth-century orientalists.

The excavations were due to begin on Monday
morning. The way on to the site was blocked by a
picket, largely made up of Palestinian protestors. It was
amongst these people that Segal had positioned himself,
holding aloft a banner that read *Yesodot Mikdash – New
York Money Destroying the Homes of Old Jerusalem*. The
reference is to the shadowy organisation which is reputed
to have helped with the financing of many recent
archaeological activities in Old Jerusalem.

An IDF soldier approached Segal, who said to him in
Hebrew: 'You'll have to break my arms too, brother,
because I'm not moving.' A scuffle broke out and arrests
ensued, including that of the iconoclastic writer whom
so many Jewish residents of Jerusalem have come to
detest. He was released later on bail.

'The *Jerusalem Post* describes it as a scuffle,' Jack said.

'I was there, boy, not you. It was a battle.'

'Suits you anyway, Josh. You look like a pirate.'

'Exactly what I am,' he said smiling. 'So what's been
happening?'

'People have been getting divorced and dying, that's all,'
Jack said. 'After my mother, Toni Inglish. Then my friend
Jonathan Hamble. Then Harry Trench.'

'At least you finished the film.'

'And we're all seeing it tonight,' Martine said. 'It was good
of you to come over for it, Josh.'

'I certainly wouldn't have missed it.' Josh was looking
carefully at Martine's belly as he spoke.

'There may have been many deaths, Jack, but I see that new life is also on the way. When's it due, out of interest?'

'July.'

'A child of the English summer.'

'We're getting married, Josh,' Martine said. 'Next month. It'll be a quiet ceremony, but we'd like you to come.'

'I'll be the cantor,' he said. 'What are you doing, Jack?'

'A critical biography of Pelikan.'

'He has a contract and an advance from the British Film Institute,' Martine said emphatically. 'I knew if he would only start writing again, everything would fall into place.'

'It's not much of an advance actually,' Jack said.

'We'll be all right,' Martine said, looking at him severely.

'Yes,' Jack said and smiled briefly. 'Yes, we'll be all right: Martine says so.'

'You can earn some money today, anyhow,' Josh said, as he drank off his coffee and stood up.

'How?'

'We're both interviewing Percy Hardinge at his flat in Whitcomb Street. For *Life* magazine. They're doing a special feature on the world's greatest living archaeologists. It's all been arranged.'

'Thanks for letting me know in time to do some preparation then, Josh.'

'Don't need any. All we need is this tape recorder. And to get there in one hour's time. Unless of course you'd prefer me to do it by myself.'

They went on the tube to Embankment Station, then walked past the National Gallery to Whitcomb Street. Above a Greek barber's was the two-storey home of Sir Percy Hardinge.

'Know what you're going to ask him?' Jack had said.

'You don't have to ask Percy anything. You just introduce yourself. He asks the questions for you.'

Jack sat in a large armchair and looked about him at the statues and the prints. It was like one of the smaller rooms in the British Museum. And on the shelf a whole line of Ishtars and Inannas – it was after all the old man who had started Jack off with his obsession in the first place. Josh was fiddling with his tape recorder on the glass table, muttering into it to make sure it was taking his voice, then playing it back. Sir Percy came in and inquired politely whether they'd rather have coffee or whisky. Jack asked for coffee, Josh for whisky. When they were all sitting down, he returned. Dressed as always in tweed jacket and pullover, with his old college tie knotted precisely in a double Windsor. His thin hair was still slicked back, the same hawk-like precision of features quickened his bony face. He pointed to the scar on Josh's forehead.

'Is that an archaeological wound, Mr Segal?'

'I won it fighting for the honour of my people,' Josh said.

'Whom were you fighting?'

'My people.'

'And you, Mr Goodrich, I seem to remember they told me you'd become an advertising copywriter.'

'You'll be relieved to know I never was much good at it, and now I've stopped completely.'

'He's a reformed character,' Josh said, taking a drink of his whisky. 'Now he's just an impoverished hack like all the rest of us. He's working on the biography of Miro Pelikan.'

'Well, Mr Goodrich and Mr Segal,' Sir Percy said, sinking back into his chair and sipping his own whisky. 'What a compliment that life should bring you both back like this to talk to the old man on his last lap. You're the two I remember best.'

Josh started the recorder and Sir Percy reminisced. He seemed to remember the dimensions and dating of every object he had ever pulled out of the ground. It was as though he had been pulling children from the rubble. Jack found himself looking out of the window to see the sun breaking momentarily through April clouds. Sir Percy's sing-song voice continued its trek through the past.

'I'm an old man and I've fought all my battles. I feel like shaking hands with my enemies now. I always disapproved of Freud, for example, as you know. He was certainly no scientist. He was, I fear, much better at inventing myths than at properly describing them. He was so ready to *overwrite* the testimony placed before him. Why people paid him with such alacrity to erase so entirely their primary text and replace it with a secondary, or even a tertiary one, baffles me to this day. But there are certain concepts he employed . . . Projection, for example. I simply can't help using that particular notion of projection. And on that basis I've had to reconsider Ishtar and her role. I sounded off so much about her over the years that it's a little embarrassing to say I might have been completely wrong after all, but there we are.

'None of us is going to argue about the fact that Ishtar is associated with fecundity and prostitutes, male and female, and is constantly portrayed as murderous. Gilgamesh certainly thinks she is murderous, and a most dangerous lover. But if we take one step back towards her devotees, the *istaritu*, we find *they* were not murderous. Very much the contrary. All the evidence suggests that they lay on their backs, or bellies, sucking beer through a straw and receiving the desires of men in the hostels set aside for that purpose. In one sense they were honoured for this: in that characteristic reversal we spent so much time talking about at Lancaster, the things held sacred are also the things profaned. Anathemata. These people had, according to the Sumerian conception of life, lost their destiny. The normal relations which were expected to bless a life were not theirs and could not be. They served all and could therefore be dedicated to none in particular. Except of course to the goddess. They were universalised – put at a universal disadvantage so that they could be of universal advantage – to men, that is, whose lives had not been so dedicated. (This distinction seems to unite the conception of whore and celibate priest, oddly enough, but I wouldn't want to take the analogy much further than that.)

'Now if a man lost his virility on the field of battle, he put it down to the malice of Ishtar. He was no longer of any use to her devotees; and they were no longer of any use to him. It's surely hard here not to employ at least some of the categories of psychology. There were certainly murderous rituals in the culture of that time, though I wonder if we might not have exaggerated their frequency. There is a curious glamour accrues to murder after the passage of the years. I personally have no doubt that the Sumerian, Akkadian and Babylonian cultures, all put together, were nowhere near as murderous as Europe during this century, which should at least give us some pause for thought.

'If Ishtar is the projection of men's desire, and the projection too of their fear, then the relative powerlessness of her devotees in prostitution, combined with the astonishing power accorded to her in poetic and liturgical formulations, provides a curious study, and one which is perhaps not so far removed from many of our present concerns.'

'You mean she may have been innocent after all?' Jack said, startled by what he was hearing.

'Like all of us she probably started out innocent. Maybe she *was* simply a neolithic fecundity figure, an icon of life and enchantment, called on to help renew humanity. Once she is written over, though, she becomes someone else, as we all do. A lifetime in archaeology has taught me that much. All the desire she provokes returns as the danger and hatred and murder ascribed to her. In *Gilgamesh*, her danger finds its context in the love between the hero and his brother Enkidu. Ishtar was the patroness of abominations, so who actually read the text of those abominations that her person embodied? Who read the delight in warfare that became so clear in her recorded features? Such writing goes into the skin, like a tattoo.'

'Like Orpheus in the Billy Rose Garden in Jerusalem,' Josh said quietly. 'In Zadkine's sculpture he's covered in poetry. He's inseparable from the text of himself. He's already disappearing into his own words, coming apart as the myth has him do.'

'Or those black schist figures in the British Museum,' Jack said. 'The Egyptian ones, remember. Covered with cuneiform. There's one whose lap is just a mass of pictograms. It's his life story, chiselled into his loins.'

'Maybe we're still not so different in that respect either,' Sir Percy said as he looked from Josh to Jack and then back

241

again. He'd never see these boys of his from Lancaster again, he knew that — fate had sent them to say one last goodbye to him. Already the years had chiselled away at them too: they weren't boys any more.

'Well, perhaps we all *do* have our life story cut into our loins,' Sir Percy said finally. 'I suppose that's one way of describing what Freud was on about, isn't it, however wrong-headedly? Except that we keep the story well hidden in our clothes these days. That's our modern propriety. So that the clothes end up deeper than the skin. That's what all modern pornography seems to be about to me: people wearing their skin as though it had been stitched together for a fashion parade. But even Ishtar had to divest herself of all her accoutrements at the gates of hell before she could meet death face to face. Maybe we've forgotten how to die, in precisely the same way we've forgotten how to be naked. The Mesopotamian cults at least had dignity.'

They drove over to Phil's, to drop Louise off before they went to the NFT. In the car both Jack and Josh were subdued.

'Just look at us, Martine,' Josh said. 'Two weary writers after a hard day in front of the tape recorder.'

'You're going back, Josh? To Jerusalem?'

'Have to,' he said. 'At least until they won't let me in any more.'

'I'd like to go to Jerusalem,' Louise said. 'That's where Jesus lived, isn't it?'

'It's where he died,' Josh said. 'A lot of people go there to die, though only the ones called Joshua actually seem to get crucified. But you could come and see me there, Louise, while I'm still alive. When you get older, that is. When you've left school and can travel by yourself.'

'She'd have to be an awful lot older, Josh, if I'm sending her to stay by herself with you,' Martine said. 'Say about sixty.'

●

They sat in the dark of the auditorium. When the titles

came up and they could read the words *A film by Miro Pelikan and Harry Trench, Script by Jack Goodrich*, Martine took his hand in hers. The andante from Beethoven's String Quartet in A Minor was already playing and the camera was moving across the graveyard so that it could stare up at the house in Cloth Fair. Jack registered again how understated it all was. He remembered hearing Harry murmur, as he edited, 'Ah, Miro, how still you taught us all to be. How slowly the truth develops in the dark.'

Ashley moved through the film, unrelentingly, obsessively. Whenever he went to a window, the scene was lit in such a way that he only ever saw his own reflection in the glass, along with the images of Ishtar from the table and the shelves. As for the illegal transactions, one simply saw the hands at work — money placed in one hand, statuettes and books in the other. Pelikan so seldom probed the face with his lens that when he occasionally did, Ashley's eyes startled with their sudden intensity. And for his journeys into the past, the camera simply focused down on to illustrations in those precious stolen books as the strings on the soundtrack swooped. And that was all that was needed. As Harry had said to him one day, Pelikan's films were a great compliment to the human imagination.

And when finally the shadowy figures came for him, the criminals whose terms he was no longer prepared to meet, one never saw them, only their shadows and the shadow of Ashley against the wall as they beat him to death. And the last shot simply locked on to the one statue of Ishtar that they'd missed as they cleaned the place out. She looked on at it all, at the murder and the mayhem before her, as she had for thousands of years.

'It was powerful, Jack,' Josh said in the car as they drove back. 'Your book of the dead was powerful. Now I'm curious to read your book of the living.'

Josh had to sleep on the sofa. In the morning Jack woke as usual at six, feeling mildly nauseous. There was a constant knot of anxiety which formed through the night in his stomach. He could only untie it by getting up early and working. He had to finish this book – he had to deliver it on time, as he had promised. With each day that went by, he grew more convinced that he could do it, and started to feel a little better.

He padded in quietly to the living room and sat down at the desk. The marble egg, the polished granite pyramid and the terracotta head of Ishtar all stood there on the edge near the window. He wondered what Ishtar's expression really meant. Could it be that the frenzy in her eyes was as much bewilderment as voracity? That she was simply astonished at what people were doing in her name? Whatever she was saying, he needed these talismans about him. He looked up to the street. Already London's busy feet had started clattering along the pavement, headed this way and that. *The Babylonish Captivity* Pelikan had called his time in Vichy France, and Jack was using that title for his chapter heading. The strange thing was, as Pelikan also said, how you could come to justify it, explain it, even enjoy it, this staying alive in intolerable conditions. This collaboration. Josh turned suddenly in the dark behind him, and Jack walked over to the sofa and pulled the sheets carefully over his friend's sleeping body. Then he went back and started on the next sheet of Pelikan's scribbled text. It depressed him sometimes how hard it was to decipher his writing. Martine came in behind him in her nightgown with a coffee. She put her hand on the back of his neck and yawned.

'Just remind me, would you,' he said, half-whispering so as not to wake Josh, 'what does *témoin* mean? *Témoin de nos temps?*'

'Witness, Jack,' she said sleepily, as he ran his hand over his own shiny scalp before turning and gently rubbing her growing belly. 'Witness to our time.'

When Enkidu dies, Gilgamesh has seen death in his own brother. He watches as the worm begins its labours on the beloved body, that wild man whose savage appetite was tempered only by his overwhelming love. Then the hero of the stone tablets learns how intolerable death is, what a stink of corruption hovers round the sweetest flesh, and so he goes in search of immortality. But too much of him is mortal. Like the apostles, he sleeps when he should stay awake. And so he must return, having acquired neither immortality nor endless youth, to the land of loss and lamentation. Gilgamesh must start to learn how to die. In that, perhaps, lies his true heroism.

PERCY HARDINGE, *Archaeology*

By the time the daylight enters our little room in the dark, our lens has already closed its eye again.

MIRO PELIKAN, *Film*